Mari J.

Love & Domination

DuBois Publishing
Cambridge

Published by DuBois Publishing 2020

ISBN: 978-1-913410-05-6

Cover design: DuBois Publishing © 2020

First edition 2020

DuBois
publishing

www.duboispublishing.com

dedicated to
David Franks (RIP) & Jocelyn Glegg (RIP)

Acknowledgements

I'm grateful to family and friends, Cambridge Writers, and readers from The Romantic Novelists' Association's New Writers' Scheme for all the support and help I've been given in writing this book.

Mari Jane Law, March 2020

Prologue

Unable to face anyone, Perdita Riley slipped down and crawled under the table. She heard the swift goodbyes of the embarrassed guests and the closing of the front door. Frank, her rescued cat, ran in and sidled up to her. Wishing she could disappear, she edged to the far end of the table and sat with her legs crossed, shielded by the deep drop of the tablecloth. Burying her fingers in Frank's black fur, she stroked him. But the action, which often soothed her, didn't work this time. Besides, it wasn't long before Saul returned to the room. He stopped by the table. Would he realise she was there? Would he hear the beating of her heart? Frank's purr?

Perdita thought back to the day which had altered everything and had led to this point. It wasn't the beginning of her story, but it was the day her landscape changed.

Chapter 1

early March

Perdita glimpsed her reflection in the bathroom mirror. If she'd been attacked by an over-ripe tomato, she wouldn't have appeared much different. But peering at her blotchy skin and swollen eyes was not going to help with either Setback Number One or Setback Number Two. She splashed her face with water, smoothed down her brown bob and went back to the sofa to bury herself under her duvet and think.

The doorbell rang. It was too early for the post. Squeezing her eyes tightly shut, she buried herself deeper under the bedding. But the doorbell pealed again.

'Perdita?' A male voice sounded through the letterbox. And she recognised it. 'Perdita, we know you're in there. We heard you moving about.'

Damn. What had happened to privacy? Although Luke and Gavin were the closest thing to family she had, taking her under their wing from the day she'd moved into the flat in Clifton, she didn't want them to see her like this. Nevertheless, she donned her dressing gown, padded to the front door and opened it a crack.

'Hi,' Luke and Gavin said in unison, smiling brightly at her. They were dressed ready for work: Luke in fitness instructor gear, and Gavin, an undertaker, wearing a smart dark suit.

'We're worried about you,' Luke said. He was bigger than Gavin, taller and broader.

'We heard you crying last night,' Gavin explained. 'And, if it's a matter of life or death, you have both of us calling so you can take your pick.'

Opening her mouth to comment on the lack of sound-proofing between the floors of the flats, and to say she was okay and that she didn't need any assistance, she suddenly blurted, 'Can you find me a job?'

Gavin's eyes widened. 'Oh, we're going through a bit of a quiet patch at the moment so we're not recruiting. Must be all the government health drives.' Gavin sniggered, but changed tack when he noticed a tear had fallen onto her cheek. 'Oh. Sorry, Perdita. Whatever happened?'

'We're coming in,' Luke said, pushing gently past her. 'We got up early specially to see you. We've got twenty minutes.' He fiddled with his sports wristwatch, and Perdita guessed he was setting the countdown timer. Being late for work would be unacceptable.

She removed some financial magazines from an armchair for Luke to sit on and dragged the duvet over one end of the sofa to make room for Gavin. The half-opened blinds were rattling, and it felt like there was a gale working its way around the room. Perhaps that was why Frank had retreated to her bedroom.

'You'll catch your death in this temperature.' Luke strode to the window and shut it fast.

'At the moment, that's an appealing prospect.'

Luke relaxed into the armchair. 'Now, tell us what's happened.'

'I got fired,' Perdita said in a wobbly voice. That was Setback Number Two which had happened only yesterday and had coincided with Most Humiliating Experience Number Two. Getting the boot had certainly felt like a humiliating experience. And losing her only source of income was definitely a setback.

Luke raised his eyebrows. 'What on earth did you do to get yourself fired? I've never known anyone as conscientious and devoted to their job as you – apart from myself and Gavin, of course.'

'I think, on reflection, that I invited Mike to fire me.' Mike Loader was her boss at F&Z Financial Planning, a Bristol-based company that offered monetary advice and services. As Luke's eyes bulged, Perdita added quickly, 'I was just trying to change company policy so that we didn't offer high-risk investment products to clients like Violet Freestone.' As Perdita noticed Gavin frown, she added, 'You know, the elderly client I told you about.' Gavin's face smoothed. 'Well, I told Mike that I didn't think I could do the job anymore. He said, "Perdita, you're one of our best!", but I told him I wasn't anymore because I wasn't happy about some of what I was expected to do. At the end of the day, he called me into his office. He said he'd discussed me with the board and they'd decided not to renew my contract. If I couldn't commit fully to the job…' She broke off, her throat tight, her chin trembling and her eyes welling up with tears.

'Then what happened?' Luke asked, elbows on his knees, hands supporting his head.

Gavin offered her a tissue and Perdita blew her nose before continuing her tale. 'Mike said I had to leave immediately, because of security and client confidentiality. Lucy, the floor secretary, gave me a cardboard box for my things...' The conversation that had followed with Lucy was not something Perdita wished to think about right now, it being related to Setback Number One. 'I've got a few weeks' pay left – until the contract ends...'

'I wish you'd talked to us before you talked to Mike,'

Luke said. 'If you'd landed a job offer with another firm before you'd had that chat you'd have been in control of when you left.'

'I know.'

'I could finish work early and give him a piece of my mind,' Luke offered, his back straightening and his hands working into fists. 'In fact, I'd really like to.'

'No! You mustn't. It's over.'

Luke edged forwards in the chair as though ready to spring into action. 'I think you should consider consulting a solicitor. And do you belong to a union?'

She shook her head. 'I don't want a solicitor, and I don't belong to a union. I can't do that job any longer: I don't believe in it.'

Luke stared at her, concern in his eyes, and then checked his watch. 'We need to go. And you need to shower, get dressed and go out. It will make you feel better.'

'Yes, treat yourself to something nice,' Gavin said. 'And tonight, we'll get a takeaway and help you thrash out where to go from here.'

As Luke and Gavin stood up, Perdita shepherded them towards the door.

'Wear one of your lovely new outfits, and put some makeup on,' Gavin suggested as he hugged her goodbye. 'It will help cheer you up.'

'We're cutting it fine,' Luke said, checking his watch and tapping his foot, 'because you haven't agreed. We don't want to lose our jobs too.'

'All right,' Perdita said, not wanting the boys to worry about her, 'I'll go out.' She said goodbye, closed the door and then lowered her gaze to where her hands were tangled anxiously with the rope belt over her belly. When should she tell them about Setback Number One?

Chapter 2

Saul Hadley sat at his colossal desk staring wide-eyed at his middle-aged client. Mr Matthews looked weird, like a scarecrow. He sounded weird too: perhaps Mr Matthews only had a pet snake to chat to at home?

'Ssso where do we go from here?' Mr Matthews enquired.

'Er… from what you have told me, Misster Matthews...' Oh no, Mr Matthews' turn of speech was catching, '…I think we have a cassse of consstructive dismissal.' Saul regarded the outline of what was nearly Mr Matthews' skull, his face was so emaciated. 'I need evidence for the eventss that you have mentioned, any relevant paperwork.' Distracted by Mr Matthews' skeletal wrists protruding beyond the cuffs of his ill-fitting suit, Saul wondered if he should have offered his client some biscuits, to feed him up.

Mr Matthews got to his feet, promising to drop in what was required. After shaking his bony hand, Saul watched his client's retreating figure with relief.

Although it was now approaching lunchtime, in practice, it was catch-up time: stacks of paperwork had been growing into tower blocks over the past weeks. Since the crisis with his aunt, Violet, Saul had spent more time at the hospital than his solicitors' practice. Now that she was home with him again, he had returned to work full-time but worried she would not manage well with the scant support that had been organised. Violet could be as stubborn as they come and had refused further help that he'd offered to pay for. If she'd still had her savings, she wouldn't have needed to worry about him using his own money for her care. It was all the fault of that damned woman, Perdita Riley.

Perdita's face had haunted him the past few weeks. Even in his sleep, she would taunt him with that sweet smile of hers. But, as he tried to get hold of her to give her a piece of his mind, she would slip out of his grasp and vanish.

It had been only that morning he'd rung F&Z Financial Planning in a final attempt to be put through to Perdita. When Mike Loader had come on the line, he'd briskly informed Saul that Perdita no longer worked for the company. Saul had asked why, and Mike had informed him that, unfortunately, they'd had to let her go as she was unsuited to her job. If that wasn't an admission of wrongdoing, Saul didn't know what was. It hadn't been a surprise to find out that she couldn't be trusted; he'd suspected it all along.

He remembered his first meeting with her, appearing like butter wouldn't melt in her mouth with her clear fresh face and large doe eyes, looking uncertain and vulnerable, and how his heartbeat had been strangely affected. But she must have been putting on an act. Although Violet had refused to discuss details of the appointments she'd had with Perdita, Violet had obviously been taken in by her as she'd never stopped singing Perdita's praises. Telling him how sweet Perdita was and how she had to be one of life's innocents. Innocent his arse. He'd had enough clients who'd been caught out by unscrupulous financial salespeople to understand how they operated. And today had proved, once and for all, that Perdita was no different.

With a file opened in front of him, Saul did his best to concentrate. Rachel, the most reliable and efficient secretary he and his legal partner, Bruce, had ever had, placed a mug of black coffee on his desk. As Saul scanned the conveyancing document, he gestured his thanks. Logging into the practice's professional account on his laptop, Saul checked that the funds for the purchase of the sale had been released to him by the client's lender. Then he wrote a confirmatory email to the anxious client to let him know. As he clicked on 'send', he raised the mug to his lips.

The coffee was scorching. As he spat it out, dark liquid sloshed over him. 'Damn!' Saul flicked at his tie. What kind of impression would he make to his important new client that afternoon if it looked like he needed a bib?

Rachel looked up in surprise as he strode towards her, tugging at his tie and then flinging it into the waste paper bin by her desk.

'Oh!' Rachel exclaimed.

'I need a new one.'

'Would you like me–?'

'No. I need some air.'

There was a department store close by. He found a space in the car park at the rear of the shop and then hurried down the alley towards the main street. Shoving open the double doors at the front of the shop, Saul marched inside. Men's ties, he saw, were located directly across the aisle from women's hats, belts and scarves.

Having bought a close copy of the tie he'd worn that morning, Saul discarded the packaging at the till and looked for the nearest mirror to guide him. As he pulled the knot into place, a flash of red and gold in the reflection caught his attention.

'Well, I'll be...' he muttered under his breath as he caught a glimpse of the chin-length mousy brown bob and long red coat. Saul stared. He worried that the apparition might suddenly vanish if he blinked. Was it real? Was it really her? Slowly, he turned. And there she was.

The office could wait a while, he decided; revenge could not. This time, Perdita Riley would not escape.

Perdita was lightly fingering a red and gold paisley scarf before slipping it around her neck in front of a mirror. She liked it but wasn't at all sure that it suited her. Anyway, it was a purchase she shouldn't make considering the circumstances. She ought to have gone to a different area of the shop but, every time she'd got close to that area, she'd had trouble breathing. It was as though there had been an invisible force-field designed only for her: everyone else could safely pass but, if she tried, something bad would happen.

So she'd ended up by women's hats, belts and scarves. That other kind of shopping would have to be put on hold for when she felt braver. But would she find the courage before her waistline started to pop buttons?

After sliding the scarf free from her neck, Perdita

replaced it on the shelf. She wanted to go home. Turning, she noticed that a man with dark-brown hair, who had to be well over six feet, was about to career into her. Something about him seemed familiar. She stretched out a hand to steady him, but he snatched his arm away and glared at her with gunmetal eyes. Frozen, she just stood there and then felt the clutch of his hand on her shoulder.

'Get off me!' She flung out an arm to shake him away.

'I need you to come with me. You owe it to me. You owe it to–'

What the–? 'No way.' Quick as a flash, Perdita headed for the exit. She felt a sharp tug: the man had grabbed the loop at the back of her coat. And then he must have overbalanced as she was suddenly falling and... 'Oomph,' she said, as she landed on top of him. For a moment, she could only feel relieved that she hadn't landed on her belly.

The man hadn't let go of her belt loop and her coat was being pulled tight from behind. 'Let me go!' Why her? Why was he attacking her?

'Believe me,' he rasped, 'I have no dessire to–'

'Then why pull me over?' she said, through gritted teeth.

'I'm not letting you get away this time.'

This time? What was he on about? She scrambled to her knees and discovered he hadn't relinquished his hold on her belt loop when she felt herself being hauled upwards. She would have preferred to have sacrificed the stitching for her freedom.

Catching hold of her arm, he said, 'Jusst come with me. One hour of your time.'

Although she tried to pull away, it was no good, his

grip was sure. And what was it with his 's's? 'Let me go!' But he didn't relax his hold. Why didn't someone come?

'We have unfinished business to discuss, as you well know.'

What was he talking about? He must have mistaken her for someone else. But then a tiny frisson of doubt crept into her mind. Did she know him? But, as soon as she registered that there was definitely something familiar about his face, it was gone. If she'd seen that deadly scowl before, she would have remembered. 'Let me go, I say!'

Two nervous-looking female shop assistants and a bulky man in blue overalls who looked to Perdita like he could be a heavyweight champion – even though she couldn't see any rippling muscles – came into view. Muscle Man, as Perdita thought of him, couldn't have been more than forty. She spotted patches of pink scalp visible between the black strands of hair. As he placed a restraining hand on the man's shoulder, Perdita noticed it had a black heart tattoo with the word, 'Mum' written inside in fancy lettering.

'What's going on?' Muscle Man asked in a gruff, grating voice.

Relief.

But Perdita heard her assailant say, with assured proprietorial tones, 'My wife's not well. I've come to take her home.' Then, to her horror, he added, 'When she forgets to take her medication she gets confused and wanders off. If it hadn't been for a neighbour spotting her and ringing me at work...' He shook his head as though he carried the universe on his shoulders.

Onlookers would be taken in by the loving

exasperation evident in his tone. Was *he* on medication? Was he playing out a fantasy of an imaginary family life? Or was she on some trick show? She glanced around for give-away cameras but hope that the scene had been manufactured for TV died when she failed to spot anything suspicious. 'He's lying! I don't know him.' She dangled her left hand in front of her and wiggled her ring finger. 'Look. No wedding ring.'

'Of course not,' he agreed pleasantly. 'We haven't had time to replace it since you lost it last. I wish you'd stop taking it off when you wash your hands but you do scrub at them so and insist they're not clean with the ring on. I think you should take one of your pills right away. You don't want to go back on that ward again.'

To her dismay, Perdita watched Muscle Man's hold on her assailant's shoulder loosen. With her arm still gripped, Perdita felt herself being led further towards the doors. It was a public kidnapping and no one was willing to help her. But she *wouldn't* let it happen. 'I honestly don't know him, and he does *not* know me!'

Muscle Man stepped in their path.

'Don't know me?' her assailant asked, his voice apparently bemused. 'The father of our three children? Perdita, don't you think it's time you accept you need help?'

'How did you...?' She didn't know how he knew her name but he did. And, judging by the effect on everyone else, they knew he'd come up trumps. There was again that fleeting insistence that perhaps she did know him but, like a butterfly, it quickly disappeared.

Momentarily, something flickered in her assailant's eyes as though he, too, was surprised at the effect knowing her name had had on her.

Muscle Man took a step back. 'Is that your name?'

'Yes, but that doesn't mean...' She had to stay calm. 'Will someone call the police? They can sort this out. I want the police.' Despite her attempt at speaking firmly, there had been a tremor in her voice.

'Perdita, we've bothered them once too often, don't you think?' Her assailant continued to propel her closer and closer to the exit. 'Insspector... Dalgliesh won't take too kindly to another public disturbance – it would be better to come home quietly, without police escort, this time.'

Although she'd heard the name Dalgliesh before, she couldn't place it. She looked about her for signs of recognition on the faces of the people standing by – but they didn't seem to notice anything amiss. Surely, Saul had plucked the character from a book? But the name of the author did not spring to mind. Then the people who'd gathered around started to shake their heads in pity.

'The woman's mad...'

'Fancy that. I almost believed her...'

'Imagine what he has to put up with...'

'The poor kids...'

'Call the police! Please!' Perdita shrieked as she was half pushed and half flung through the doorway – opened for them by Muscle Man.

'I am so sorry about this,' her assailant said to Muscle Man, his voice only slightly strained as Perdita writhed in his grasp. 'Honestly, she's not like this all the time. Once I get her home, she'll feel much better.'

Chapter 3

Elliott Bletch nodded at the husband and carefully let the door go. He would have gladly married a woman as good-looking as Perdita but not with the insanity that went with it. He admired her husband for sticking by her. Now that's what he called love. He hoped, one day, to find it too. Someone Mother would like. That would be perfect.

He put the episode out of his mind, and began to concentrate on selecting a gift for Mother's Day; he would give it before they went for lunch at The Berkeley Square Hotel's Square Kitchen – their preferred dining venue. He and his mother had been given life membership of The Square Club when his dad, who had been head chef, died from a heart attack while presiding over the grilling of two sea bass fillets. When Elliott was not dining out at The Square Kitchen, he enjoyed basic pub grub – occasionally at The Dick Wittington in Westbridge as he was the landlord's go-to plumber and heating engineer.

Looking past menswear, Elliott headed towards women's hats, belts and scarves. Now *that's* pretty, he thought, as his gaze fell on a red and gold paisley scarf that wasn't neatly folded like the others. The material felt good between his fingers. He looked at the label. Silk. Yes, Mother would definitely approve: she liked to look smart. And it made him proud to be seen with her.

Outside in the alley that led to the car park, her assailant stopped and turned to face Perdita. The scowl had all but gone. 'I won't hurt you, I promise. I'm...'

Perdita stamped her stiletto heel down hard on his foot. She must remember to thank Gavin for telling her to dress up.

'Aah! I'll promise... not to hurt you... if you promise... not to hurt me,' her assailant whimpered hoarsely, relaxing his grip for a moment. Then he held her more firmly than before.

Time for another attack. And it wasn't difficult with all the adrenaline pumping around her body. She'd read something about people becoming superstrong and being able to carry out amazing feats when under stress. And she had two lives to fight for now.

'I'm... Vi–' he began. 'Ugh!' He bent over and gasped for breath. 'That... hurt,' he croaked, cupping his crotch with his free hand.

Obviously, her angled rear kick had reached its target. Goal to Perdita. With a few more offensives, she might disable him enough to escape. And then she'd go straight to a police station. 'You're hurting my arm,' she protested as his grip was even tighter now.

'Probably nothing to what a certain part of my body is experiencing.' Limping out of the alley and into the car park, her assailant aimed his key fob at a silver Mercedes. The car lights blinked. 'As I said... I promise... not to hurt you, I'm ...' Just as Perdita was about to swing her fist behind her in the hope that it would connect with the man's jaw, she heard him add, '...Violet Freestone's nephew. Saul Hadley.'

She gasped, relaxed her hand and all the fight left her, faster than a deflating balloon. Her mouth went dry and her cheeks burned. 'What do you want?' But she could guess. And perhaps it wasn't such a bad idea.

He let her arm go. 'A visit. And I'm really ssorry if I hurt you.'

She rubbed her upper arm to show that it was sore and was surprised to see genuine regret in his expression. When they approached the rear door, Saul opened it, and she climbed in before realising it probably hadn't been one of her better decisions. Wouldn't the front passenger seat have been more appropriate? She had an impulse to climb out the other rear door but knew he'd catch her. Then he joined her, his body next to hers... his thigh touching hers. The door was shut and they were close enough for her to hear his breathing.

'Do you have a speech impediment?' she asked. It was the blush that did it. He looked quite sheepish now, quite harmless.

'No,' he said. 'Just a blip. It's temporary.'

'Do you have a pet snake?'

'No.' His blush deepened. 'Can we stick to business?'

'Do you usually conduct business with a woman in the back of your Merc?'

'First time.'

'Me too. I don't like it. I want to go home.' She only half meant it. It was time she did the right thing and faced the music. Although she wanted it to be to a tune of Violet's choosing, not Saul's; he was angry with her. She could tell.

It felt too intimate sitting here with his gaze boring into her. But, as it continued to bore into her, his anger appeared to melt, and his whole demeanour softened. Worryingly, she felt her muscles relaxing in sympathy, and she had to stop herself from leaning towards him. It had been hard to believe that all the generous words

Violet had used to describe Saul were true, but he looked so different now that perhaps they were. She glanced down. Her fingers were plucking at her dress through the opening of her coat.

'Now look at me, Perdita. Really look. And then you'll see that you will be safe with me,' he said, his warm man-scented breath fanning her cheek.

She wasn't sure what was happening to her, but Perdita felt certain the last thing she should do was to look at him. From the sound of his deep voice, the feel of the puffs of warm breath on her as he spoke and that manly scent still detectable through the sharp lemon of his aftershave, Perdita knew his face could only be millimetres away.

But he was silent with expectation and, inching her chin upwards, she met his intent gaze and felt again the pull of attraction she'd experienced when Violet had introduced him. And she was going to fight those unwelcome feelings. She'd learnt from the Tony experience, hadn't she? It would not be at all sensible to be taken in by another good-looking guy.

But Perdita could smell the zing of his after–shave as Saul leaned over her and could detect the pressure of his thigh next to hers and, despite herself, her heartbeat quickened again. He really was the most attractive man she'd ever come across.

'Do you believe that you're safe with me?' Saul asked gently.

'Yes,' she whispered.

'And you understand why I have questions for you? Why I want you to see Violet?'

Of course she did. Looking away, she stared out of the window at the passing traffic.

'Violet left messages for you,' Saul said. 'And you

didn't answer any of them.'

Perdita flinched.

'You haven't got receptionists to say you're not available now.'

'I wasn't available.' She'd hidden in the toilets. It had been cowardly, but she hadn't been able to cope with Violet at the time.

'Later today, if you come home with me, you will understand why I acted as I did, why I became a brute of a caveman.'

Facing him again, she said, 'Presumably not because you want to share your cave with me?'

He snorted. 'No.' His expression said it all: why on earth would he want to share anything with her? Then he looked shamefaced as though realising he'd been offensive.

'Okay. I was wrong not to return Violet's calls. And I'm really sorry.' She bent her head to study her hands, pinching and stroking her fingers as it was too difficult to look him in the eye. All she'd had to do was to return Violet's calls, but she'd been in too much turmoil; she'd just found out about Setback Number One.

'And you agree to come with me, to see Violet now?' His tone was coaxing, almost seductively soft. And there was that lemony zing again.

Which made Perdita wonder what it would feel like to have him pull her close and kiss her, and she almost gasped at the image it made in her mind. What was wrong with her? First Tony and now Saul? When her gaze met his, she saw him falter. Was that an answering spark of temptation in his eyes? But he shifted away.

'Let's go,' he said.

Perdita walked around to the passenger seat as Saul limped to the driver's side and got in beside her. As he steered out of the car park, she glanced to her left and saw Muscle Man with a store bag standing by a blue van watching them go. The name, Elliott Bletch, was painted on the side panel as were the words heating and plumbing and emergency callouts. Now she felt embarrassed and ashamed by the whole scene in the store and wished she'd recognised Saul straightaway. Then she would not have made such a fuss. Then she would have understood that he was angry with her. He had every right to be. She was angry with herself.

Waves of nausea and light-headedness reminded Perdita of her empty stomach; she should have had breakfast. As they approached Clifton Suspension Bridge, she hoped she would be offered food at Violet and Saul's home.

Chapter 4

the previous autumn

The last time Perdita had been in Westbridge was in November, when she'd made her final visit to Violet. When the work was complete, Violet had brought them tea and home-made biscuits.

'Now that we've got business over, you can tell me all about yourself,' Violet invited from her armchair opposite.

Perdita stiffened. She didn't want to admit to Violet that she led a very staid and uneventful existence. 'Oh. There's nothing much to tell, and I really should be going.' She placed her empty tea cup on the low table in front of her.

Violet checked her watch. 'Oh, do stay a while. Surely, you're not off to see someone else after me?'

Perdita smiled. 'I do have evening appointments too.' Sometimes. But not today.

'I hope they pay you well for these long hours.'

'It certainly pays my rent – and I have a special loan to repay. I wouldn't have been able to afford to go to university without it.' She was paying the money back to the orphanage fund as quickly as she could, though it meant that she couldn't build up savings of her own.

Perdita was about to get up when Violet asked, 'Tell me, do you have a man in your life?'

It was exactly as she feared: it was getting too personal. 'Oh... no. I'm far too busy for that.' Perdita gave what she hoped was a carefree laugh but it came out too shrill for nonchalance.

There had been three men and three dinner dates. Memories of each flashed through her mind. The dates had all ended with emergency calls half-way through the meal. Man Number One had his house broken into. Man Number Two's baby–sitter had to be carted off in an ambulance as she'd eaten peanut butter by mistake and was in the throes of anaphylactic shock. And Man Number Three had the misfortune to have a meteorite strike his roof.

Each time, Perdita nodded sympathetically saying that of course she understood. When she hurried home from dinner with Man Number Three, she switched on the news to get a glimpse of the gaping hole in his roof. But she was too late; the news flash must have already been shown.

Violet smiled an all-knowing smile which Perdita did not warm to at all, guessing some advice was coming her way. 'A woman has to make men notice,' Violet explained. 'In my day, we weren't shy about wearing pretty clothes.'

Perdita glanced down at the serviceable skirt and blouse she was wearing and wondered what was wrong with them. She was at work, not at a party.

'Think of it like a flower needing to attract a bee. The ones that need bees to help them pollinate are bright and colourful.'

And smell nice? Perdita suppressed an urge to stick her nose into her armpit. 'You think that's the problem? That I'm not pretty enough?'

'Not at all, my dear. But you don't show yourself off to the best advantage. Make men notice you.'

Perdita pictured the other women in the office who

teetered on impossibly high heels, showed off proud generous breasts and pirouetted between desks, emphasising their tight-fitting skirts hugging perfectly-formed buttocks. The men would track their movements around the room while they sat at their desks making calls. But Perdita had never noticed any man track *her* movements.

Perhaps her clothes were a little dull and shapeless. Her coat was the only bright piece of clothing she had – plucked from a rail in a charity shop. Violet's words echoed what Luke and Gavin had said when they were on the subject of finding her a partner. If she didn't make some drastic changes to the way she lived her life, she would end up like Violet: never having been pollinated. She wanted marriage and children; a family life.

Violet added apologetically, 'Have you considered wearing makeup? You have beautiful eyes. With a hint of mascara, a dash of eyeliner, and perhaps some shading on your lids, they would be stunning.'

Perdita frowned. 'Oh, I have. Just not to work.'

Violet nodded kindly. 'When then?'

When indeed?

'Remember,' Violet continued, 'if you make the most of yourself, you won't need to do the chasing. But do make sure you choose the right bee out of all the bees your beautiful petals might attract. Someone who is ready to settle down, has his career on track and can offer you a nice place to live. Someone in the same position as my nephew currently is, for example.'

Perdita knew who she'd pick if she could.

'I found a treasure of a man,' Violet sighed, 'but two months before our wedding, he was killed by a runaway car. The driver had forgotten to engage the handbrake before getting out, and it was on a bit of a hill. By the time it reached my Arthur, it was going quite a pace.'

Perdita felt desperately sad for Violet. 'How tragic.'

'He was the one for me. And you must be sure to find the person you are meant to be with. You must take opportunities as they arise.'

Perdita murmured, 'Yes,' while thinking of Tony. But would he ever notice her? And had it been her lacklustre appearance that had put off Burglary, Anaphylactic Shock and Meteorite? She agreed with Violet; she did need a makeover.

Violet accompanied Perdita to the hall a few minutes later, picking up a shawl and wrapping it around her shoulders as Perdita opened the door.

'Thank you, my dear, for looking after my interests so well.'

'As you know, I'm not at all sure about–'

'I know, dear, you explained it earlier. But it's what I want.'

At that moment, a large car, headlights blazing, drove in and turned in front of the house. A bright security light automatically came on.

'Oh. It's Saul,' Violet exclaimed, taking hold of Perdita's arm rather too tightly for comfort, preventing her from going down the steps.

Seeing the pleasure light up in Violet's sky-blue eyes, and finding it hard to politely escape Violet's grip, Perdita knew she'd have to delay her departure.

As Saul approached the house wearing an unbuttoned heavy coat over his suit, briefcase by his side, Perdita could make out that his hair was perhaps a few shades darker than her own. When Saul reached the bottom of the steps, his inquisitive gaze took her in.

She didn't know why, but she felt uncomfortable and wished she'd managed to escape ten minutes earlier.

'Perdita, this is my nephew, Saul. Saul, Perdita.' Violet's voice was filled with pride.

Saul reached the top step. He towered above her, and she could see he was the most gorgeous-looking man she'd ever clapped eyes on.

Violet released her grip, and Perdita was now free to stretch out her arm. 'Hello. I'm so pleased to meet you.' She found his hand to be large and warm, and she smiled up at him.

'My aunt has spoken a lot about you.' His words were innocent enough, presumably for Violet's benefit. But Violet didn't have the benefit of seeing the unexpected chill in his grey eyes. Perdita felt sure he disliked her.

Saul was still clutching her hand, and the touch of his flesh was unnerving her. She wasn't used to prolonged contact with a man, and his lack of emotional warmth unsettled her. By the time she stumbled back to her car, she had trouble getting the key in the ignition; it had been a very awkward encounter, being attracted to someone who was not in the least attracted to her. That was one man she didn't want to meet again.

As Perdita hadn't a clue how she was going to spruce up her act, she decided to consult a personal shopper at a department store in Bristol city centre almost a week after the meeting with Violet. Bracing herself with shoulders thrown back and head held high, Perdita approached the enquiry desk. When she explained that she was looking for help choosing new clothes, the woman asked if she had an appointment.

'I didn't realise that I…' It was hard to keep her

shoulders back and her head high in the face of adversity.

The woman consulted the diary. 'I'm fully booked today, but I do have a trainee who could help you. I would, of course, oversee her choices to ensure that they are suitable.'

'Sounds good.' Shoulders were firmly back again.

'There will be a charge for this service which is fully refundable on any purchases you make.'

Perdita agreed to go ahead. After paying the required fee, the woman said, 'If you wouldn't mind taking a seat, I'll let Carol know she has a customer.'

When voluptuous Carol emerged from the changing area, clipboard in hand, Perdita wondered whether she should ask about buying a push-up bra. Her assets were minimal compared to Carol's. And she looked confident. Unlike Perdita who, over the past few days, had developed an inferiority complex so deep that she had convinced herself that she was the most unattractive single woman this side of the universe.

Beaming, Carol took the place next to Perdita on the sofa and introduced herself. 'If I could just take some details first...' When the formalities were over, Carol said, 'Now, what is it that you would like help with?'

Perdita wasn't sure where to start or how much to admit to.

'Perhaps you're interested in having something new as a general face-lift to your existing wardrobe or for a specific event?'

This was easier; she didn't have to admit to losing confidence in her entire wardrobe or, indeed, in herself. 'It's for a specific event.' And, she thought, for a specific male target. 'It's a work conference. In a hotel.'

'And is dress quite formal then for this conference?

People don't dress down for it?'

'Oh no. The men are in suits and the women have heels like long spikes.'

'Would you like to try on some high-heeled shoes? A good outfit is all in the attention to detail, you see. It has to fit together perfectly. It's no good trying on trousers with low heels if you later decide to look for higher heels.'

A frisson of excitement snaked through Perdita. Carol seemed to know her stuff.

'What colours do you normally wear?' Carol asked.

'Oh. There are no specific colours I go for. If I like the look of it, and it fits, I buy it.' Perdita tapped her chin. 'Perhaps that's where I've been going wrong?' Having been brought up by nuns who always wore the same dull habitual garb, Perdita's own clothing hadn't seemed particularly important. Until now.

Carol produced a swatch book. 'For your colouring,' she said, flicking through the pages, 'I think these would be the best options.' She pointed to oranges, browns and greens. 'Patterns where any of these colours predominate would really suit you, particularly as you have such dark-brown eyes. Cream and beige are good as neutrals for a base to build on.'

Yes, Perdita could run with that.

'We suggest clients stick to having only three colours in an outfit as a general guideline. Two colours can make an outfit look a bit contrived – although this can sometimes work well such as when you put black and white together. But that's quite a sharp, dramatic look and a third colour can soften it if you want a more feminine look. Just adding a brightly-coloured scarf could do the trick.'

Perdita's heart was racing with excitement, and she

wished she'd brought a notebook. Here was a whole new world opening up before her, one that her schooling had failed to prepare her for.

'More than three colours can be over-powering,' Carol went on. 'But it all depends on the complete look. Sometimes it comes down to trying different things out and seeing whether you like the effect. We encourage clients to experiment with clothes.'

'Can you do that for me? Experiment?' The word experiment conjured up time in the science lab with test tubes, dangerous chemicals and explosions. It didn't sound safe to her.

Carol nodded. 'That's what we do. When you've chosen the basic look, I'll find some accessories to complete the outfits.'

An hour later, Perdita left the store, her bank balance almost in the red. She'd bought two pairs of shoes she would need to practise stilt-walking in; plain dark-brown trousers that, with the shoes, made her appear incredibly leggy; a brown fitted jacket flecked with green and burnt orange that nipped in, emphasising her waist – as well as her bust, without the additional scaffolding she'd feared she'd need; some cream blouses and two patterned dresses that, Carol had told her, flattered her figure. She didn't like to think of the belts, scarves and bag she'd also bought; extravagance such as this made her feel guilty.

But hey, soon she would be ready for Operation Tony.

Chapter 5

December

Perdita was standing at the conference hotel bar holding a glass of white wine, waiting; Tony always came here before his speech. She was wearing her super-long brown trousers, white shirt and flecked jacket, and shoes she'd practised walking in until she could glide along. When she glimpsed her reflection in the mirror behind the bar, she felt she was looking into the eyes of a stranger. But then she remembered the makeup lesson she'd paid for and the hours of practise after. If Violet Freestone were here now, would she tell Perdita she'd blossomed into a beautiful brightly-coloured flower?

'Hello. I don't remember seeing you here before. You're new, aren't you?' It was a voice she recognised.

Spinning around, Perdita came face to face with Tony and his startling topaz eyes that were... admiring her. Aware of the hot flush that had suddenly come, she wondered if her foundation would disguise it. 'Hi... No... I've been here before.'

'I'm sure I would have remembered someone as beautiful as you.' He held her gaze longer than he needed to and then turned to the barman to order a glass of red.

She took a gulp from her glass. 'How long have you been a speaker at events like this?' she asked when he'd finished the transaction, at a loss for anything more scintillating to say.

'Too long.'

'Then why...?'

'It's well-paid, and a man has to do something. Now, at the moment I'm far more interested in you. Tell me how you came to work in the financial planning and sales sector.'

So, Perdita told him about her mathematics degree and wanting to use her skill with numbers to help people. It had also been the first job she'd been offered. Because she'd been mindful of that loan that needed to be repaid, she'd taken it. Other students might have had homes to go back to, but she'd had to start earning as soon as term was over so that she could afford somewhere to rent.

'Listen,' Tony said, 'I hate to break this up, but I need to get ready for my speech, and there are one or two people I must see before I get on the podium. Save me a place at the dinner table, and I'll join you later, all right?'

Dazzled, Perdita nodded.

All through Tony's speech, Perdita gawped at him. He commanded the stage and made the subject sound exciting. When his glance fell on her, her heart skipped, and she felt like he was talking only to her. It was so important she got it right, that she didn't mess it up. She hoped that Tony wouldn't get a phone call during dinner to warn of an imminent alien invasion, or some other humungous calamity.

Once the speech was over and the clapping underway, Perdita hurried out of the conference room and sallied along the corridor, achieving quite a pace despite her stilts. In the dining room, she claimed two seats at a table close to the door. She eyed the opened bottles of wine and reached for the white. This was the new, redesigned Perdita who could handle a glass or two.

Leaving her jacket hanging on the back of her chair and her delegate folder on the chair next to it to save a place for Tony, she joined the fast-growing queue at the hot counter. With a plate of chicken casserole, rice, and some mixed vegetables, she weaved her way back to the table.

'Where did you rush off to?' someone said behind her. It was a man she worked with. 'We're all sitting over there,' he said, pointing. 'You can come and join us if you like.'

Perdita saw that there was only one place remaining. 'Perhaps later?'

He shrugged. 'Suit yourself.'

There was no sign of Tony. His was the only vacant seat at her table now and everyone else seemed to know one another.

When Tony finally arrived carrying a plate of food, he said, 'It was mad back there. So many people wanted a chat. And I can't refuse. I'm being paid to be here.'

'No, of course not,' Perdita agreed. She hoped her colleagues hadn't seen her wave him over. She knew what office gossip was like.

In between mouthfuls of ricotta tortellini, Tony regaled her with amusing stories of conferences he'd been to where there had been hitches. He described the last-minute panics that occurred behind the scenes and how he, and others, had put things right. Then he grinned at her. 'You know, I've been drinking you up ever since I saw you. You have a lovely smile; quite endearing.'

A warm bubble of contentment rose inside her and

grew to bursting point. 'Oh. Thank you.' It was unlikely that the aliens would invade this evening.

Later, when Tony suggested they returned to the bar, Perdita was feeling she would go anywhere with him, even to the men's loos, just to keep on chatting. She ordered another white wine, and Tony insisted on paying for it. By now, she was very light-headed and not just from the booze. Tony kept showering her with compliments, and her crush was ballooning into something far more substantial. Was this what love was like? And could it happen so quickly?

Looking down, fearing she'd spilt some of her wine, she saw the tips of her new shoes peeping out from the hem of her trousers which made her think of flowers, bees and Violet. 'There's something I'd like to ask your opinion on.'

'Yes?'

'I'm concerned about an investment package a client opted for.'

'It's terribly noisy in here,' Tony remarked. 'Come to my room where we can talk it over properly.'

'Oh.' Should she?

'Look, there are one or two people I must have a word with about tomorrow. Go up to the sixth floor and wait for me by the lifts.'

'Umm.' Why not? 'I'll drop my folder in my room first then.'

'Okay. I tell you what; make it half an hour on the sixth floor, by the lift.'

Perdita scurried back to her room and checked her appearance. And her armpits. She didn't want to smell bad; it might put a bee off. She hoped that, tonight, Tony would kiss her. That was not something he could do at the bar, in front of all those people. And she would be far too embarrassed to let that happen. But in the privacy of his room… that would be nice. Better brush her teeth.

When she stepped out of the lift at the sixth floor, she was alone. It was impossible to keep still, so she stilt-walked. When she felt her armpits becoming damp, she flapped her arms like a chicken to help keep them dry. It was then she remembered that hotels had security cameras in the corridors. Glancing up, she saw there was one winking right at her. Imagining the security guards bent double in laughter, Perdita forced herself to stand still. Studying the motion of the lift by watching the glow of the digital display above it, she finally saw it approaching the sixth floor. The lift stopped, and Tony appeared.

'Sorry to have kept you waiting.' He gave an apologetic smile before swinging to his left.

More nervous now, Perdita reminded herself that he was doing her a favour. There was no harm in going to his room. Probably many business chats took place in hotel bedrooms.

As though Tony could read her mind, he said, 'The bar is no place for a serious chat.'

'No,' she agreed with a quiver in her voice.

'My room's the last on the right.'

As soon as Tony's door was opened by a swipe of his room card, Perdita's gaze was drawn to the massive bed. His television was larger than hers, and it was wall-mounted; the TV in her room took up space on the desk. And he had a sofa, whereas she had just an armchair.

'How about another top up?' He pointed to the small fridge under his desk. Before she could answer, he turned away saying, 'Sit down while I get sorted here.'

He opened the mini-bar and selected a couple of small bottles. 'Here.' He tossed her a small bottle of white wine.

But she didn't open it straight away. She felt like she'd already had enough, and perhaps he wouldn't notice if it remained on her lap for a while.

As he sat down beside her, he asked, 'So, what's the problem?'

'I've got an elderly client who had £25,000 to invest. I asked her if she was risk-averse but she wouldn't answer until I'd explained about the difference between high, medium and low-risk investments. Even though I advised against it for her, she chose a high-risk investment that specialised in the Far East.'

'Did you warn her that they were for long-term investments only? That, in the short term, she could lose money?'

'Yes. I warned her that she could lose a great deal of money, and then she asked if she could also make a great deal of money, and I agreed that it was possible. She said that she had all she needed to live on, and the investment wasn't for her future – she was old, after all – it was for her nephew. He would be inheriting it, and it could mature over the long-term. But I have this niggling feeling that I shouldn't have mentioned high-risk investments at all. I feel uneasy every time I think about it.'

'The emphasis is on the client making an informed decision, not on you deciding it for them. You can't make certain packages available to some clients and not to others. Now, if she'd said she was very risk-averse, then you could have only mentioned the low-risk products. But that isn't what happened. You didn't do anything wrong.' He took hold of her hand and started to stroke it. 'Stop worrying about it.'

The touch of his hand on hers, and the feel of his fingers caressing her skin, brought on fiery feelings, trails of unusual sensations skating through her.

'I'm so pleased I met you,' he said softly and slowly bent his head to kiss her.

She almost pulled away. Had there been garlic in his meal? Perdita had discovered advice given in a women's magazine she'd glanced at in her dentist's waiting room, and she'd practised kissing her hand when she'd got home. But this was the first opportunity to actually connect her lips to a man's. Were people meant to enjoy this? Intent on getting it right, she found it hard to relax.

So, when Tony broke off, she unscrewed her little wine bottle and took a swig. She felt out of her depth but then wasn't this what she'd been looking for: to finally have a proper relationship? And who better with than Tony, whom she'd fancied like mad ever since she'd first seen him? The kissing was bound to get better.

Before she realised it, the rest of the little bottle of wine was inside her, and she felt like she was floating. Tony suggested they move to the bed, and she thought it would be more comfortable kissing him while lying down. The room didn't feel safe, it was wobbling. But lying next to him wasn't much better; it was as though the bed had set sail.

Sometime later, they were lying on their backs under the duvet Perdita had pulled over her when Tony had removed her clothes. She was in a kind of stupor, not quite sure what had happened or what she felt about it.

'That was your first time, wasn't it?' Tony asked.

She put her hand on his. 'Yes.' She shut her eyes for a moment to see if that would ward off the dizziness.

He pulled away. 'Shit. Why didn't you tell me?'

Perdita frowned and turned to him. The room spun and then settled down again. 'What do you mean? Are you meant to give a number before you... with someone? You didn't tell me any number.'

'Don't play dumb.'

He was staring at her in the dimmed light and she didn't know what to think.

'Jesus, you're serious. It wasn't a joke.'

'Joke? Why would I joke about something like this?'

'Have you ever had a boyfriend?'

Perdita shook her head, carefully. It felt like a fragile egg.

'You are on the pill?'

'Why would I be on the pill?'

'Fuck.'

'What's wrong? Didn't you use... something?' Should she have asked him? She'd assumed, as he was in control, he knew what he was doing. What would she know about those kinds of things? And did that mean there might be... consequences?

'Fuck.'

'Was it your first time too?'

Tony stared at her. 'No. Of course not. Are you mad?'

Stung, she said, 'I thought perhaps you didn't know about these things either.'

'You are mad. Completely and utterly mad.'

'Next time? We can use something next time?' She wanted to appease him. If they hadn't done it right this time, they could ensure that they got it right the next time. Isn't that how these things worked?

Tony didn't answer. Then, a few minutes later, he said, 'I'm getting some shut-eye. I have a busy schedule tomorrow.'

The fact that Tony turned his back to her suggested he didn't want to speak anymore. He hadn't told her to go, so she didn't. She didn't think she was capable of moving anywhere. Perhaps they could continue the conversation in the morning?

This was not how it was meant to be, Perdita was sure. In romantic films, men usually held a woman after he'd made love to her. Was it that she hadn't known what to do, how to please him? She'd felt awkward and embarrassed and had let him get on with it since he had obviously known where to touch, where to put the... thing. With a few tears escaping her eyes, she shut them and willed for sleep.

In the morning, she awoke with a headache and felt sick. For a brief moment, she was disoriented and didn't know where she was. Then she remembered. She reached out for Tony but his side of the bed was empty. She squinted about the room expecting to find him. 'Tony?' There was no answer from the bathroom. He was gone, and she didn't belong here.

Scrambling into her clothes, stilt shoes in her hand, she walked sedately back to her room. After taking a couple of paracetamol, she showered and put on the sage-green dress that emphasised her curves – or so Carol had said. Grabbing her folder and a pen, Perdita hurried to the dining area that was laid out for breakfast to find she was probably the last to arrive. There were few people left at the tables and those that were glanced up as she came in. There was no one she recognised.

Opting for just toast and marmalade, Perdita ate it reluctantly, still feeling a little queasy. But the combination of toast and hot black coffee seemed to revive her, and she was just about ready to face another talk. That was, until she spied Tony stroll past the open doors with a red-haired woman she'd noticed him with in the past. At lunchtime, Perdita waited miserably, with a spare seat beside her, for Tony to join her. She'd only taken a few mouthfuls of her pasta when she saw him follow a blonde woman and sit at her table.

Initially, Perdita was affronted. Then it gradually dawned on her what a fool she'd been. Why had she believed that the love at first sight she'd witnessed in films could possibly have happened to her, Perdita Riley? The nausea she'd felt earlier returned, and she had to leave the table. It was all she could do to walk with her head held high and her tears held in check… until she reached the privacy of her room and an anguished sob escaped her lips. Having the man, to whom she'd given up her virginity, avoid her and ingratiate himself with other women, showing her just how stupid and naïve she'd been, was the absolutely most humiliating experience of her life.

Unable to contemplate remaining in the hotel while Tony was still around, Perdita packed her things. Using the programme to judge when everyone would be safely in the conference room, giving her a free exit, she made for the lift. Reception was deserted; it couldn't have worked out better. But, having stowed her case in her car boot, Perdita recalled she hadn't returned her key card. As she was going back in through the swing doors, Tony was on his way out, phone in hand.

Damn. Why hadn't she checked whose turn it was to take the podium? 'Tony…', she began frostily, expecting to tell him exactly what she thought of him.

But he tapped his phone as he whooshed past. 'Alien invasion.'

As if she would believe that one.

As soon as Perdita got home, she went to bed. Frank was delighted to see her, and she buried her face in his fur as he purred in her ear. Luke and Gavin had been feeding him while she'd been away, and she texted them to let them know she could take care of Frank that evening. She didn't want to see them or anybody else. She was going to hide away.

Shame overcame her. How could she have behaved like that? How could she have let Tony...? Why had she thought him such a great person when she hadn't even known him? And the experience hadn't even been pleasant. Was Tony laughing at her? Telling the other women about her? How could she ever face him at one of those conferences again? Perhaps, if she reverted to how she used to dress, he wouldn't recognise her?

By early evening, her throat hurt every time she swallowed, and her face and pillow were wet. Alcohol had clouded her judgement, and Tony had taken advantage of her. But she'd let him... Silent tears escaped the corners of her eyes.

Chapter 6

January

Perdita had had a very uneventful Christmas, still licking the emotional wounds from her disastrous encounter with Tony. But on New Year's Eve, she'd picked herself up, dusted herself down and had told herself that life went on and that there were many more bees in the world that weren't called Tony Crawley. Feeling heartened, Perdita would have celebrated with some wine but, bearing in mind she was a bit under the weather from a stomach upset, she thought she would give it a miss. In fact, since the boys were spending the evening at the gay club where they'd first met and wouldn't be coming home until the early hours, and other neighbours, Faith and Hope, were with their parents, Perdita just snuggled up in bed to watch TV.

The day after New Year's Day, she was due back at work and her radio alarm woke her, blaring out the tragic news of the earthquake that had hit Japan. Her eyes shot open. Those poor people losing lives and homes... And then she thought of Violet.

As she tugged on her work clothes, she felt that awful feeling again. Did stomach bugs go on and on like this? Her gut instincts whispered the answer, but Perdita did not want to listen to them; she didn't like what they were whispering. And she didn't like the word she'd thought of in Tony's hotel room: consequences.

However, with her head down the toilet bowl, she

knew she did have to admit there was definitely a problem. But, until she knew for sure, there was hope, wasn't there? She didn't want to go to work; she wanted to be alone and not have to pretend that everything was normal when it wasn't. But then, it wasn't a normal day anyway because of the earthquake.

Luckily, the snow that had been falling during her drive to the office wasn't settling and her tyres gripped the road without any apparent difficulty. Whether because of the earthquake or the weather, people had come in early as the car park was almost full.

In the office, the phones were already jangling, and her colleagues were jabbering into mouthpieces. On her monitor, as she took her share of the calls, she watched as share prices fell. It seemed that stock was in free fall. With the reporters widening the scope of their coverage on the significance of the earthquake for people in Japan and their businesses, it would not be long, Perdita guessed, before Violet knew.

It was as though the stock was Perdita's own as she clung on to the slim hope that it would all work out, that the devastation would not be as great as initially feared and that the aftermath would not be nearly so terrible. Unfortunately, there was nothing to suggest it wasn't every bit as damaging to the economy as she'd dreaded.

Many of her colleagues looked like they were going to take their lunch break at their desks instead of sticking to their usual habits. But when Perdita saw her boss, Mike, make for the executive floor to have his lunch at his usual time, she sneaked out to her car. She fired the engine and headed towards the anonymity of the closest superstore.

Inside ASDA, she headed to the pharmacy and found

what she wanted on a display shelf. As soon as she'd paid for a suitable kit, she scurried towards the ladies' toilets and locked herself in the first cubicle. Her hands were shaking as she opened the box. Inside were an instruction leaflet and a detector stick. The instructions were in tiny print.

Someone tried her door. Couldn't they see the engaged sign?

'Are you going to be long? I'm desperate,' a commanding female voice the other side of the door said.

'Erm. I'm not sure,' Perdita told her. 'What about the other loos?'

'Taken and out of order. Please hurry. You must have been in ages. You have to be first out.'

'I'll do my best. Only one more paragraph to go.'

'You're reading?' the woman said in a disbelieving tone.

'It's all right, just instructions. And I need to be in here to carry out those instructions. It will be quicker if you keep quiet so that I can concentrate.'

The woman huffed.

Lucky, Perdita thought, that the woman didn't puff as well or the door might come down just when Perdita was in the middle of her test. She opened the sterile packaging, did what the instructions told her to do and then operated the flush. 'Keep back, I'm coming out,' she warned. She didn't want the woman to collide with her stick so she held it aloft like a wand.

'Huh.' The sturdy woman waiting on the other side almost pushed Perdita out of the way to get in.

The re-opening of the same cubicle door coincided with time up, and they were the only two left in the room. Perdita scrutinized the strip. The woman approached, wanting to wash her hands, and Perdita hid the detector stick behind her, hoping the woman hadn't spotted the bright red lines in the display confirming the reality of her setback.

'If you don't want a child, you shouldn't play grown-up games,' the woman told her as she shook her hands above the sink and then headed for the dryer.

'The rules weren't explained to me properly,' Perdita countered. 'I had no instructions.'

The woman huffed again.

Back in her car, Perdita was having trouble breathing. Setback Number One was not happening to her.

Now those were the most comforting words she'd said to herself all day. She said them again. Setback Number One was not happening to her. How could it be? She wasn't ready. She wasn't married or engaged. Recalling her reproduction lessons in school, Perdita remembered that the nuns had talked about flowers and bees just like Violet Freestone had done.

She was a flower. There had been a bee, and then he'd flown away. It was a much more palatable way of looking at Setback Number One. Quite how soon after Most Humiliating Experience Number One pollination had actually occurred, Perdita wasn't sure because she didn't know how long it took for a seed to be formed. But she did know that this particular kind of seed took about nine months to germinate. Which would take her to sometime in August. It was still too hard to picture herself with a seedling, so she didn't. But what she did know, was that the seedling would not grow up an orphan like she had.

Thinking of Setback Number One was making Perdita's heart race and her breathing strained as though she was being crushed by… Tony on top of her. That presented a very unhelpful picture and she was almost wheezing as she fought for air. She shut her eyes and thought of a pretty flower. No, a beautiful brightly-coloured flower. And there was a breeze. It was waving in a gentle breeze. Which made it look happy. Then Perdita added a hillside with lots of grass to the picture and decided it was complete. There wasn't a bee in sight. And she began to feel better.

Chapter 7

March

Perdita was jerked back to the present as she realised they were now on the edge of Westbridge. Then Saul turned right, past The Dick Whittington pub, into Westbrook Lane. Soon, the Merc's wheels were crunching the stone chippings on the sweep of the drive. Clumps of yellow daffodils were starting to show along the edges.

Saul brought the car in line with the familiar stone porch of the double-fronted house and switched off the engine. 'I just have to call the office to tell them I'll be late back.'

She took a couple of deep breaths to centre her feelings and fight that ever-present nausea. With luck, Violet didn't blame her for the loss of her savings any more than Perdita blamed Violet for Setback Number One.

When Saul finished his call and opened the driver's door, Perdita opened the passenger door, and they stepped out in synchrony. Her heels began to sink. Tiptoeing clumsily, she headed towards the safety of the steps, grabbing one of the fat pillars as soon as she was within reach.

'Please wait here while I warn Violet,' Saul said once they were inside, and he entered the same room she'd sat in during her visits last year.

The smell of wood polish reminded her of the serenity she'd felt in the chapel of the Convent of the

Divine Heart of Jesus, attached to the orphanage. It was somewhere she'd felt close to her mother and had spent many hours in. But with her heart pumping at twice its normal capacity, Perdita didn't feel at all serene now. She swiped aside memories of the past and thought about what was to come.

She imagined that a guillotine had been erected in front of the disused fireplace and that a masked executioner would be waiting for her. As the door Saul had gone through opened, Perdita swung around.

'You may come in now.' Saul's face was unreadable. Was he the executioner?

Perdita went in. The pale-yellow walls and bright-yellow curtains were as before, but now there were nets at the windows and the floral sofa had gone. In its place was a bed. Violet sat in the large bay of the window in her armchair but she had a Zimmer frame in front of it and a table at her side laden with a child's trainer cup, tissues and a small brass hand-bell. An alarm pendant hung around her neck. Perdita knew from the drop of Violet's cheek, and the droop of her lip, that she'd suffered a stroke. When Perdita threw Saul a reproachful glance for not warning her, he just stared back accusingly.

Perdita went to crouch by Violet's side and gently touched her arm. 'I'm so very, very sorry.'

Violet gave a little nod as though to thank her, and her gaze became urgent. But Perdita could not understand why. Was it anger? She could understand if it was anger. But it didn't seem like it especially when Violet put her hand over Perdita's.

'Shall we talk in the kitchen?' Saul's lips were flattened into a grim line. It made her think of the executioner again.

The sun was streaming through the kitchen

windows, as though spotlighting the worktop piled high with dirty dishes and the cooker hob stacked with unwashed pans. She felt the crunch of food on the floor and heard a tacky sucking under her shoes as she approached the pine oblong table. The room smelt stale. It turned her queasy stomach, but there was a half-eaten packet of Rich Tea biscuits on the worktop that would relieve the queasiness.

As Saul was pulling out a chair to sit down, she lowered herself onto a chair opposite while throwing another glance towards the biscuits. If she didn't eat soon, she might be sick. 'When did it happen?'

'Two days after she found out. Late in the evening.'

Perdita felt wretched.

Saul held his head in his hands. He looked exhausted. Perdita had an urge to comfort him, but when he said, 'I want to discuss compensation,' the urge dissolved. The way he was watching her, his eyes full of blame and dislike, made her shrink inside.

'I have no money.' Perdita raised empty palms. Keep calm and unemotional, she told herself.

'Then I will sue you.'

'I could report you to the police for assault and abduction.'

'The courts would be sympathetic towards me. There would be mitigating circumstances.' He seemed confident of his ground.

'You cannot sue for a circumstance which could not have been foreseen,' Perdita replied, thinking of the earthquake that had caused the problem, hoping she was right.

'I could sue for malpractice.' Saul's voice held an unmistakable note of victory.

Could she rely on F&Z to give her legal assistance?

She felt sure they would be obliged to defend her. In any case, she'd done nothing wrong – even though it felt like she had.

'It is in your code of ethics,' Saul said, 'that an adviser should only recommend unit trust products if they consider such a product suitable for the client's needs. You invested my aunt's money in a high-risk unit trust, specialising in the Far East, that was expected to pay off only in the long-term. My aunt is in her seventies. She did not need to save for her old age; this already *is* her old age.'

'Your aunt particularly asked for a long-term investment with a high return so that you would have a greater inheritance.'

'I don't need an inheritance. I make enough money to support myself and more. Besides which, Violet only had her savings and nothing more to call her own.'

'She has this house.' It was in the paperwork Perdita had had to fill in, and Violet had signed it.

He gave an unpleasant laugh. 'No, she doesn't. The house passed to me when my parents died.'

'But she told me the house was hers...' Staggered, Perdita could not complete the sentence; now she understood the extent of Saul's fury.

'You could have invested in something safer – you didn't have to lump twenty-five thousand into the one hole-ridden basket!' he snapped. 'What was your incentive? Employee of the month for striking the most deals?'

Perdita sprang to her feet but quickly sat down again as it had made her feel dizzy. 'You're being unfair.' She'd never pushed for a sale if she'd thought a product was unsuitable. And she'd advised Violet to go with a low-risk unit trust. It had been Violet who'd badgered her into agreeing to the high-risk investment.

'Am I being unfair? Am I really?'

'Yes.' Perdita couldn't help her gaze flicking towards the Rich Tea biscuits. Hadn't prisoners, years ago, at least been offered bread and water? 'As I said, she did tell me the house was hers. And she said that she didn't need her savings – they were to be for you to inherit.'

'You expect me to believe that? And what about when she tried to call you? And you refused to take those calls? Was that fair?'

It had been such a struggle just to turn up to work after she'd taken that special test. When the calls had suddenly stopped, Perdita had found more excuses not to ring until it had become inappropriately late to do so. 'It was cowardly of me not to talk to Violet,' Perdita admitted. She felt sure he wouldn't want to know about the nights she'd lain awake, overwhelmed by guilt. 'If you were so unhappy about Violet's investment, why didn't you make a formal complaint?'

'Violet would not discuss it after the initial shock.' Saul frowned. 'Why do you keep looking behind me?' Saul twisted round. 'Are you judging me for the mess?'

Perdita licked her lips. Her mouth was dry. And her tummy was rumbling.

Saul caught the action and must have heard the gurgling. 'Were you looking at the biscuits?'

She nodded. 'Would you mind if I had a few? With some water? I haven't eaten since yesterday.'

Saul nodded and got what she wanted.

After a large gulp from a tall glass of water, Perdita began to eat. The first biscuit tasted wonderful. So wonderful, she wasn't sure whether to do the polite thing and offer one to Saul or just keep the rest to herself. In the end, she nudged the packet closer to the centre of the table but kept it within easy reach. It was up to Saul if he leaned across to grab one.

'Because of you,' Saul said, 'Violet suffered a stroke and lost her savings. She refused to let me get a full-time carer, at my own expense, and will only accept the help Social Services can provide on their stretched resources.' Seeming to sense Perdita's puzzlement over how Violet could refuse such a request when she couldn't speak, Saul said, 'Violet can print words on paper.' He pointed an accusing finger. 'It's your fault she's in this mess.'

'I could help out, after work or on weekends,' Perdita offered. 'I'd like to, really I would.' She didn't want him to know she'd lost her job and the sooner she found another to enable her to pay her rent the better. She was on her third biscuit and the nausea was receding.

Unblinking for a few moments, Saul said, 'She really needs someone with her all of the time–'

'What are you suggesting? That I give up my job to look after her?'

'Have you forgotten your job has already given *you* up?'

'How...?'

There was a glint of satisfaction in his eyes. 'I called your office this morning in a renewed effort to give my low opinion of you, and Mike Loader was happy to tell me you are no longer in their employ. And we all know what that means.'

'I kind of resigned yesterday – I said I couldn't do the work anymore – and he asked me to leave straight away. It's their policy apparently when someone's not happy in their job.' She felt cornered, and he must have known it; she wished she could wipe the smirk from his face.

'You expect me to believe you left of your own free will?'

They hadn't had to call security to get her to go, had they?

Saul must have noticed her hesitation. 'I didn't think so.'

'I did tell Mike that I couldn't do the work anymore. And,' she said hotly, 'I offered to help look after Violet, remember? It was my idea. But now you're using that offer as some kind of... retribution.'

'Don't be so melodramatic. I just honed your idea into something far more equivalent to what you owe.'

He'd deliberately led her into the trap, knowing the whole while she had no job. She pursed her lips and tilted her chin defiantly. 'What you are suggesting is utterly ridiculous. How would you expect me to live? I wouldn't even be able to pay my rent.' Perdita almost choked on the words – and the fourth biscuit. Thinking she should insist on leaving, she then recalled the lengths Saul had gone to getting her here. He would only haul her back.

A fleeting memory of a lesson at school fluttered into her mind. Historically, when men kidnapped women, didn't they have to marry them afterwards? She wondered whether there was some ancient law about it that was still in force today. A sudden image of dragging Saul to the altar, his ankle shackled to hers, with armed guards bringing up the rear, prodding him forward, pleased her immensely. Not that she'd have him, of course.

'Would you like to share whatever it is that seems to be amusing you?' Saul asked truculently. 'I can't imagine what you have to find funny in all of this.'

'I just remembered part of a history lesson.'

'Does it have some bearing on the matter?'

'I wouldn't know without seeking independent legal advice.'

'I could save you the trouble. I'm a solicitor.'

'I said, *independent*.'

He tightened his lips. 'We're digressing. And I've got to get back to work. Move in here – then you would have no expenses. And, as I have a holiday coming up, I shan't have to cancel it. It would be fair reparation to Violet, don't you think? Then I might be persuaded not to sue you – we've already established you contravened official guidelines.'

'You mean you have,' Perdita snapped, but worried over the point. She always was a worrier even when something wasn't her fault. Surely F&Z's legal department would deal with Saul if he were to sue despite her no longer being an employee and despite Violet having lied?

'If you feel unable to agree to my terms,' Saul warned, 'in addition to suing you, I'll take Violet's story to the *Bristol Post*. The human-interest angle would feed a journalist's appetite for a bad luck story. And you would be unemployable in the financial sector…'

Perdita didn't like the idea of her name being in the local paper. But, presumably, a journalist would have to verify facts before undertaking a defamation of her character. And there would be no damning facts to find as all the paperwork was in order. But did she want to risk it?

'They say Violet may well make a near-full recovery, given time and effort. Stay for a year and I won't sue – or I'll take the story to the paper.'

Perdita was almost totally convinced that Saul was bluffing, but his threats did still scare her. If she agreed to move in, she need not worry about them or the fuss that might ensue if he were to carry out his intimidation tactics. In fact, it was rather a good idea. 'Did the notion ever occur to you that, if you'd asked me very nicely, I might have agreed to move in anyway?' After all, she had Setback Number One and Setback

Number Two to consider.

He stared back with disbelief written all over his face.

Having no means of supporting herself had put her in a very weak position. Could she help herself while at the same time be helping Violet? Perdita had to consider the malaise she'd felt of late, the difficulty in getting herself out of bed in the mornings, her perpetual tiredness, the sudden bouts of nausea. Living with Violet meant she could create structure in her day and rest when Violet rested. It would be no hardship to look after Violet. Overwork, irregular meals and vomiting had kept Perdita skinny; she'd been losing, instead of gaining, weight.

She scrunched up the now empty biscuit packet and put it on the table and then drained her glass. Instead of feeling trapped, she saw possibilities – a safety net, a kind of rescue even though the rescuer didn't realise it. And if Saul thought he'd got the better of her... well, time would tell. 'I'll do it,' she said.

Saul's eyebrows shot up, and his eyes bulged. 'Well, er… let's tell Violet.'

Violet watched as Saul pulled up a chair next to her while Perdita sank onto the bed appearing weary. As Saul outlined the plan, Violet's spirits began to lift. It would do no good now to reveal her long medical history of high blood pressure or that she'd deliberately misled Perdita over the ownership of the house so that Violet could be considered suitable for that high-risk investment. If Perdita knew these things, she might decide not to move in after all, and Saul would think his aunt a very silly woman indeed with regard to her savings. That was why she'd tried so hard to warn Perdita that Saul might get in touch and to reassure her that it hadn't been her fault – as well as asking her to keep it secret about the house. But Perdita hadn't returned her calls.

If Perdita really had no job at present, as Saul just said, they would be giving her a year's break from the grind of everyday tail-chasing. Lots of things could happen in the space of a year, even with her stubborn and proud nephew. Neither had a clue of the trouble she'd gone to, to find a suitable wife for Saul. All those appointments she'd sought with various organisations until she'd found the right woman...

So far, Saul's dalliances hadn't amounted to even a hint of marriage. The only girl who'd got remotely close had been Teri and look how that had turned out! Violet had quickly seen that the girl was duplicitous, unprincipled, and a devious cow. Saul had learned about her true nature the hard way. Violet knew it had been a bad blow for him, and he'd avoided women after he and Teri broke up. Perhaps having Perdita here, and seeing his practice partner's baby that was due later this year, would shove Saul in the right direction. Violet wanted grandnephews and nieces before she died. Time, for her, was running out.

Sensing the animosity between Saul and Perdita, Violet thought it was just as well she couldn't speak. It let her off the hook.

'Well, what do you think, Violet?' Saul pressed. 'Will you have Perdita come and help you out?'

Was he mad? Of course she wanted Perdita to stay. Dimwit. She gave the biggest nod she could. If it all worked out, it would be £25,000 very well spent.

When Violet nodded in agreement, Saul smiled. But it was not a smile Perdita warmed to considering it was laced with triumph. To cap it all, he actually rubbed his hands together. He'd switched from being goggle-eyed in surprise at her agreeing to his terms to confident and smug in no time at all. Was this down to Violet's approval of the scheme – and, therefore, of his actions?

'Well,' he said, 'it seems you're moving in.' He stood up.

Perdita felt that pompous bubble of his must be burst; and she would do her best to be the one to grab that privilege. 'What guarantee will I have that once I've given up my flat, you won't throw me out the moment Violet can fend for herself?'

'My word.'

'Uh-uh. I don't know you.'

'You mean you don't trust me?'

She blinked in surprise. Did he think he deserved her trust?

'Okay,' Saul agreed, his palms held up in surrender. 'I'll draw up an Agreement. Twelve months to clear the debt.'

'I have little savings. Not enough to live on.'

'Do you really think I'm that gullible? You must have had a high income.'

'I'm not lying.' She didn't want to tell him that all her spare money had gone to repay that university loan from the orphanage's benefactors.

'All right. I'll cover the costs of keeping your car on the road. And give you pocket money on top. I'll even pay your National Insurance contributions.'

'There are other conditions.'

Saul laughed. 'I don't think you're in a position to...' Then he seemed to think better of what he was going to say. 'Go on then. What do you want?'

'I don't want to be the focus of malicious gossip in the village.'

'It's a town,' Saul snapped. 'It's got a town hall.'

As though he hadn't interrupted her, Perdita continued, 'Tell people I'm a friend who has offered to help out.' She'd no wish for wagging tongues – and being shunned over what had happened to Violet's savings. And when the... town... saw her ballooning out, ready for lift off, as they one day would, she guessed what ideas might get into their heads then.

'Some friend.'

She ignored the barb. 'And show me some respect. And I'd expect any visitors that come to the house to show me respect too.'

'Respect has to be earned. And I can't be held responsible for how others perceive you.'

'Yes, you can – it depends on what you tell them. And I shall respect *you* when you've earned it.' Hearing a sudden noise, Perdita flicked her gaze to Violet who was giving a lopsided chuckle.

'I'll be as polite as I can until you prove you are worthy of more.'

'Same for you,' Perdita retorted. Why did he think relationships were one-way streets? She might be inexperienced with men, but she'd garnered much from living in an orphanage. She looked forward to Saul realising, sometime in the future, that he should never have invited a stranger into his home; he was going to get rather more than he bargained for.

'Shall I show you where you'll be sleeping?' Saul asked.

She scowled. How long would that take? But she supposed it would be good to know that he wasn't planning to shove her under the stairs to sleep.

Chapter 8

Back at her flat that evening, Perdita was ready with copies of the Chinese takeaway menu when the boys came around. She'd been steeling herself to tell them the news about moving in with Violet. They'd brought beers, but she declined. She opted for apple juice and handed them tall glasses as they popped open two cans.

'How was your day?' Luke asked as he poured beer into his glass.

'Before I tell you about it, I need us to put the takeaway order in.' Perdita handed them copies of the menu. 'Sit.'

'Do we get doggie treats if we do as we're told?' Gavin asked.

'No, but you do get to hear an interesting story.'

When the order had been put through, she joined Gavin on the sofa. Luke had chosen the armchair he'd had that morning and was regarding her keenly, glass in hand.

'Now, I need you to stay calm because I think you might get overexcited and not listen.'

'We're listening,' Luke said.

Gavin nodded his agreement.

'This morning, I went out as you told me to. But it was a bad idea because I was kidnapped. But don't worry, I'm here now, and I'm safe.'

'We can see that you're here, and you're certainly safe with us. But what makes you think you were kidnapped?' Luke asked quietly.

'Because a man got hold of me, wouldn't let me go and dragged me to his car.' She'd decided the experience was worthy of the title, Most Humiliating Experience Number Three.

Luke catapulted to his feet, sloshing beer over his hand and onto his jeans. 'Have you been to the police? How did you manage to escape?'

'I haven't been to the police because, when he explained why he did it, I decided that I deserved it. And I didn't escape. He let me go.'

Luke sank back down, frowning. He placed his glass back on the table and found a tissue to dry his hand.

'Were you actually kidnapped today?' Gavin asked, taking a slurp from his glass. 'Or has losing your job upset your mental balance?'

She guessed that Gavin was trying to make everything into a joke. But she wasn't ready to be cheered up.

'Explain what happened,' Luke said. 'Then we'll have a better understanding of what you mean by the word "kidnap".'

She told them what had happened in the department store and, later, in the car park.

Luke looked at Gavin before saying, 'I believe we can confirm that is definitely called kidnapping. What kind of Neanderthal is he?'

Perdita was thinking that, if Saul were a Neanderthal, he was a very attractive one. And weren't Neanderthals the original cavemen? She wondered what his Ice Age cave would have looked like.

'Who was he? And what did he want?' Luke asked. 'Why did he let you go?'

'He's called Saul Hadley, and he's Violet Freestone's

nephew,' she said. 'He was very angry with me and wanted me to see Violet.' She described the state she'd found Violet in and how Violet had reacted to her presence. She decided that she would save Luke's question about why she was let go until later.

'Caveman blames you for Violet's stroke,' Luke said. 'But it doesn't sound as though she does.'

Perdita blinked at Luke's moniker for Saul – it was as though he'd read her mind about Ice Age caves. Come to think of it, Saul had referred to himself as a brute of a caveman, and she decided the nickname suited him well. She hoped Luke stuck with it. 'No, she doesn't seem to.' She shared the conversation she'd had with Saul finishing at the point where Saul demanded she move in with him and Violet.

Luke was breathing heavily. 'He is an absolute, utter bastard. We'll cancel the takeaway. Pay what we owe. And get you straight to the police. Who knows, there might be CCTV footage of him abducting you.'

'Please listen to the whole story before you get overexcited,' Perdita said. Then the doorbell rang. 'That'll be the food. I'm really hungry. And it's come at just the right point in my tale.' She headed to the door, pretending not to notice Luke and Gavin exchanging incredulous glances.

She spread out the containers on the coffee table and brought in pasta bowls, spoons to serve and chopsticks. Then she sat on the floor at the head of the table, leaving a side each for Luke and Gavin. Frank thought he'd been invited too, but Perdita whisked him up and shut him in the kitchen with some fishy biscuits. When she began to load her plate, Luke and Gavin got stuck in as well.

'I told Saul I'd do as he asked.' Perdita thought it best

to slip that in while Luke and Gavin were distracted by the food.

'I think,' Luke said, 'you need to tell us what you just said again as I don't think I could have possibly heard right.'

'I didn't hear right either,' Gavin said. 'But if it turns out we did hear right, we'll have to get you tested under the Mental Capacity Act.'

'I'm here now because Saul said I could go if I promised to come back, and look after Violet.' They gaped at her. 'I'm moving in with Saul and Violet.'

'Are you mad?' Gavin squeaked. 'They're complete strangers – and you did nothing wrong. Luke, we need the number of a psychiatrist.'

'Violet's not a complete stranger.'

'Caveman certainly is,' Luke countered as he picked another sweet and sour chicken ball and poured over some sauce. 'You know, we've always known you're a bit different to other girls, and that's fine, we are okay with different. But I don't think we appreciated quite how different you are. And it's a worry.'

'Mike confirmed I'd done everything correctly. Nevertheless, I feel like I have done wrong, and I need to make amends having seen Violet broken like that.'

'Violet's bad choice and bad luck are responsible,' Luke said. 'Not you. What kind of a man is he, dragging you out of the store and lying to all those people? You don't owe him anything. He owes you. There's no need for you to go there. You could sue.'

'Where would I get the money to do that? And what judge would look upon me sympathetically when he or she finds out what the root of the argument is about? Uh?' She busied herself picking up a few extra slices of marinated lamb.

'Why did you agree to his ridiculous terms?' Luke asked. 'I say that because I'm desperately hoping there's more to this than loopiness.'

'Because it suits me to. And I wasn't a complete pushover.' She repeated the conversation she'd had with Saul about wanting to be treated with respect and her thoughts on moving in.

'What do you mean by... ' Gavin asked when she finished, '...he should never have invited a stranger into his home? Do you intend to bump them off?'

'No, that would be illegal. Besides, I really like Violet. And I'm sure she really likes me. She looked delighted when we told her that I was going to move in with her.'

'You're a numpty,' Luke said.

'I have no job. It will solve my rent problem.' But not the problem of the loan. She would have to phone Sister Margaret about that.

'But you'd get another, easily,' Luke assured her.

Perdita waved her chopsticks at the boys. 'The passion isn't there anymore and employers would pick up on it.' She helped herself to some more lamb. So far, the boys hadn't tasted any of it. She put her chopsticks down; she had to tell them. 'Besides, I've been... pollinated.' Luke and Gavin's expressions were blank. Perdita examined her hand. 'Remember when you commented on my new clothes?'

'Y-es,' said Gavin.

Luke was looking into the middle distance with a slight furrow between his brows as though trying to recall something.

'Remember I told you the reason I'd bought new clothes was because Violet had said bees are attracted to beautiful brightly-coloured flowers?'

Luke's brow cleared. 'You're pregnant.'

'Pollinated sounds nicer,' she said. 'Gentler.'

Gavin gawped at her. 'Well, go and tell your GP you've been pollinated and see if she can make better sense of it than we could. You know, you're not doing a good job of convincing me that you're sane. And I'm not going to use that word. You are pregnant, Perdita, and you are going to have a baby.'

Perdita was finding it hard to breathe. 'I'm not... This isn't...' Unpleasant sensations were star-bursting their way through her body. And tears spilled from her eyes. Nevertheless, she wanted the boys to understand, so she tried again. 'What you said... Can't be happening to me... Not married... All alone.' She was drawing breath now like a croaky seal and worried the lamb would come back up and bleat at them.

'Gavin, what you said wasn't at all helpful,' Luke admonished, as he moved closer and put an arm around her shoulders. 'Perdita, can we take it that you're not exactly happy with the situation?'

She nodded, hiccupped, found a tissue, dabbed her face and blew her nose, avoiding Gavin's gaze.

'Is calling yourself pollinated a coping mechanism?' Luke asked.

'I don't know. All I do know is that what Gavin said is happening to me isn't happening to me.'

'I'm sorry,' Gavin said.

'Shall I come with you to your doctor to talk about it?' Luke offered.

Feeling much more centred now, she took a deep breath, and that made her feel better still. 'No need. All I had to do was show her the special stick I'd taken into the toilet with me to do the test, and she understood.' Feeling that the danger had passed, she mustered up some inner optimism and smiled at the boys through blurry eyes.

'Well,' Luke said, taking his arm back, 'we don't want to give you any more panic attacks, so we will use whatever terminology makes you feel most comfortable, won't we, Gavin?'

'I'm not sure that losing touch with reality is a good thing though,' Gavin commented. 'We know you're a bit different. I was just trying to help you be a bit more norm–'

'Perdita is a bit different, and it's something we love about her, isn't it?' Luke gave Gavin a hard stare.

'Absolutely,' Gavin said.

'Now tell us,' Luke encouraged, 'how you have come to be... pollinated.'

Gavin's eyes were close to popping out of his head. 'You don't have a boyfriend. How on earth did you manage it? You don't strike me as a one-night stand woman.'

'Oh, I'm not a one-night stand woman,' she said. 'But it was just the once.' Luke rolled his eyes. 'I didn't know it was only going to be the once. Men don't book the next session until after the first, do they? I understand that now.'

'Session?' Gavin exclaimed. 'It's not therapy.'

'Tell us what happened,' Luke urged.

She took a deep breath. 'It was at the last work conference. I bought the clothes especially for it because a man whom I had a crush on was going there. He'd never noticed me before. But this time he did. Straight away. I was waiting for him at the bar – it's where he always goes when he's down from his room after dropping off his luggage.'

'You were staking it out? The bar?' Luke asked.

'Yes.' She shifted uncomfortably. 'He told me I was beautiful, and he couldn't understand why he'd missed noticing someone as beautiful as me.'

'You are beautiful,' Gavin said. 'We could have told you that. You don't have to go and sha–'

'What then?' Luke asked.

'He spent all evening with me.' She couldn't meet their gaze. 'And then I spent all night with him.' Scrunching her face in embarrassment, she added, 'But he was upset with me. In the morning, he'd already left. When I went down to breakfast, he was chatting to another woman. And at lunch time, he sat with a second woman. He didn't even glance my way.'

'How did someone as sweet as you upset him? Did you laugh at the size of him? Rubbish his technique? Tell him it was over too soon?' Gavin asked.

Feeling a fiery heat in her face, she suspected she looked like a bottle of tomato ketchup. 'I didn't tell him my number.'

'Your... number? Phone number?' Gavin asked. 'If you refused to give him your mobile number then of course there wouldn't be a second "session". How could there be?'

She shook her head. 'He told me off afterwards for not telling him that he was my first... but he didn't tell me whatever number I was.'

Luke rubbed his jaw with his hand and only briefly glanced at Gavin. 'You were a virgin? And he didn't like it?' Luke asked.

'No. He didn't.'

'Perdita,' Luke said, 'he's a creep. He just used you.'

'I know.'

'Next time,' Gavin said, 'let's hope it's with a man who appreciates the gift of virginity.'

'What are you talking about? She can't be a virgin again,' Luke snapped. 'Although, next time, I too hope it will be with someone who appreciates you, Perdita. Loves you even.'

'How did a creep like him get you preg– pollinated?' Gavin asked.

'Yes,' Luke said, 'what happened about the... er... pollen?'

'He thought I was on the pill, and I thought he was using... something.'

Luke shielded his eyes with his hands for a moment.

'It's called a condom, Perdita.' Gavin was shaking his head.

She winced.

When Luke glanced up again, he was wearing an expression of disbelief. 'You didn't think to check? Didn't you feel that he wasn't wearing one?'

'How is it meant to feel?' Perdita knit her brows with the effort of trying to recollect how it had felt when Tony had entered her. But all she could recall was the shock of having something plunged into that private place and how bewildered she'd felt right up to the finale of uncomfortable piston thrusts. All else seemed to have escaped her notice.

Gavin said, 'You didn't touch him, did you?'

'Touch him? Well, of course I touched him.'

'Down below,' Luke said. 'Did you hold him, touch his private parts?'

'Of course not!' Then, more softly, she said, 'Was I meant to?' The stunned expressions on both their faces told her the answer. 'I haven't done it before. I wasn't expecting to do it, and I wish so much that I hadn't,' she wailed. 'And now I find I didn't even do it right.'

Luke and Gavin shifted closer and put brotherly

arms around her. 'Didn't you have any sex education?' Gavin asked.

'Yes,' she said, nodding enthusiastically, 'I know all about stamens, pollen, stigmas, pistils and ovules.' She plucked some more lamb from the dish and then boldly picked up the container and scraped the remainder into her bowl. Luke and Gavin had hardly touched their food.

'I mean human sexual education,' Gavin said.

'Oh. Kind of. In biology, we were told to read the section on sexual reproduction ourselves.'

'Did you?' Luke asked.

'Yes. I also know all about the sperm, the ovum, fertilisation and the embryo.'

'It sounds purely from a scientific point of view.'

'In our school,' Gavin commented, 'we had bananas–'

'Our school was more into oranges,' Perdita said. 'More vitamin C I think.'

'That's not what I–'

'No practical information was given, was it?' Luke said as he raised his eyebrows at Gavin. 'It couldn't have been.'

Miserably, she shook her head. Catholic education clearly had drawbacks.

'What are you going to do?' Luke asked.

'Practise?'

'I meant,' Luke added firmly, raising an exasperated gaze to the ceiling, 'about the... pollination.'

'More to the point, what's he, the man you, erm, with... going to do?' Gavin asked.

'I don't know.'

'You have told him?' Luke asked.

'No.' She laughed awkwardly. 'He wouldn't be interested. Obviously, he's the love 'em and leave 'em kind. I... I'd seen him with lots of women at these conferences, but I didn't see him kissing any of them. But then he didn't kiss me in public either. How was I to know he got up to... things... with them?' Perdita paused to frown at the boys. 'You know, that's really boosting my confidence, you guys looking up to the ceiling like that. I know I've been an idiot, but there's no need to rub it in.' They had the grace to look chastened. 'Anyway, I don't want Tony to know. He knew there'd been a risk of pollination because neither of us used... anything.'

'So, we're the only ones who know?' Luke asked tentatively.

'Uh-uh. By Monday, the whole office might know.'

Luke sighed. 'It feels like we have to prise every bit of information out of you. It's hard work. Can you just tell us – simply, mind – in a way that we will understand how come the *whole* office might know by Monday?'

'Only if you carry on eating. The food's getting cold.'

'What about you?' Luke asked. 'Aren't you having any more?'

'That's okay,' she said quickly. 'I'm done.'

Gavin tapped the side of the empty lamb container with his chopsticks. 'Only because there is none of this left. What was it?'

'Oh, it wasn't very good.' She picked up a prawn cracker and then another.

'So, you thought you'd protect us from eating substandard food by gobbling it all up?' Luke asked.

Luke had summed up what she'd wanted to say admirably. She nodded.

'Pull the other one, Perdita,' Luke said.

Abashed, she said, 'Sorry, guys. I just couldn't resist it, and you weren't eating. Now come on, eat up while

I explain.' She didn't mind what they ate now. The lamb had been absolutely scrumptious. How come she'd not realised before how great it tasted?

As they helped themselves to more food, her thoughts flew back to her final ten minutes at the office and landed on her conversation with Lucy after Mike had said it was best she left immediately.

'I was packing the box Lucy had given me with all my things when Lucy said she wanted to wish me luck. With...' Perdita pointed to her belly. 'Apparently, she'd heard me being sick in the toilet a few times, and she didn't believe me when I said I'd had an upset stomach. She seemed quite concerned, but when she asked about who the father was, I knew I just had to get away. She guessed I was on my own, and I asked her not to tell anyone. She promised not to, but I don't know if she will keep that promise.'

'Could Lucy find out who the father is from the other people who were at the conference if she starts asking them questions?' Luke asked.

'They might guess who the father is if she were to mention it although we weren't seen leaving the bar together, and I pretended that I left the conference early because I had a migraine. But if they guess then Tony might find out.'

'Does Caveman know?' Luke asked.

'That's just it, he didn't ask a single personal question about me. That's what I meant when I said he shouldn't have invited a stranger into his home.'

'You didn't tell him?' Luke was incredulous.

'Would you if he'd been so heavy-handed with you?'

'Depends on what he looks like,' Gavin commented. 'What does he look like?'

Wistfully, she said, 'He's absolutely gorgeous. The

most attractive man I have ever met.'

'More attractive than this Tony guy?' Gavin asked.

'Yes,' she said dreamily and thought again of the time when she was in the back of the Merc with Saul. Each time she recalled the scene, she remembered that small moment of indecision before Saul told her to get into the front passenger seat. What would his kiss have felt like had he given in to temptation?

'How can you say that,' Luke demanded, 'when he's been such a bastard?'

'Mm?'

'I said, how can you say he's gorgeous when he's been such a bastard?'

'Oh. Well, just because he's easy on the eye, it doesn't mean I like his personality. That definitely needs some work.'

'Perdita,' Luke said, 'you don't have some mad idea of changing him? Men like that don't change.'

'But he's not always like that. He's lovely towards Violet. She can't fault him. He and I just got off on the wrong foot. And I hope to make him see that.'

'Luke's right. Cavemen don't have it in them to change,' Gavin warned. 'It's not part of their genetic make-up. But I'd certainly like to meet him. Especially if he's as gorgeous as you say.'

'Hey,' Luke said. 'You're with me. Aren't I gorgeous enough for you?' He flexed his toned biceps.

Grinning, Gavin gave a sexy wink. 'You are one fit guy. But one can do a spot of window shopping without buying. And since I've never known Perdita to be involved with any man it's quite something to be told in one evening that there are two men in her life. The first man's got her... pollinated, and the second one has demanded she move in with him. Aren't you curious?'

Then Gavin turned to her. 'There isn't a third man in your life that you've been keeping quiet about?'

What did he take her for? 'No!'

Luke thought for a moment and then said, in a very serious tone, 'Perdita, we're the nearest you've got to brothers. I think that we should help you move in so that Caveman sees that you are not unprotected, that you have big strong men who will look out for you.'

'That's it!' Gavin said. 'We can tell him that if he messes with you, he will have to mess with us too. And he'd be welcome to. Any time.'

'Strictly no flirting? He wouldn't take you seriously as my protectors if you do.' The possibility that Saul might think that either Luke or Gavin was her boyfriend sent a tiny thrill through her. How would Caveman Saul react?

Chapter 9

Luke and Gavin were fantastic: they'd spent time on Saturday going to supermarkets, greengrocers and off licences in search of strong cardboard boxes while she'd sorted through her things assigning some non-breakables to bin liners or large carrier bags. By Sunday morning, Perdita was ready to load her car. After her first trip down the stairs with a bag of bedding, she knocked on Luke and Gavin's door.

'Ready?' she asked as Luke's head appeared.

'Yes. Gavin called the big boss woman yesterday to ask if he could borrow one of the company cars. We could probably do it in one go, with three cars loaded up.'

'You mean two cars and a hearse?'

'Yes. And if Caveman gets uppity with you, we could offer him a ride to the graveyard. Bet that would shut him up.'

Just then, Perdita heard the sound of a car's engine. Glancing out of the glazed entrance doors, she watched as the gleaming hearse pulled up with Gavin at the wheel. Then Luke emerged from his flat dangling his own car keys wearing one of his tight white T-shirts with green cotton shorts. Perhaps she should have swapped her grey baggy top and loose-fitting jeans for something more flattering?

The entrance door to the flats opened, and Gavin joined them. 'Ready then?' He was wearing chinos and an open-necked shirt. Perdita felt dowdy. She wished she could go back upstairs and change. She felt at a definite disadvantage.

'Just say which things are fragile, and leave the rest to us,' Luke said. 'Because you're fragile too.'

'That's right,' Gavin agreed. 'You're not to do any lifting or carrying.'

'Hey, I'm fine, I'm–'

'No, you're not.' Gavin grinned. 'You look pasty. Done in.'

She'd spent half the night crying – having to leave hadn't really sunk in until most of her things had been packed, and she felt skittish about moving in with Saul and Violet. The bravado she'd felt on Friday had done a runner, and she didn't know whether she'd find it again.

Faith from the other downstairs flat came out. 'I'd like to wish you luck. Do you need some extra help?'

'No,' Perdita said firmly. 'It's all under control, thanks.' Faith's shoulders relaxed with what looked like relief. Faith's sister, Hope, had been ill for years, and Faith took care of her in addition to working full-time.

Faith put out her arms and gave Perdita a hug. 'Best of luck now from both of us – Hope's still asleep.'

'Thanks.'

Very quickly, all three cars were filled. Frank's cat box was secured with the front passenger seat-belt, and he meowed piteously while reaching with a paw through the bars of the hinged door. Then he began to headbutt it. 'There, there,' Perdita whispered reassuringly while stroking his fur through the bars. 'We aren't going to see the vet. He's had your bits, and there's nothing more to worry about.' But she was worried. Very worried. And if it didn't work out, she'd have nowhere else to go…

She started the engine of her blue Renault and led the way with Luke driving behind her in his red Ford and Gavin behind Luke. As they drove through Clifton, Perdita noticed, in the rear-view mirror, a couple of old men respectfully remove their caps and then stare uncomprehendingly as they saw that the hearse was not carrying a wreath-laden coffin but her bagged and boxed possessions. Then they were driving past Clifton Down to the suspension bridge where they would cross the River Avon and head towards Westbridge.

Later, turning into the gravelled driveway, Perdita saw Saul's silver Merc. It stood bang-opposite the front door. Had he parked at the extreme corner of the driveway, there was a chance that all three cars could have at least driven beyond the property boundary. Just as she decided to get out and find him, he was there on the steps, in denim jeans and a red polo shirt, looking down at her.

Then Luke was running past her Renault. He bounded up the steps, presumably introduced himself and then, the traitor, he was shaking hands with Saul. What had happened to solidarity? What had happened to nick-naming Saul Caveman and threatening to take him to the cemetery if he messed her around? Male hormones. Perdita didn't think she would ever get to grips with them. Saul popped back inside the house only to reappear straight after with keys in his hand. Luke gave her the thumbs-up sign.

With the Merc moved forward and tightly parked by the bushes that shielded the property from Westbrook Lane, there was plenty of room for the extra cars.

When she got out, Saul said, 'Is it your funeral or

mine?' as he nodded towards Gavin and the hearse which was pulling into view, blocking the entrance.

Perdita sniffed at his quip. Gavin got out and was approaching where she stood with Luke and Saul. She introduced them. 'Well, you've already met Luke. This is Gavin. Gavin, this is Saul.'

'Good morning,' Saul said. 'Have you brought the hearse on the off-chance it might be needed? Who's going to be the victim?'

'Look, mate,' Luke warned. 'You need to know that Perdita is not alone.'

'I can count,' Saul said.

'What I mean is, if you mess with her, you mess with us.'

'That sounds rather like a threat to me. You'd better be careful.'

'And that,' Gavin snarled, 'sounds like a threat to me and you had better be careful.'

'Boys!' Perdita snapped. 'There's work to be done.'

'Go on then,' Saul said mildly to Luke and Gavin.

'I can count too,' Perdita said. 'And there are three men here.' She looked pointedly at Saul.

He gave a brief snort. 'I've got work to do.' Taking the steps two at a time, he disappeared into the house.

What an arrogant, supercilious, pompous...

'Well,' Luke said, 'since Caveman isn't coming out to play, let's get on with the job.'

'It's the room at the top of the house. The attic room actually.'

Luke frowned. 'How many flights is that?'

'That will be my problem when the time comes,' she hissed, worrying they might be overheard. She doubted the enemy would be far away.

'Well?' Luke said, 'Are you going to show us the way

or stand there daydreaming all morning? You won't be very happy if we put all your stuff into Caveman's room.'

Immediately, she had a mental picture of lying in Saul's bed; and she wasn't alone. She pushed the unsettling image aside. She did not feel at all lovey-dovey towards Caveman Saul and she was mourning the loss of her flat which was down to him. She'd not expected to feel this bad about it, but it had been her first very own home. Her only proper home.

'Perdita?' Luke said. 'Do not go gooey-eyed over Caveman. Even though he'd be a tremendous catch.' Luke shot a look at Gavin. 'Did you see those muscles rippling in his arms as he walked? And that broad back and tight arse?'

Dragging her thoughts back to the here and now, Perdita spat, 'I wasn't going gooey-eyed over Caveman and you promised not to flirt with him.'

'I'm not but–'

'You'd like to,' Gavin finished understandingly. 'I think we'd both like to.'

'I would too,' Perdita admitted in a weak voice, 'but only if he were a much nicer person.'

Luke and Gavin turned incredulous eyes towards her.

'I've come to the conclusion,' Luke said, 'that we really don't know you very well. First you liked this Tony guy without realising what a bastard he is, and now you're after Caveman. What about his awful treatment of you? Does that not ring warning bells?'

'I looked up that number. I'm saving it until it's needed,' Gavin warned.

Perdita threw him a venomous glance. 'He was protecting Violet's interests. He cares about her. But it doesn't mean I like his character, does it? That's what you guys were just doing, admiring his body but not his personality. And, right now, as a person, he's most unappealing.'

Luke sighed. 'Take us to your room. Now.'

'Yes, sir.' Perdita saluted. 'Then I'll come straight back down to make sure you don't take up the boxes that are to go into the garage.' She'd marked them with her red highlighter pen. Saul had assured her that the garage was free from damp.

The boys got stuck in as though doing a work-out. Up and down they went without a pause. The pile of boxes on the gravel destined for the garage grew – the boys were going to move them last – and the cars emptied rapidly.

When they were done, Luke handed Perdita and Gavin a bottle of water each and drank from a third himself. 'Mustn't get dehydrated,' he said. 'You're still looking peaky,' he added, regarding Perdita thoughtfully. 'You know, flowers do need plenty of water and fertiliser especially–'

'I know, I get the message,' Perdita cut in.

'Sh,' Gavin warned. 'Caveman alert.'

The crunching steps got louder, and Perdita turned.

'All done? I'd like to take my car out.' Saul jingled his keys.

'Yes, we're done,' Luke said. 'But before we leave, we want you to understand that we are Perdita's protectors.'

'Perdita's virtue is perfectly safe with me,' Saul said smoothly.

'Good,' Gavin said. 'It doesn't need any more poundings.'

Perdita's jaw slackened.

Luke laughed, Perdita guessed, to cover up as he

draped his arm over Gavin's shoulder. 'What Gavin means is we just don't want her sweet nature to be taken advantage of. We're protective of her just like you are with that aunt of yours.'

'Sweet nature...?' Saul repeated.

Perdita was about to protest but then realised he'd only had Friday to judge her on – sweet mode had been disabled during the time she'd spent with him. She decided it was best to retrieve the last box from her car now, while the boys were still here, since Saul was in such a sour mood. Having won the fight, he should have been jolly and friendly; a good sport. It made her despise him.

Reaching into the Renault, she unbuckled the seat belt and grabbed the cat box. It was heavy, and she rested it on the ground. Frank kept trying to dig his way out, and his whiskers were quivering as he sniffed the air. Plus, he was making a fair racket. Perdita tried to soothe him.

'What the...?' Saul exclaimed.

'May I introduce you to Frank?' Luke said.

With his hands on his hips, Saul said, 'What's it doing here?'

'Didn't she tell you?' Luke said in mock innocence, 'that she came with *responsibilities*?'

Perdita gasped – was Luke referring to more than one responsibility?

Saul spluttered, 'You can't bring a cat here.'

'Erm...' Perdita glanced at Frank as he tried to chew the bars and then met Saul's gaze with maximum defiance. 'I already have.'

'We need to shoot off now, Perdita. Let us know how things go,' Luke said. 'Any problems and we'll come back.'

That should keep Saul well-behaved. 'Thanks.'

Each of the boys gave her a big hug and then waved as they walked back to the cars. They ignored Saul.

'This wasn't part of the agreement.' Saul pointed at the cat box. His gaze was locked on hers, challenging.

'He's with me, and you did not forbid me to bring a pet.' She glared at him.

'You'll have to find somewhere else for it.'

'There is nowhere else. This is my home now. He stays.'

'Why can't your parents have him?'

'Because they're dead.' Perdita picked up the cat carrier and started to walk.

'I'm sorry, I didn't know,' Saul said.

As Perdita turned, she saw his hands drop from his hips to hang loosely by his sides, his car keys dangling from a finger he'd hooked through a metal hoop. She fixed him with a burning gaze. 'What would you have said if it was a husband I'd brought instead of a cat?'

Saul lifted his head sharply. 'But you're not married?'

'No.'

He put his keys in his pockets and eyed her keenly. 'Aren't you curious as to whether I'm married?'

'No.'

'I'm sorry I dragged you here.'

Looking him in the eye, Perdita said, 'Really? A bit late for regrets now.'

'Yes, but I am sorry. It was the best option for Violet.' The unexpected softness in his voice confused her. 'Your cat can sleep in the garage. There's a window that can be left open, so he can get in and out.'

'No,' she said rebelliously. 'At least, not until I can be sure he won't run away. He can stay upstairs with me. He's excellent at using a litter tray. I'll put it in the en suite.'

As Saul turned towards his car, he stopped and looked at her again, sharply. 'Is there anything else I should know?'

She almost began to laugh hysterically but quashed the bitter bubbles of mirth before they could grow and pop. 'You should have asked that question before you made me come here, made me give up my flat, my home. You'll have to take me as I am now.'

Saul nodded. 'Ditto.' His tone was hard.

As soon as Perdita had lumbered upstairs with Frank, she started to unpack. When her stomach rumblings were powerful enough to register on the Richter scale of seismological activity, she made her way downstairs. Violet was alone in what was now her bedroom, and it became apparent that Saul had not returned. Perdita laid out a cold spread using what she could find in the fridge, which wasn't at all impressive, and hoped bread and cheese and a couple of tomatoes were not indicators of how Violet and Saul usually ate.

Just as they were finishing, Perdita heard the front door open and close, and then Saul appeared carrying three pizzas. He took in the scene and said they could have them in the evening. Perdita glanced at Violet; they'd eaten all the bread and all the cheese. And both tomatoes.

'I think I saw a tin of soup in the cupboard,' Perdita said. Why go to a supermarket and only come home with three pizzas?

It was as though she'd spoken aloud as Saul said, 'Oh. I've been in the office and just grabbed these on the way home. I should have…'

Yes, you should have, Perdita thought. He could at least have made sure there was food in the house, gone to some effort before her arrival.

'The soup will be fine,' Saul said. 'I didn't think. Tail-chasing… makes you less efficient.'

Was that meant to be an apology? 'Would you like me to go shopping tomorrow?' She wasn't going to offer to heat up his soup. She was here to look after Violet and that she had done.

But Saul didn't expect her to. He'd already found a small saucepan, the opener and the can. She wasn't sure whether to remain seated at the table with Violet, to start clearing up or to excuse herself to continue sorting her room out and reassuring Frank. She'd shut him in the en suite in case stress led to an accident.

'Thank you for getting Violet lunch. I appreciate you taking the initiative.'

Was this praise? Gratitude? 'No problem,' she snapped. Wasn't she now the house slave?

'How's it going upstairs?' Saul asked.

Why did he want to know? Was he gauging how soon he could fit the yoke and get her to work? She wasn't an ox. 'I should be finished late afternoon.'

'There's a TV in the second living room, opposite where Violet's sleeping.'

Perdita tilted her head, expecting him to say more. Was he going to list the location of all the appliances in the house?

'Feel free to make use of it.'

Was this his way of saying the second living room would be hers to use while he and Violet would watch the TV in Violet's room? 'Does anyone else use it?'

'Not at the moment.'

So, she would be relegated to servants' quarters. A pat of her hand made her turn towards Violet who was pointing between the two of them. 'I can watch TV with you?'

Violet nodded and gave a wonky smile.

Perdita threw Saul a triumphant look, and he reddened.

'What I meant was, you can have your own space, you don't have to miss–'

'There's catch up TV,' Perdita reminded, 'if there's something I really want to see.'

'I think you misunderstood–'

'You were being kind? I'm sorry, I hadn't noticed.' Then Perdita felt mean as Saul directed wounded eyes towards her. As she was about to apologise, she saw his jaw clench, and she changed her mind. She mustn't forget he was the enemy.

By the time Saul called her down to eat pizza, she'd tamed the chaos in her room and found homes for almost everything. And, because Frank was scratching at the carpet by the door to the stairs to do a spot of exploring, she'd had to shut him in the en suite again.

There were three different kinds of pizza: pepperoni, margherita and vegetable. Saul was expertly slicing them with a pizza wheel. 'I didn't know what you liked. So I played safe and got a selection,' Saul explained.

Trying to make up for earlier, since they were going to have to rub along somehow, she said, 'Thank you. I like them all.'

Saul saw to Violet's every need. Was this a discreet way of training Perdita to help Violet when he wasn't around? If so, Perdita was impressed by both his tact and attentiveness. But what if the mellow fuzz that started to grow as she watched Saul engage with Violet was false, just like it had been with Tony?

She was so deep in her thoughts that when Saul spoke to her, she jumped. Her hand jumped too and the pizza piece she'd been holding flicked over her shoulder and onto the floor. 'Oh, sorry.' She scrambled to clear it up. When she sat down again, Saul pushed the serving plate towards her and, guiltily, she took another slice, regretting the waste of the previous one. 'You were saying?'

'I'd like you to come to my study at eight o'clock tomorrow morning so that we can discuss your role in more detail. I don't expect you to start helping out until then. You can have the evening to yourself.'

Did he want her out of the way? She couldn't tell, but she thought it would have been kind if he'd invited her to spend the evening with him and Violet considering she was among strangers and he'd forced her out of her home. She finished her last mouthful. 'I'll go then, if I'm not needed,' she said, feeling unwelcome and alone.

Chapter 10

The next day, Perdita breakfasted in her room from her stash of Rich Tea and her drinking bottle she'd filled the night before. Now she was taking in the green expanse of the garden from her attic window while stroking Frank's head as he sat on her lap. He sauntered closer to her face and yawned, displaying his sharp teeth and ridged palate. Perdita turned her head away as a whiff of fishy breath came towards her – it made her stomach lurch. Ugh. Now he was purring, almost into her mouth, while kneading her breasts – and it hurt. Gently, she released his claws from her jumper and turned him to face the window. But now Frank's bottom was facing her, and his tail was swishing her cheek. Perdita pressed on his hind quarters, and he settled. And so did her stomach.

Scanning the garden below her, Perdita thought her new home was a lovely setting for bringing up a seedling. But she was unlikely to be here long enough for that. She forced herself to picture a more urban lifestyle – where there were buildings, shops, cars and buses to be seen from her bedroom window instead of trees, shrubs, grass and daffodils. But having to face the future in an unknown place without support was a daunting prospect. She felt suddenly nauseous and had to push the unsettling thought from her mind.

Yesterday, she'd taken her empty boxes to the garage. The bespoke floor to ceiling wardrobes and shelving that followed the line of the eaves held all her spare bedding, clothes, shoes and many other things. There was a cupboard in the en suite shower room where she'd put all her makeup and toiletries. She had the whole of the attic space to herself and the floor area was considerable.

Checking her watch, Perdita discovered it was time to go to Saul's study which was along a small corridor to the right of the kitchen.

The door to the study was ajar. Tapping away at his laptop, Saul only acknowledged her presence with a lift of a finger. She sat on a green armchair opposite and took in the walls lined with what looked like heavy-duty law books.

When Saul finally glanced up, Perdita gave him a forced smile. He didn't return it. Prat. Couldn't he try to make the best of things? Otherwise the next twelve months would become intolerable.

'The carer will come around nine,' Saul said. 'She'll get Violet up. Someone also comes in the evening to help prepare Violet for bed. So, there is no need to help her with personal care. I've taken tea and toast to her already and will every day – except when I'm away on holiday. And there's a gardener, Jim, who keeps things neat outside. A cleaner comes in weekly. Although she's been off sick, she's due back soon. I'd like you to keep the house tidy and superficially clean. And to shop, cook and keep Violet company. Help her with her exercises – the physio and speech and language therapists can teach you what to do when they visit. The housekeeping money is on the worktop in the kitchen in an envelope – I'll need receipts for every transaction.' He fixed her with a penetrating stare.

Perdita pulled her brows together and stared back;

she was not a thief. He'd been so unfair to her. With a quivering voice, she said, 'I'm calling you out. You're a bully.'

As though she'd slapped him, Saul seemed dazed and lost for words.

'I'm not an insect to be squashed every time you see me, I'm a person with feelings. And you just keep trampling on them. You got what you wanted, I'm here. You won the battle. But you're not a gracious winner.' When Saul broke the stare (goal to Perdita), she said, 'You're assuming I can cook. Is that because you expect a woman to be born with a mastery of culinary skills or because you have faith in my versatility?'

'Can you cook?' he snapped.

'You mean in an oven rather than a microwave?' She injected a dash of awe as though the thought of using a traditional oven was a shock to her. Of course, she could cook; she was a dab hand at it. While at uni, the students she lived with shared the cooking, and she was used to preparing meals and baking cakes. And she'd often cooked for Luke and Gavin and Faith and Hope. She'd loved entertaining and the family atmosphere it had brought to her lonely flat. But why let Saul know?

He looked concerned. 'I thought...'

'Yes?' Would he admit to stereotyping? Sexist attitudes? Was he a caveman through and through?

'Never mind.' He passed her a sheet of A4 paper. 'Here's the Agreement. Read it, and we'll sign it tonight.'

Perdita saluted. 'Yes, sir.'

Saul paused gathering what he needed from the Davenport desk but then quickened his pace, grabbing at various papers as though he was desperate to leave. Having shut the lid of his laptop, he loped out.

Perdita stayed. After a short while, she began to talk

in a very low pitch, but by no means lowered volume, to the empty chair opposite – she'd done some drama in school and knew how to put on voices. 'Well, Perdita, I do hope you enjoy your stay here – there's no reason why we can't be friendly and put our differences behind us. Do you have anything you'd like to say?'

Replying in a saccharine voice, Perdita said, 'I'd like to thank you for being so warm and welcoming, treating me as though I'm one of the family. It was so kind of you to make a special effort in helping me settle in yesterday, getting my things upstairs and reassuring me there would be no further animosity between us. Tell me, how did you come to be such a considerate and caring man?'

'I gather I inherited those characteristics from my mother.' The deep wry response came from behind Perdita.

Whirling around, embarrassment burned her cheeks.

'I see you have a sense of dramatics. Is that how you managed to get your sales?'

It was like locking horns as they stared at each other. 'There you go, bullying again.'

Saul's eyes blazed for a moment, and then the fire went out as though she'd thrown the contents of an ice bucket at him. 'You're absolutely right. I have been a bully, and I have trampled on your feelings. I should have been kinder and more welcoming to you yesterday. I'll try to do better.' He picked up an envelope from his desk and tapped it against his hand. His eyes had softened with remorse. 'It's been hard lately and... the thought of losing Violet... I haven't always acted rationally, and you've been caught up in my anguish. I'm not usually so unkind.'

He left without another glance in her direction. A

short while later, she heard him exit the house and the sound of a car engine. And she could breathe again.

After consulting Violet about her proposed menu, Perdita left her listening to the radio and set off to find the shops. Westbridge town proper began at The Dick Whittington pub that was at the corner of Westbrook Lane and High Street, a narrow climbing road that wended to the right as the shops came into view. D. Murphy Family Butcher was about half-way along High Street.

The butcher was around thirty or so with carrot-coloured hair, pale skin and freckles everywhere, including on his hands. He was wearing white trousers and a white shirt protected by a red apron. While Perdita gave her order he eyed her curiously. In a town this small, Perdita supposed, the locals would recognise any strangers.

'Half a kilo of minced lamb and... six small lamb chops,' the butcher repeated as he handed first one and then the second bag to Perdita; she'd decided it made sense to shop for two days. 'On holiday?' he asked.

'I'm helping to look after a lady who's had a stroke,' Perdita said.

'Oh, yes?'

'Violet Freestone.'

'Of course. She's lived here a long time. I was at school with Saul. Know the family then?'

'Slightly. I'm in between jobs at the moment, so it suited me.'

'Ah. My cousin's in the same position.' His smile appeared sincere and understanding. 'I'm David by the way.'

'Perdita.'

'That's an unusual name.'

As she didn't want to explain, she just agreed with him.

She was fishing in her bag for her purse when David added, 'My wife, Catherine, will take the money.' He pointed to the counter at the end of the shop she'd not noticed where a woman with long brown wavy hair sat smiling at her. Perdita went over to pay.

'It's a friendly town, very welcoming. Anything you need, just let me know,' Catherine said with such warmth, Perdita was taken aback.

'That's so kind. Thank you.' It would be good to have a friend here.

Once she'd used the zebra crossing to get to the greengrocers, she visited the Spar next door. Just as well she'd brought plenty of Frank's food with her as she would have been unable to carry more. She returned to the house feeling like a pack mule. As long as she didn't look like one...

After they'd had sandwiches for lunch, Perdita brought two armchairs into the dining room from the second living room together with blankets in case the breeze had a chill in it; she'd opened the patio door. Violet listened to the afternoon play on the radio while Perdita cleaned the kitchen. When she'd finished, she returned to the dining room and switched off the radio. 'Violet, I'd like us to be friends. I think it's important that we are. For both of us.'

Violet's chin dropped briefly and was jerked up again. She wanted to be friends too; that was good.

'I am truly sorry about your money. I should never have agreed to–'

Violet tossed her head to one side and then the other.

'You don't blame me then?'

Violet gave another awkward shake to her head.

'Saul doesn't believe me about not knowing the house was his. You didn't tell him that's what you told me?'

Violet made what Perdita took to be the distorted sound of, 'No.'

She wanted to understand. 'You could have done, before you'd had your stroke, but you didn't want to, is that it?'

'Es.'

'I'll take that as a yes. I presume you'd rather he didn't know? Otherwise you would inform him using that pad and pen of yours.'

'Es.'

'Why is that, Violet?' Perdita put on her thinking hat. 'Is it that he wouldn't have asked me to stay if he'd known the truth? Wouldn't want me to stay now?'

Violet made her eyes very big and stared at Perdita with both sides of her mouth downturned instead of just the side that had been damaged from the stroke.

'You might well look guilty,' Perdita admonished. Should she be furious with Violet rather than with Saul as this had basically been the crux of her losing her flat and being forced here? But no, Violet had not made Saul kidnap her or force her to stay or behave like he had when she was moving in and again today. 'Saul doesn't think at all well of me, and that's because of you. I'd like you to think about telling him the truth. I'm here now, and I don't intend to leave, so you needn't worry about that.'

Violet raised her hands to cover her face and shook her head.

Squinting, Perdita studied the body language. 'Are you trying to tell me you can't face telling him?'

Violet nodded and lowered her hands.

'Think about it. It would make my life easier as Saul

is not being very nice to me, and I don't like him. It is stressful living with someone you can't stand.' As Violet didn't say anything, Perdita said in an upbeat tone, 'Well, we will have to try to get you better. Strict rules about your physio and speech therapy, okay? We'll have a regular time that you do these things each day, and you can chill out in between. How's that? And the rest of the time we'll try to have some fun.'

Violet stretched out her good arm and gave Perdita's hand a gentle squeeze.

Two hours later, just as the alarm on the cooker sounded, Perdita heard the opening of the front door. By the time Saul entered the kitchen, having changed into a T-shirt and jeans, the food was on the table and ready to be served.

Trying to avoid gawping at his broad chest and strong-looking arms, Perdita wondered why Saul wasn't married. Perhaps dealing with acrimonious divorces had curdled his desire to get hitched? He seemed to be short on trust. As she looked up, Perdita noticed Saul's surprised expression. She guessed he'd expected the kitchen to be in disarray and the meal either not ready or burnt. Then he approached her, bringing forward the hand that had been behind his back, and passed her a prettily wrapped box of chocolates. 'Peace offering to say sorry.' Saul was leaning in, and Perdita realised he was about to kiss her cheek. But a sound by the door startled her and, as she turned to look, his lips connected to hers.

They stepped away from each other. She touched her lips, stunned by the intimacy of his mouth on hers. Saul touched his lips at the same time. She felt bewildered by unexpected and unaccustomed feelings and saw bewilderment in his expression also.

'I'm s-sorry,' Saul stuttered. 'I was aiming for your cheek.'

'I thought I heard a sound, which is why I turned my head. And I was startled, which was why my lips weren't as together as they might have been.'

'Let's forget it,' Saul said. 'I hope you like the chocolates.'

'Yes, let's forget. And thank you.' Impulsively, she stood on tiptoe to kiss his cheek. But he turned his head and their lips were conjoined again.

They both gasped and took a step back.

'There was a sound by the door…' Saul explained. 'And, as I was startled my lips weren't… Like yours hadn't been.'

Flustered, Perdita placed her chocolates on the table and went to investigate. Violet was on the other side of the door with her Zimmer frame. 'Let's prop this open,' Perdita suggested.

While Saul greeted Violet, Perdita folded some newspaper to wedge underneath the door. Being busy helped her cope with what had just happened. His skin had only touched hers for a brief moment… twice… so why did she feel like it had been for a lot longer, and why was she replaying it in her mind, recalling his lemony scent and how the kisses had felt?

'So, you can cook,' Saul said when she'd finished with the door, indicating the moussaka-filled dish.

'You haven't tasted it yet. The proof of the pudding...'

'I'll reserve judgment until later then.'

They took their places at the table. 'I think that's best. And then you can give me ten out of ten.' She wasn't sure why she'd said that, but perhaps it was because she wanted him to acknowledge he'd underestimated her.

'A modest young lady, aren't you?'

'Credit where credit's due, please.' She began

dishing out generous portions.

'You ran out of credit long ago.'

Ouch. Goal to Saul. She aimed hurt eyes at Saul, and he looked away, heat suffusing his cheeks. Goal to Perdita.

'Sorry, that was only meant to be a quip. It sprung to mind, and I just let the words out.'

Perdita looked at the box of chocolates next to her. It would be better to make a joke out of it. 'Perhaps you need to keep your words on a tighter leash? Otherwise you might feel obliged to buy me another box of chocolates.'

Saul smiled gratefully.

Violet was managing to eat with only a spoon in her left hand as the food was quite soft.

'Perdita? You've done great today,' Saul said awkwardly.

'Thanks,' she said, 'but there's no pudding. Unless you'd care for tinned peaches?'

Saul grimaced. 'I'll give it a miss.'

'I ran out of money, and I couldn't carry any more. I'll drive to a supermarket tomorrow if you give me more – the cupboards are bare.'

'I would have repaid you if you'd used your own money, you know. I had no more cash to spare.'

'I know you would have repaid me, but there was enough money for today. I didn't want to go to the cash point because I haven't much money in my account – it's two weeks until I get paid.' Perdita hadn't meant to sound critical, but, judging by the sudden spark of anger that had just crossed his face and the tight clenching of his jaw, she knew she'd infuriated him. Too bad if he didn't like the truth.

'You'd have had to have fed yourself during those two weeks anyway – so I don't know why you keep impressing upon me that you're virtually penniless.'

Perdita played with some grains of salt that had spilt onto the table. 'My landlord insisted I paid him another month's rent up front before I left because I'd not given notice, and my contract was for another three months – hence my deposit has gone too. He let me off the last month's payment as he said he'd probably find someone else by that time.' Now she raised her head, wondering if he suspected her of fibbing.

Dragging his long square fingers through his dark hair, Saul answered, 'I'm sorry I didn't believe you, and I'm sorry about the rent, but surely you have savings? For someone who concerned herself with the financial security of others, you seem to have taken none of your own advice – which is rather difficult to swallow.'

Perdita examined her nails. They were back on that dreadful subject.

'I don't know what to make of you,' he commented. 'You annihilated my aunt's savings and refused to take her calls – which suggests you're either amoral or incompetent or both. And you accepted the blame by coming here – but you have an indignant air as though you're the innocent party, and I'm the guilty one.'

Why should she explain herself now? He hadn't wanted to listen to her on Friday. 'I can't help you there. You must be free to make up your own mind.'

'I was wondering... although your parents are no longer around, do you have any other family you'd like to visit you? As you pointed out yesterday, this is your home too now, and I want to respect that.'

'I have...' she was about to say she had no one and then a thought occurred to her. 'There's a Sister I'd like to invite.'

'Well, you'd better invite her to Sunday lunch then,' Saul said. 'And I'll be here to welcome her.'

Chapter 11

mid-March

Perdita checked the leg of lamb she'd liberally sprinkled with rosemary, nestled amongst carrots and parsnips. There was a second tray of garlic potatoes which were now beginning to crisp. Delicious aromas permeated the kitchen and wafted all over the house; even when she'd nipped upstairs to change into a white over-shirt, leggings and ballet pumps, she could smell the food. The prospect of tasting it made her mouth water. But if Sister Margaret didn't come soon the precious lamb might become dry.

Turning her thoughts to Frank, Perdita worried about him breaking his side of the bargain, having been let out for the first time. She'd allowed him out to sunbathe on the lawn on the understanding he would come back in when she shouted his name. He'd sat so contentedly on the grass, cleaning himself, she'd thought he would be safe from running off. But now he'd disappeared. Thinking Violet might have spied him crossing the driveway, Perdita tapped on Violet's door and walked in.

The window by Violet's chair was wide open and there was Frank, curled up on her lap.

When Saul joined them, Perdita said, 'Look how Violet's stroking Frank. With her weak hand. Did you open the window, Violet?'

Violet nodded and gave a lopsided grin.

'I didn't set this up,' Perdita said defensively.

'I can see that,' Saul said. 'He's clearly a very welcome guest with Violet.'

'But?'

Saul waved his hands vaguely about, and she guessed he was worried about the carpets and furniture.

'I'll limit where he goes in the main part of the house and how long he's in for,' Perdita assured him, delighted with the victory of being able to have Frank in the communal areas at all. Goal to Violet. Or would it be to Frank? Perdita took Frank upstairs and re-joined Violet, Saul having disappeared somewhere, just as she heard the sound of a car approach. When a nun emerged in full uniform, Perdita ran towards the hall, but Saul must have heard the car too and was at the front door before her.

'Good day to you. I'm Sister Margaret,' Sister Margaret said cheerily in her Irish accent. 'So good of you to welcome me to your lovely home.'

Clearly thrown, but recovering well, Saul stretched out his hand. 'Hello. I'm Saul Hadley. You're very welcome. Do come in.' He glowered at Perdita.

As Sister Margaret stepped into the hall, she gushed, 'I'm sorry now, if I'm a little late. Didn't I get talking to Father after Mass, and it's rather difficult to get away when that happens.'

'No, not at all.'

'And here's Perdita!'

'Hello, Sister Margaret.' Perdita approached to kiss her. After introducing her guest to Violet, who had joined them, Perdita excused herself to return to the kitchen. She heard Saul's slow measured steps behind her making her feel she was being stalked by a wolf.

When she straightened up, after delving in the oven, she saw Mr Wolf was watching her with eyes hungry for answers.

'Why didn't you tell me your so-called *sister* was a nun? And don't say it was because I didn't ask.'

'You haven't exactly told me anything about yourself,' Perdita pointed out.

Saul sighed. 'I don't understand what's going on. You and Violet have been the best of friends all week. But I fail to see how so much rapport could have evolved on so short an acquaintance. What's the mystery?'

'There is no mystery, Saul. It's about you seeing the truth.'

'Which is?'

'That's for you to find out. You don't believe the things I say.'

When they were all seated at the dining table, Sister Margaret said grace, and then they started tucking in, including Violet, as Perdita had cut up her food for her while Saul had continued serving. Sister Margaret wanted to hear for herself about what Saul did for a living, how long Saul's family had lived in the house, about Westbridge and what had happened to Violet's health. Then she said, 'I am glad that Perdita has such a grand home and such kindly people to live with. I expect you're glad of her offer of help?'

There was a taut silence before Saul said awkwardly, 'Yes. Of course. And so is Violet.'

'Whatever Perdita agrees to do is based on conscientiousness and generosity, as you'll no doubt agree, Saul?' Sister Margaret continued blithely.

Saul coughed. 'I don't know that I'd go that far. Did she tell you she lost my aunt's savings?'

'Now that doesn't sound like Perdita at all. She's

always been so careful, especially when it comes to other people's money.'

Saul glared at Perdita. 'Perdita's version is, no doubt, different to the way I see it.'

Sister Margaret's eyes widened. 'And what would her version be?' When Saul didn't reply, she smiled, patted her mouth with her napkin and placed her cutlery on her plate. Then she sighed. 'Well that was grand indeed,' she said, apparently happy to forget her last question. 'You certainly didn't learn how to cook at the orphanage, did you, Perdita?'

Perdita shook her head, remembering meals of lumpy mashed potato and soggy boiled cabbage followed by semolina or runny rice pudding, all of which she'd loathed.

'What orphanage?' Saul asked politely, with barely masked vexation.

Sister Margaret glanced at Perdita with an open mouth.

'The Orphanage of Saints Peter and Paul attached to the Convent of the Divine Heart of Jesus – it houses orphaned Catholic children.' Perdita felt skewered by the sharp look of reprimand Sister Margaret gave her – for not properly explaining her presence to Saul, presumably. 'It's where I was brought up.' Perdita, too, relinquished her cutlery and placed her hands neatly on her lap.

'Oh?' Saul assumed an attentive air.

It was all the encouragement Sister Margaret needed. 'Well of course you must know that poor Perdita is an orphan. When her dear mother knew she was dying she asked that Perdita come to us as she was familiar with our work. I had already bonded with the child, when Perdita was a tiny baby you know. And so, after her poor mother died, may she rest in peace, I was the one who comforted the little mite, though she was far too young to understand the terrible loss she'd suffered.'

Had the nun been closer, Perdita would have given her a small kick under the table. Instead, she coughed, tapped her knife against her plate and made exaggerated sweeping gestures with her napkin, with no success. Sister Margaret's gaze was studiously aimed at Saul's face.

But Saul must have noticed her antics as Perdita saw him suppress a smile as he cleared his plate. The line of conversation was not what she'd expected, believing that Sister Margaret would just sing her praises rather than reveal her crumple buttons.

'She's like a daughter to me, and we became extremely close. Maureen Riley chose the name, Perdita – the lost child – because of the dreadful sadness she felt, knowing she was to be separated from the daughter she loved so much.' Sister Margaret shook her head sorrowfully. 'So terrible for Maureen to know she would die months after giving birth and for Perdita not to be able to remember her mother–'

'Sister! I'm sure Saul and Violet aren't interested in my past.' Saul and Violet were watching Sister Margaret with rapt attention. Although Perdita had told Violet a bit about her background, she'd not gone into details. She never did.

'On the contrary,' Saul said, 'I'm very interested. You are living with us, so we should get to know you better.'

'Of course, you should. As I was saying,' Sister Margaret said, 'although the other children had been so unkind about Perdita's name, she'd felt that by renouncing it, she would renounce the love her mother had for her.'

Just as Violet popped her last morsel of food into her mouth, Perdita sprang up to whip the things away. Too bad if anyone wanted more. Her eyes had stung warningly the moment Sister Margaret had begun talking about her mother, but now tears over-spilled, and she didn't want Saul to see. She had never needed her mother as much as she needed her now, and, lately, she seemed to cry so easily. By the time she laid an apple crumble, a bowl of soft brown sugar and a jug of double cream on the table, her face was schooled into indifference, and, thankfully, the topic had changed to the weather.

But Sister Margaret resumed her reminiscences when Perdita returned to the table. 'Perdita has always yearned for a home of her very own – and her own family of course. Although we'd looked into adoption, to give her a home and family life, we'd decided that the wrench of separation from me, having lost her mother, would be too great at that time. And later…' Sister Margaret shook her head as though she'd said too much, 'well, that's another story. Don't you know, it was a big sacrifice for Perdita to give up her flat, it being her first home of her very own.'

'Please, Sister!' Perdita protested. Sister Margaret had switched the emotional tap back on. Perdita cringed with embarrassment as she sniffed and wiped her face.

'Perdita, as you know, I don't normally talk about your past but you need to be more forthcoming, let people in, when you are living in their home. I realise that you had not told these kindly people to expect a nun, am I right? Or that you were brought up in an orphanage?'

'Violet knew,' Perdita defended, and she saw Saul give Violet a sharp look.

'And don't you think you owe Saul an apology for not explaining today?'

Miserably, Perdita nodded. 'I'm sorry,' she said.

After the apple crumble, Perdita served coffee. And then Sister Margaret said it was time to leave. 'Thank you for a wonderful meal, Perdita, and thank you too, Saul and Violet, for your kind hospitality. It was a great pleasure to meet you both, and I'll rest easy now, knowing that Perdita is with such good people.'

Sister Margaret took Perdita's arm as they walked towards the front door. 'Now, about the loan, dear. It was never a condition that it should be repaid to your own detriment and, at the moment, you need money for yourself to live on, so don't be giving it another thought. Not even when you've finished here.' Sister Margaret patted her hand. 'Your circumstances have changed, Perdita, and the benefactors who fund the loans do understand these things.'

Flushing, Perdita peeped up at Saul. He was staring hollowly at her. No doubt, now he understood why she didn't have any savings.

While Violet rested in her chair by the patio door, Saul helped Perdita clear up. They worked in silence until it was done, and then he said, 'I'd like you to come to the study.' His voice sounded flat, defeated.

He pulled aside a Renoir print to reveal a safe and spun the combination knob. The lock clicked. Saul extracted a sheet of paper which she recognised. Tearing it into two, and then into two again, Saul said, 'You're free to go.'

Speech failed her until the brunt of the shock receded. 'Go? Where to? How dare you sweep aside your commitment to me?'

Saul's hands flailed helplessly. 'I thought this was what you wanted – what today had been about.'

'When I have nowhere else to go? I am staying!' As Perdita glared at him, Saul's expression relaxed in relief. 'Besides which, Violet needs me.'

It was as though Saul had forgotten her reason for being there and then disliked that reason once he'd rediscovered it. 'Violet... Yes, of course, I'm grateful if you look after her until she can cope on her own.' Saul straightened his shoulders. 'But as far as I'm concerned, you may go as soon as you've found another job.' He walked towards the door, leaving Perdita feeling more forlorn than ever.

'Saul?' Her voice caught huskily just as Saul's back was disappearing into the hallway.

He stopped but didn't turn around, his hand resting on the door jamb. 'Yes?' Saul's tone was icy.

Perdita shivered. 'Can't we start afresh, be friends? I am sorry. About lunch.'

Saul strode towards her, eyes aflame and his lips pressed into a line. 'You deliberately set me up, deceiving me about your *sister* and subjected me to a series of enlightenments you could have explained yourself; *Sister's* not so subtle reprimands were most unwelcome and now you expect us to be *friends*?'

Perdita had wanted Sister Margaret to show Saul that he'd invited a decent person to live with him and Violet, that his character assessment of her had been inaccurate. And Sister Margaret had done that. But she'd also revealed Perdita's weaknesses – which Saul had correctly interpreted as a hefty slap on the wrist. 'I'm really sorry.' He must hate her now and that was the opposite of what she'd set out to achieve.

'As you're willing to stay to fulfil your obligations, it means I shan't need to cancel my holiday.'

'That's convenient.'

As an afterthought, most probably inspired by Perdita's sarcasm, Saul added, 'And next Sunday, I'd like to invite a friend to lunch. And it's to be roast chicken.' Saul was eyeing her carefully. 'I take it your culinary expertise does extend to poultry?'

'I prefer lamb,' Perdita said hopefully. Would the smell of roasting chicken make her vomit? The craving for lamb, and revulsion for chicken, had been affecting her ever since she'd found out about Setback Number One.

'I've noticed. I wondered if perhaps you were working your way, page by page, through *The Lamb Lover's Recipe Book*.'

Perdita brightened. '*The Lamb Lover's*–?'

'There's no need for excitement,' Saul snapped. 'I made the title up.'

'I really don't like chicken. I'd prefer to roast lamb.'

'I want chicken. Fiona prefers it.'

Who was Fiona? An instrument of revenge for today? Unwillingly, Perdita gave a show of capitulation. 'Then chicken it shall be.' But she wasn't going to eat it, and he couldn't make her. Blinking back tears, Perdita groped her way up the stairs to the seclusion of her room. It had all gone very, very wrong and she didn't think buying him a box of chocolates would help put it right. But she could give it a go; she'd accepted his chocolate apology so perhaps he would be big enough to accept a chocolate apology from her.

Chapter 12

The following morning, Perdita drove Violet to a quiet café in Clifton. Whilst they drank their coffee, Perdita intended to get the lowdown on Fiona.

'Violet, who is Fiona? Is she Saul's girlfriend?'

Violet tossed her head to the side.

Good. Perdita hadn't forgotten those accidental kisses in the kitchen – although slushy thoughts about Saul were probably incompatible with keeping a pertinent secret from him. 'Does she often come to lunch then?'

This time, Violet's left shoulder was raised in a shrug.

'She sometimes comes to lunch? With you both?'

'Es.'

Perdita's tension reduced a notch. If Saul and Fiona were serious about one another she doubted Violet would be present at their meetings; they would want to be alone together. 'What does she do?' Was she a hot shot solicitor? A barrister?

Violet made some hand gestures.

'She reads a lot?' Drat. Legal people had to do that, didn't they? Read things?

Violet took to pen and paper. By the time she'd written the third letter, Perdita exclaimed, 'Librarian. She's a librarian?'

'Es.'

Well, that wasn't so scary then, Perdita thought, picturing a slight woman with glasses who was a bit timid. No, make that a lot timid. And some problem with her appearance such as... one eye in the middle of her forehead? Then she gasped. Would the topic of conversation be around books? Highbrow ones? No, no, that wouldn't do. She couldn't recall any highbrow books she'd read unless she counted compulsory texts for school exams. Would they count as highbrow enough?

Jerked out of her musings by a nudge, Perdita looked at Violet whose left arm swung slowly across her body. She was cradling an imaginary...

Perdita gulped and gawped at Violet. 'Oh.' Perdita felt stupid expecting to live without detection. 'It was a mistake,' she confessed sadly. 'But I wouldn't have it any other way now. It's just me and the bump.' And, perhaps, Saul? No, he was far too grumpy. Were he to find out her secret, he'd likely send her packing pretty sharpish. She'd best stick to her original plan and steer clear of confiding in him for as long as possible.

Violet pressed Perdita's hand sympathetically. She didn't see any point in mentioning the fact that she'd taken Violet's advice and that it had worked: she'd attracted a bee, but it had been the wrong kind of bee. Would Saul have made a better bee? Of course, he would have, she was sure of that.

Leaving Violet in the café, reading a magazine, Perdita nipped out to search for the most exclusive box of apology chocolates she could reasonably afford. She was going to give them to Saul this evening.

In the afternoon, back in Westbridge, Perdita went to David Murphy's. As well as buying meat for the next couple of days, she decided it made sense to put in an order for the weekend.

When David spotted her entering the shop, he

grinned. 'Hello. You're looking very well today. Is the weather cheering you up?'

Perdita returned his smile. 'Probably. It feels like summer's come early.' A shame it wouldn't last.

'And what can I do for you?'

Perdita asked for minced lamb and lamb steaks and then said, 'Could I order a large roasting chicken to be picked up Saturday, please?'

'Chicken? Not lamb?' David queried.

'Chicken,' Perdita said. 'By request.'

'Ah. And for yourself?' He grinned, conspiratorially.

'Oh, no lamb this weekend, thanks.' She knew he must think her odd.

David leaned forward, checked the door for looming customers and whispered, 'Doesn't the baby want some?'

Perdita gasped and invoked the beautiful brightly-coloured flower waving in a gentle breeze, on a hillside with lots of grass. Glancing nervously to the paying counter, she saw Catherine Murphy smiling broadly at her.

'Catherine and I have talked about your only buying lamb and we came to the same conclusion,' David said. 'We are right, aren't we? It's a craving?'

'It's a secret,' Perdita whispered, looking from one to the other.

'Catherine and I love secrets.'

When Perdita went to the counter to pay, Catherine said, 'I know you're not well-fixed at the moment as you're helping Violet out. Is there anything you need? Our two have out-grown so much now and, although we haven't ruled out having a third, you're welcome to borrow what we have.' Catherine looked over at David with a sexy smile, and he winked back at her.

Perdita was moved by the offer. 'I don't know what to say. That's so kind of you. Thank you. But are you sure? What if you suddenly... need them?'

'Then we'll cross that bridge when we come to it,' Catherine said firmly. 'I can ask around too. Some people are bound to have their families complete. Father O'Connor could put a request in the parish newsletter.'

'Oh, no, I don't think that would be a good idea! Then it wouldn't be a secret.' It was far too soon for Saul to find out.

'Well, perhaps nearer the time, after you've told everyone. Father O'Connor won't mind a bit.'

That evening, when Violet had settled to watch TV in her makeshift bedroom, Perdita ventured down that short corridor to Saul's study with her gift. She'd heard him come home from having had dinner with friends and wanted to give him the confectionery as soon as possible, to get the awkwardness out of the way. And while Violet was out of the way. It was easier to eat humble pie without a witness.

Saul invited her in when she knocked. She was surprised to see him standing at the window instead of toiling at his desk. And he was still wearing his work clothes. In her mind, she'd planned to sit opposite him and then reveal the treasure behind her back. Now she had a greater distance to cover. Keen to get the tough deed over with, she picked up the pace. But, as she approached, she stubbed her foot against the leg of his desk and screamed as she flew towards him, dropping the chocolates to save herself.

As she landed against him, she felt him fall onto the windowsill. He must have put his arms out instinctively to save himself, but she didn't see how grabbing her buttocks would have helped as she'd been the cause of the mishap. As long as Saul didn't topple to either side, she was probably stable enough locked between his thighs. Her forehead was pressed against the double glazing and her fingers were clutching his shoulders.

'I'm sorry,' Saul said. 'Will you be safe if I let go? I tried to catch you.'

'Yes,' she mumbled in his ear. His neck felt warm and homely and smelt of lemonade. She had an unaccountable urge to run her lips along his skin.

Saul removed his hands from her bottom, but she'd no idea what he'd done with them; all she knew is that they weren't on her. Much more appropriate.

'I tripped,' she said. 'This wasn't meant to happen.'

'I gathered that.'

She couldn't move. But the pain in her breasts instructed her to get up. She pushed on his chest with both hands, feeling the warmth of his body through the thin material of his shirt. The pressure on her chest eased, but she was no closer to standing upright despite exploring the possibility by twisting first to one side and then the other – she was still captured between his legs and her feet were far behind her.

It seemed Saul was stuck fast too as her weight was pinning him down. And now that she was pushing her upper body back, her pelvis was rammed hard into his. She knew this because whatever he had in his pocket was digging in and she'd not noticed it before.

'I came to say sorry for yesterday,' Perdita told his mouth. 'And I brought a peace offering.'

'This is what you call a peace offering?' Saul said huskily, the scent of coffee mingling with the lemon.

When his soft lips met hers, he kissed her gently, sensuously, and her knees almost gave way. Why she was kissing him back, she didn't know. It seemed her body didn't care. Saul's arms were tightening around her now. But she resisted, with a stronger press-up on his chest, to save her sore breasts. Immediately, Saul broke off kissing her and relaxed his hold.

'I'm sorry,' he said. 'I... got carried away.'

'I don't know how to get up,' she told his mouth. It was easier to pretend the kiss had never happened.

'Perhaps if you slide down, bend your knees?'

'I don't think that's a good idea.' If she were to bend her knees her head would be in Saul's lap. And that thing in his pocket might hurt her face; the longer she was pressed against him the harder it felt. Besides, she would be too close to his bottom and dangly bits.

'Okay, I'll push you up by your shoulders. If you bring a foot forward and keep your back straight, you might be able to manage to get upright.'

Although Perdita succeeded in regaining her freedom of movement, she felt bereft now that her body had lost contact with Saul's – and her lips had lost connection with his. It was now his turn to get to his feet and, as soon as he saw the box on the floor, he picked it up and held it in front of him as though hiding that thing in his pocket. Should she warn him he could damage himself? Best not to, if it was clandestine; he was entitled to some privacy especially considering the fact that she was hiding something from him. She'd pretend she hadn't noticed.

'I... hope you like chocolates,' she said, unable to meet his eyes. Did he think badly of her because she'd kissed back?

'I do,' Saul said warmly, although there was a note of strain present. 'It's actually the first time a woman has bought me chocolates.' He made an adjustment to his trousers behind the box. She wasn't surprised; she knew just how uncomfortable that thing was.

'Not even girlfriends?'

'No. It tended to be the other way around.' Saul was a bit fidgety on his feet now, and Perdita wondered if they itched. She made a similar action when she was trying to scratch her bare soles on the carpet.

'Not buying you chocolates was mean of them,' she commented just to show she was a superior kind of female, one much better suited to being his girlfriend than his previous conquests. 'And you're the first man who's bought me chocolates... Am I forgiven? For Sunday?' As she finally forced herself to look up, she noticed Saul eyeing the doorway.

'Er, I think that would be best. If you'll... er... excuse me, it's been a hot day. I need a cold shower.' Saul scarpered taking the gift with him.

She hadn't realised he had such a sweet tooth. Then she wondered what he would look like in the shower and whether there was enough room for two.

Chapter 13

When Perdita heard the rapping at the front door the following Sunday, she was busy in the kitchen with the windows flung wide open. Not only was it a warm day, but the oven was belching out heat laden with sweet cloying aromas that threatened her breakfast of Marmite on toast with a thick layer of marmalade on top. Reluctantly, she made her way into the hall. There, she reluctantly witnessed Saul's welcoming embrace of a woman whose face was so made-up the slightest brush against her would leave a coating. Perdita wondered if Fiona's face was like walls: rendering and then two – or was it three? – skims of plaster. Perdita had seen it done on TV on one of those home renovations programmes.

The creamy mounds of Fiona's magnificent breasts threatened to overspill the cut of her tight-fitting dress that had eye-catching crimson roses against a white background. And her heels were matching red spikes, spikier than any shoe Perdita had bought. When Fiona turned to place her bag on the hall table, her straight black hair, that fell to just below her shoulder blades, swished about, and Perdita wished her hair was long enough to do that.

When Perdita had moved in with Saul and Violet, she'd been rather skinny from not eating regularly and being sick. But now she was a healthy weight and didn't look like a half-starved orphan, thanks to all her cooking and baking and eating. The old dress she was wearing today was the last of her pretty outfits to still fit without making her look like a sausage bursting out from its skin as it cooked. But, next to Fiona, she felt a frump. Round One to Fiona.

The smile Saul aimed at Fiona was full of warmth that spoke of long-standing familiarity. It transformed his face. There was something else that transformed his face, Perdita noted: two faint lipstick smudges on each cheek where Fiona had kissed with her painted red lips.

Jealousy sprouted and quickly grew into a monster. Perdita wanted Saul for herself. Her body had barely responded when she'd been with Tony compared to the tidal wave of wanton longing that assaulted her whenever she recalled Saul's kisses. Her heart throbbed painfully seeing him with Fiona and even more so when she saw Fiona regard him with a confidence that suggested a sense of ownership.

Perdita wondered if she would have felt as resentful at this moment had Saul not kissed her the day she'd given him that box of chocolates. His caressing lips had been her undoing and, with his being so friendly and kind ever since, it was like adding fertiliser to her utterly mad and unsafe feelings. The more deeply she was falling for him, the guiltier she felt for keeping her secret. But she didn't want him to send her away. And how did Fiona fit into the picture?

'Fiona, this is Perdita; Perdita, Fiona,' Saul said.

They shook hands and said pleased to meet you, exchanging plastic smiles.

Saul regarded them with a dazed expression as though trying to decide which of the two of them he preferred. Would he opt for Fiona's sharp sophistication or Perdita's more natural and cuddly appearance? How high did he rate her cooking? Could Fiona cook?

Saul asked, 'What would you both like to drink? Wine? Sherry?' as he ushered them into the second living room where there was a drinks cabinet.

Just as Perdita was about to decline a drink, Violet joined them, expertly wielding her Zimmer frame. She was getting stronger.

'Hello, Violet.' Fiona bent to kiss Violet's cheek. 'How are you? It's so lovely to see you again.' Fiona sounded genuine and sincere, and it made Perdita contrite for disliking her for no other reason than she had shared history with Saul.

When Violet nodded, Saul said, 'I think you're progressing well, aren't you? Perdita has been a great help.'

Turning to Perdita, Fiona said kindly, 'Violet's lucky to have you. I feel bad I haven't been more involved...'

'Don't be ridiculous,' Saul said. 'You're working and have your mum to look after. Has she recovered from her last heart attack?'

'Excuse me,' Perdita muttered as she left to attend to the dreaded chicken. Fiona being a ministering angel would make her even more likeable in Saul's eyes, Perdita was sure.

Holding a large bunched tissue to her nose, Perdita boiled the water in the steam pan for the vegetables. When she lifted the roasting tin out of the oven to baste the chicken, she held her breath. Happy that it was the final check before serving, Perdita removed some juices to flavour the gravy, returned the now golden chicken to the oven and rushed outside to be free of the clinging, abominable smell. How would she get through the meal?

'Perdita?' Fiona's voice was distant, but soon she emerged from the back of the house. 'Oh, there you are – I wondered if you'd like some help?' There was a subtle difference in how she'd spoken earlier and, although Perdita couldn't be sure, she suspected Fiona's tone implied the last thing she wanted to do was to help. 'What are you doing out here?'

'I was just checking on the progress of Violet's herbs,' Perdita lied before turning to go back inside and brave her Herculean task, faintness and nausea hovering.

Fiona followed, and Perdita saw her take in the pots and pans and mess yet to be cleared up from the food preparation. 'You're a proper little Cinderella, aren't you, slaving away like this?' Fiona said.

Remembering that look of ownership Fiona had cast Saul, Perdita smiled sweetly. 'Hmm, that must mean I get the prince.'

Fiona laughed. 'Taken a fancy to Saul?'

Perdita thought she heard a noise from the hallway but, when she looked up, she couldn't see anyone. 'I was just keeping to the fairy-tale theme, since you brought it up.' Perdita had no intention of naming anyone. Especially since one particular prince was probably lurking out there, listening.

'Was that why you were sacked? Because your head was in the clouds, dreaming of a fairy-tale ending for yourself?'

Perdita was stunned that Saul had broken his promise about keeping the true reason for her being there a secret. To have been discussed behind her back with Fiona stung as though she'd been attacked by a swarm of bees. For a few seconds, she could do nothing but stare in disbelief. Then she said, 'I resigned.' Round

Two to Fiona.

'I must say, I don't think Saul's description of his home-help was very accurate. You need to substitute some of that lamb I've heard you're so fond of for an extra helping of vegetables. It might reduce the household food bill too.'

Perdita gasped. Then a sudden movement in the doorway caught her attention. Springing forward, she found Saul standing there. She scowled at him and was gratified to see his eyes narrow in what she hoped was disapproval of his guest and not her. He stepped into the kitchen and handed Fiona her half-empty glass.

'Perdita seems to have everything under control,' Fiona informed Saul sweetly, back to her former self.

The gravy bubbled explosively, and Perdita reduced the heat. She stirred and then divided it into two gravy boats before saying to Fiona, 'As you came to help, you might like to carry these to the table.' Turning to Saul, Perdita said, 'And the vegetables need to be put into serving dishes and the chicken carved.' Then she went to call Violet – and breathe in some fresher air.

As Saul carved at the table, Perdita served potatoes, green beans and carrots. 'Remember, no chicken for me, please.' She'd cooked the damned meat, but she certainly wasn't going to eat it. 'I've never been able to stomach it since a bout of food poisoning.' Perdita had spent the past few days working out the excuse.

Fiona served Violet a portion of chicken that Saul had sliced off the carcass, and Perdita automatically started to cut it up. But when she turned to look at her own plate, she found that Fiona had dumped a huge piece of breast on it. At the sight of its glistening skin and white meat, Perdita felt her nausea rise to the brink of overflowing.

She charged from the dining room, roughly pushing aside her chair, and into the downstairs cloakroom. As she retched, tears spurted from her eyes at the meanness of them both but more so with regard to Saul; he'd broken her trust. And what else had he told Fiona? And had they had a good laugh over her?

After flushing the loo and rinsing her mouth under the tap in the basin, Perdita's sixth sense was sufficiently recovered to suggest that there was someone behind her, at the open cloakroom door. There hadn't been time to close it.

'I had no idea you felt so ill – you should've told me.' Saul's voice was deep with concern.

'I just don't like chicken anymore,' Perdita said tetchily. 'I'm going to my room.' She tried to push past him, but he wouldn't budge.

'Don't you want anything to eat?' Saul sounded apologetic, eager to put things right.

'I've lost my appetite. Or haven't you noticed?'

He touched her shoulder. 'I'm sorry.'

But she shrugged him off and pushed past with her head high. Round Three to Fiona. Game over?

In her room, Perdita gave way to silent tears. On Monday, she'd suspected that Saul was coming to care for her. But now her illusions were shattered, and that familiar, unwelcome feeling of aloneness washed over her. Why had she even harboured hopes that he could be interested in her – especially with Setback Number One still under wraps? She was so glad now that he didn't know; she bet he and Fiona would have had a great laugh at her expense had she confided in him.

Stupidly, idiotically, she'd become involved with another man who played around with women's feelings. Were any of them just regular blokes who knew how to be honest and straight with a woman?

Her thoughts flew to the men she knew. Well, Luke and Gavin weren't exactly straight-straight, but they were straightforward and uncomplicated. Reluctantly, she popped Saul into the 'player' category with Tony. These men toyed with women's feelings and came out unscathed every time. Although it was tempting to Skype Luke and Gavin now for some sympathy, they might insist on coming around, and it could make her situation worse; she would fill them in tomorrow in the hope that things might have settled down by then. She stretched out on the bed. It had been a long morning and preparing all that food had not only knocked the stuffing out of her but had vacuumed it out at full suction power.

Later, she was roused by a soft knock. She could guess who it was. Violet was hardly up to tackling two flights of stairs with her Zimmer frame. It was highly unlikely that Fiona would be paying her a visit. But it was wise to make sure that it wasn't the Wicked Witch of Westbridge.

Groggily, she asked, 'Who is it?'

'Saul.'

'Go away,' she mumbled, half into her pillow.

'I've come to talk.'

Perdita opened the door then went to flop down on her bed.

Saul surveyed the room. 'You've made it very – homely.'

'I despise you for today,' she commented lightly as though discussing something banal like the weather.

'I don't blame you. I despise myself.' He approached the bed and sat down next to her.

Perdita glowered, and he retreated to the end of the

bed. 'What happened to your promise not to tell anyone about the circumstances that led me here?'

'Fiona had a right to be told. I've known her most of my life. I couldn't suddenly produce a female friend she knew nothing about.'

'Did you expect me to put up with all that she dished out?' Perdita then recalled what Fiona had, in actuality, dished out to her. 'I'm not just talking about the chicken.'

'I hardly know what I thought. But today has made things awkward between us considering we've been friends from childhood.'

'And that's my fault, I suppose? Why did you ask her here? To teach me a lesson?'

Saul shrugged helplessly. 'At the time, it seemed a good idea to invite Fiona – but, of course, it's backfired on me. Like Sister Margaret's visit did with you. We both made mistakes.'

'You didn't stop Fiona needling me.'

'It wasn't that I didn't want to – but when I heard the things she was saying, I became fascinated. I realised that, although I'd known her for years, I hadn't really known her at all. And I'm truly sorry that you got hurt.'

'Mmph.'

'I regret it now. Although it's certainly made me see her in a new light. It appears Fiona's like my glamorous mother. She can be nice, very nice – but it seems only if it suits her. After you'd gone, I told her that she'd been out of order, and she apologised. She's going to write you a letter.'

Perdita was disappointed that she wasn't going to get chocolates too.

'You made a fantastic lunch today, and I'm very grateful for all your hard work,' he said softly.

Feeling her skin prickle, Perdita looked away. He was here, in her bedroom, so close. And yet so far. There was the conflict of Violet's money between them and the secret she was clinging on to. And did he really like her or, when he'd kissed her, had he been using her in the same way Tony had? Although she couldn't imagine Saul behaving like Tony, she was wary nevertheless. She and Saul had been thrown into each other's company, sharing accommodation, meals and conversations. And she felt that seeing him with Violet had given her a fair insight into his character. And she liked it. But was it safe to fall in love with Saul? And was it real this time?

'I meant to thank you,' Saul said, 'for ironing my shirts. It was quite a surprise when I went to do my washing to find them all hanging there. You really didn't need to.'

'Oh. Well, I'd already got the ironing board up, saw them lying in a heap, and I had the time. It was no bother.' Should she have left them alone? She thought he'd be pleased. Then she felt heat rise in her face. Had he guessed that she'd stroked and caressed his shirts, imagining the material was his skin?

'I am grateful. But I don't want you to be my skivvy. I can look after myself.'

She felt snubbed. She'd only meant it as a friendly gesture, and since she did have spare time, it seemed mean not to include Saul's shirts with her own and Violet's ironing. 'I know you can. I'll leave them in future.' Now he looked awkward as though realising she'd been offended.

'Let's not quarrel,' Saul said. 'Would another box of chocolates help you accept my sincere apology for telling Fiona the circumstances under which you are here?'

'And the fact you discussed my eating habits,' Perdita added.

'That, too,' Saul said.

She considered. 'I rather liked the selection in the last box you bought me.'

'Deal.'

She grinned. Fiona just got disqualified for unfair play. Game to Perdita.

Chapter 14

Saul's impression that he'd wronged Perdita had been growing since she'd moved in. The conscientiousness with which she had approached every task asked of her proved she was very capable, efficient and caring beyond expectations. The grasping individual he'd initially taken her for had not been at all in evidence. Now, having had the opportunity to compare her to Fiona, he suspected he'd made a gargantuan mistake.

Whenever he'd pictured that day in the store, grabbing hold of Perdita, pulling her to the floor – albeit accidentally, lying to that man about her being his mentally unwell wife with three children and coercing her to the car, let alone the bullying that had followed, he just cringed. At the time, he'd been so incensed by what had happened to Violet, he hadn't been able to see what he now believed was truth staring him in the face. It was time he had it out with Violet.

He found her resting in an armchair by the patio door in the dining room, looking out into the garden. He'd brought a pen and some paper and handed them to her as he said, 'We need to have a chat.'

Her eyes widened.

He pulled up a seat so that he could study her expression when he asked his questions. 'Did you tell Perdita that the house belonged to you?' When Violet lowered her eyes, he repeated the question and added, 'I want to know the truth.'

Meekly, Violet said, 'Es.'

'Did Perdita suggest you take out that high risk investment?' Again, Violet averted her eyes. He could guess the answer but he wanted to hear it from her. 'Well?'

'No.' Then she wrote: *All my fault, not Perdita's*. She underlined 'not' twice. Then she added: *I want her to stay. Don't let her leave!*

It was a bad enough shock to find out that his aunt had deceived him about the circumstances of her investment, but it was incomprehensible why she'd allowed him to force Perdita to move in when she was blameless. Violet had not struck him as a selfish person before. 'I think we should clear this up with Perdita, let her know that I know she was telling the truth that day. Then she can decide what to do with a clear conscience, whether to go or stay.' He'd been a monster and was devastated he'd got to know Perdita under such awful circumstances.

Violet grabbed his arm and aimed pleading eyes at him, shaking her head. Then, with trembling fingers, she scribbled: *Perdita wants to stay. Don't give her a reason to feel she must leave!*

Well, he didn't want Perdita to leave either. 'I'll be nice.'

The concern on Violet's face abated, but she hadn't relaxed back into her seat when he turned to go. Why had his aunt taken to Perdita so strongly when Violet had been indifferent to girlfriends he'd brought home in the past? What had Violet seen that he'd missed when he'd first encountered Perdita?

If he'd met Perdita in the usual way, such as in a pub or through work, would he have been interested then or would he have been too quick to dismiss her as a potential partner? Probably the latter. When he'd found out that Teri, his last girlfriend, had cheated on him, he'd given all women a wide berth, considering them all as unfaithful and as untrustworthy as his mother had been. And now here was a sweet kind-natured woman living with them, and he wasn't sure how to deal with the situation. When he was at work, Perdita was never far from his mind. He would picture her face with those large doe eyes and recall the softness of her mouth and the tentative way she'd responded to his kisses.

Wracked by guilt over his treatment of her, Saul decided he would prepare the evening cold spread; it would be easier to talk to Perdita if his aunt were not present. He would let Violet know that he would take her supper in on a tray.

When everything was ready, he called up the stairs to Perdita. When she noticed that only two places had been laid at the kitchen table, he explained that Violet was eating off a tray. 'She's fine,' he reassured Perdita. 'She's just having some quiet time.' On the naughty chair, he wanted to add.

Perdita went to Frank's food cupboard and retrieved a tin of pilchards in tomato sauce. In another cupboard, she found a packet of salt and vinegar crisps. As Saul helped himself to cheese and pickle, Perdita arranged the tomatoey pilchards over two slices of buttered bread. She looked up and caught him watching.

'Although pilchards are Frank's favourite treat, he won't notice if I've taken a tin,' she explained. Then she opened the bag of crisps and pressed them onto the fish. Just as he was getting accustomed to what she was about to eat, she stood up, went to the fridge and retrieved a plastic bottle of American mustard. After liberally squeezing the yellow liquid all over the crisps,

Perdita buttered more bread to place on top. He wondered how long this combination had been a hit with her and determined never to ask her to make him a packed lunch.

She must have caught him staring. 'Would you like a piece?'

He almost gagged. 'I'm good, thanks.'

'You never know how yummy something is until you've tried it.'

'I'll pass, all the same.' Saul tried to eat. His stomach churned every time he caught sight of Perdita taking another large bite of her supper, the yellow sauce oozing out onto her plate, and he wondered whether it was some kind of message about being served up chicken she hadn't wanted at lunchtime. Was this to prove to him that everybody had different palates? Well, thank goodness her cooked food was more mainstream – although there was something decidedly odd about her obsession with lamb. 'Perdita?'

'Mm?' She wiped away some sauce from her chin and dabbed at her lips with the napkin he'd provided. Then she kept eating.

'I've spoken to Violet. I know she lied to you about the house, and I know it wasn't your fault about the investment.' He'd expected Perdita to smile in relief but, instead, her eyes widened in what appeared to be fright.

'Are you telling me I've got to leave?'

'Not at all. But I don't want you to feel under any obligation to stay.' Why had Perdita agreed to help out when she'd been completely innocent? Had he scared her that much? 'I'm sorry that I made you come here, and I apologise for my inexcusable behaviour. It was brutish. I've never done anything like that before, and

I hope I never will again.' From now on, he would treat her with the utmost respect. And help her when it was time for her to move on, whenever that might be. The house would feel empty when she did eventually leave; she seemed part of the place already. She'd slotted in so perfectly with his and Violet's routine it was as though Perdita was meant to live here.

When he'd noticed that she'd ironed all his work shirts his heart had given a little squeeze. It had been such a kind and unexpected gesture, and Perdita had blushed when he'd mentioned it. But she'd seemed offended when he'd said not to do it again. He'd only meant he was uncomfortable taking advantage of her; she was here to help Violet, not act like a wife who ironed for the love of him. Then he wondered how she would act if she were his wife…

Perdita paused eating. 'It was brutish. But Violet needs me, and I said I would stay. Violet doesn't want me to go... Do you?'

'That's not the point. I want you to be free to do what you want to do. I will help you get another flat. After all, I am responsible for you losing your last place and having you suffer financially through having to leave without notice.'

Her eyes became moist. 'You promised that, no matter what, you would let me stay for a year. Are you breaking that promise?'

'No… I just… need you to know that the misunderstanding has been sorted – and I'm sorry for all those cruel things I said.' He wanted to do the right thing by her. He also wanted – no *needed* – her to stay.

Alarm had grown on Perdita's face, similar to Violet's expression earlier when she'd grabbed his arm. 'I don't want to go. I like Violet, and she likes me. And it's the first time I've lived with a family...'

'You can stay. I'd like you to. Please don't worry. You get that year.' And more...? Then Saul recalled what Sister Margaret had said. 'When Sister Margaret came, she said you'd desperately wanted a family of your own, a home of your own. How come that didn't happen?'

Perdita finished eating and took a long drink of water. 'Sister Margaret had been looking after me when my mum was too sick to take care of me herself and took me to visit my mum in the hospice. Apparently, I was as good as gold for both of them, settling easily and feeding well – but with no one else. A couple desperate to have a child were found and came to spend time with me. But as soon as they picked me up, I would start to scream. The moment Sister Margaret took hold of me, I stopped. They decided that I wasn't for them. Sister Margaret told me that babies can recognise who is holding them and so can form attachments very early on.

'I was a few years old the next time a couple wanting to adopt was found. Things were fine when they visited me at the orphanage, but when I went to their home without Sister Margaret, I started to scream and bit them.

'When I was about ten, the last couple were found. They'd adopted two children already and wanted a third.' She chewed her lip, but Saul couldn't make out the details of expression around her eyes as his own were beginning to blur. 'I had a couple of visits to their home and met the other children who were both older than me. Things at the orphanage weren't going too well, the other kids weren't being nice to me. I didn't trust those two children in the family to be nice to me either when their parents weren't around – I didn't feel safe. And I felt that if I went somewhere else to live, I wanted the attention of both parents to myself. I'd experienced Sister Margaret and the other nuns sharing their time among us, and it was never enough. Later, I regretted not trying for longer, but there was something perverse inside me that had prevented me from trying to make it work.' Abruptly, Perdita stood up, taking her plate and knife to the kitchen sink.

Saul took his plate and cutlery over as well. He'd forgotten to empty the dishwasher from lunch. 'Let me do the washing up,' Saul said. There were a few mugs from earlier to add to the pile, but he would leave Violet's things until later.

'Then I'll dry.' Perdita grabbed the tea towel.

Saul started with a mug. 'I thought Sister Margaret said you'd always wanted a family of your own? I don't understand.'

'I'm not sure I... can explain.'

'Try,' he coaxed softly, taking in her pinched face, longing to know what had caused her so much pain as to make her reject something she'd sorely wanted.

She turned away so that he couldn't see her face, but he could tell from the movement of her arms that she was drying a mug that would be, by now, already dry. 'I... It...'

He wiped his hands and placed them on her shoulders. 'I'd like to know. I'd like to get to know you better.'

She turned towards him, her big brown eyes wide with sadness. 'I don't think I realised at the time, but I was punishing myself.'

His heart lurched with compassion. He wanted to hold her and tell her that it was all right, he wouldn't judge, and that he might be able to help by reassuring her she had deserved a loving family.

'I... I'm sorry, I've got to go.' She placed the mug and tea towel on the worktop and brushed past him.

'Please, perhaps I can help?'

She stood with her back to him. 'I don't see how.'

'A trouble shared? I won't judge.'

Although she remained facing the door, he heard her say, 'It was punishment for killing my mother. She'd been expected to make a full recovery, but she delayed her cancer treatment when she discovered she was going to have me. The doctors did everything they could for her after I was born, but it was too late... They couldn't save her.' Perdita struggled to hide a sob. She fled the kitchen.

Saul heard her running up the stairs but didn't go after her. He could understand she wanted to be alone. How could she have lived her life blaming herself for her mother's death? It was natural for a mother to do everything to protect her child, and it had been her mother's decision, not Perdita's.

How could he have treated someone so vulnerable so cruelly that day in the department store? And later, forcing her to give up her home just because he willed it – and, as it turned out, for no good reason? For no reason at all. He sat down, holding his head in his hands.

Chapter 15

Two days later, remembering with remarkable clarity how humiliated she'd felt after her disastrous experience with Tony, Perdita decided some research was necessary. It had been on her mental to-do list that needed to be completed before the seedling was due. She knew she would be too busy then. For an adult woman with a bump, she was incredibly ignorant, and it was time she made an effort to fill that gap in her education. With Saul being so nice to her now since their chat in the kitchen, she had hopes that perhaps one day in the future they would be good friends and perhaps even more. She wanted to be prepared should that day ever come.

Initially, she'd considered researching on the Internet, but she didn't trust her browsing history to be properly deleted from her hard drive, and she preferred a more official, recognised source of information. Besides which, she didn't know enough about anything to know whether the advice she might read over the Internet was good.

Bristol's Central Library should give plenty of the relevant reading material and, as far as she knew, Fiona didn't work there. Unless, Perdita suddenly thought, Fiona had been called in under some cover system to deal with staff absence. For a moment, she felt panicked by the idea – imagine if Fiona told Saul about her visit and the purpose of that visit? Calm down, she told herself. Fiona was probably miles away, in her post at Westbridge Library, composing that letter of apology.

As Perdita entered the lending library on the ground floor, she did a recce of the area first to ensure there was no Wicked Witch about and, secondly, to identify the most motherly-looking librarian to help with her query. On finding no Wicked Witch, Perdita fixed on a matronly middle-aged woman and advanced towards her. 'Excuse me,' Perdita whispered furtively.

The librarian halted her task of returning books to the shelves. 'Yes?' Beady eyes were aimed at her.

Perdita stepped closer. Then she leaned right in, cupped her hand to the woman's ear and whispered to her very softly.

The librarian whispered back, 'The library isn't the best place for that kind of thing.'

'But I thought you get all information in a library.' Perdita had made the trip especially.

'But not *that* kind of information,' the librarian answered firmly, fixing her with a steely gaze.

Perdita's mouth opened and then closed.

'It's great for the biological side of things,' the librarian explained, a little more relaxed now. 'But if you want to learn about the actual act, and how to please a man, it's best to go somewhere else. We can't have those kinds of books out on the shelves here.'

'Can you help me access such information on a computer here? I don't want anything like that to be on my own browsing history, and I don't know if I would get to the right kind of sites and not have anything... inappropriate... come up.'

The librarian shook her head. 'Nothing like that can be accessed in the library. And I certainly wouldn't advise you trying to get the information over the Internet.' She leaned forward and whispered into Perdita's ear, and Perdita felt her eyes stretch open. She stared at her. 'I can't go there,' Perdita croaked. Then a wonderful idea struck her. 'Can you come with me? Please?'

The librarian looked horrified.

'Isn't it your job to help people find written information?'

'No, not like that,' was the spluttered reply. 'Only within the Library Service. What you want falls outside of that.'

'If you don't help me,' Perdita said, 'I won't know if I pick up the wrong kind of book and get the wrong kind of information. And where will I be then?' The librarian pursed her lips. 'I'm an orphan,' Perdita explained. 'My mother died a few months after I was brought into this world. I was brought up by nuns in a convent. And I don't know anything about how to give pleasure to a man in bed. Please?'

Suddenly, Perdita remembered you weren't meant to talk in a library, and she realised she'd forgotten to whisper. Glancing around the room she saw desks with people sitting at them. But the people weren't concentrating on their work; they were all gazing her way. She placed cool hands over her cheeks. Most Humiliating Experience Number...? What was she up to now? Five? That must be it as Most Humiliating Experience Number Four had happened at her first obstetrics appointment – and she didn't want to think about that now.

Decisively, the librarian checked her watch. 'I'm due a break,' she said with a sigh. 'I'll just let them know I'm taking it now.'

'Thank you so much,' Perdita said and turned to glare at the people who'd been watching and listening. They lowered their heads to look at their work.

Perdita trotted beside the librarian as she strode briskly down the street, shaking her head and muttering, 'This is very awkward. I'm not at all sure I should be doing this.'

'Please, I need help.'

The woman shook her head again.

'I do appreciate it,' Perdita encouraged.

'Is there any particular aspect of pleasing a man you are interested in?'

'Oh, I've kissed a man before,' Perdita said panting, wishing she'd worn trainers, 'I just haven't touched him. You know... downstairs.' Perdita signalled downwards.

The librarian's eyes rolled skywards. 'Where've you been living all your life?'

'I told you. Most of it was with nuns. After that – well, I don't know what happened.'

'Sounds to me like you carry your own convent around with you.'

Perdita was just about to put the librarian right and confide about being pollinated but then thought better of it. It might confuse her. And Perdita wouldn't wish to explain.

'I'll try to find you a book suitable for absolute beginners.'

'Thank you,' Perdita said.

The shop was dimly lit with multi-coloured lights. Perdita's gaze darted around the room in stupefaction. Her bemused gaze fixed on hanging displays set on boards where numerous packets of brightly-coloured things were on show. She felt heat rush to her face when she made out what some of the shapes were meant to mimic. The others she hadn't a clue about. Did they come with instructions?

'This way.' She dragged Perdita along by her arm. 'I don't have long. If you wish to linger, you can come back on your own.'

Perdita picked up the pace. Returning without a chaperone was not something she could visualise. They reached an inner room where there were shelves of books and... Perdita gawped. DVDs. But unlike any she'd seen before. These had lurid covers with enormous-breasted women on the front. She hadn't known women's breasts could grow that big and wondered about backaches and bra construction.

'Are you going to help or just stand there staring all day?' the librarian snapped.

With a start, Perdita remembered where she was and why she'd come.

Her reluctant companion was flicking through books, tutting and returning them. 'I don't have time for this.'

Perdita expected the librarian to march out of the shop, but she marched right up to a shop assistant. At least, Perdita assumed it was a shop assistant. Dressed with all that fur and the pointy ears on her head suggested she might have escaped from the pet shop next door.

'Excuse me,' the librarian said in a clear, commanding voice. 'Do you have any books that are easy for a beginner to read? And, when I say beginner, I mean an absolute beginner. For someone who's just left the convent.'

The shop assistant blinked. Perdita blinked too. That wasn't quite how she would have described herself.

The shop assistant looked at Perdita pityingly. Then she strolled to the shelves, swishing her bushy tail, and ran her finger along the book spines. She picked one out, flicked through it and replaced it. But the second one she took passed her fleeting examination. 'Try this.' She handed the book to Perdita. 'Unless your mum wants to check it over first?'

The librarian raised a questioning brow to Perdita.

'I think that's best.' Meekly, Perdita handed the book over to her "mum" who turned a few pages and looked at the line drawings.

'Yes,' the librarian agreed. 'I think this is suitable.'

'You know,' the shop assistant said, 'I do admire you. My mum would never have done anything like this for me.'

'I'm not her mother. I'm her librarian.'

'Oh. I didn't know they offered a book-finding service like this. It's amazing how modern the council have become.'

'They don't and they haven't. I took pity on her. No mother. Orphan.' The librarian turned to Perdita and passed the book back. 'You can pay for it now, and I'm off to have some lunch.'

Perdita felt panic rising. 'No. Please wait until I'm safely outside. It's far too strange in here.'

'Perdita!'

She froze at the sound of her name. Surely there couldn't be two Perditas in the shop? Surely, she couldn't have gone through the past twenty-eight years without bumping into a fellow Perdita only to discover a twin now, in this shop?

'Perdita. What are you doing here?'

She recognised the voice as Gavin's. And here he was, coming towards her holding a couple of brightly coloured tubes that could be hand cream. Thrusting the book into her companion's hand, Perdita explained, 'Oh, hi Gavin. Just helping a friend choose a book.' She avoided the librarian's gaze.

'Oh. Are you going to introduce me then? I don't think we've met. I'm Gavin.' He held out his hand. 'Hey, you must be Sister Margaret. We've heard so much about you from Perdita.'

'Do I look like a nun?' the librarian asked sardonically.

'Well, no. But then you're in disguise, aren't you? You couldn't come into a place like this without being in mufti. You know, civvies. No habit.' Gavin gave a raucous laugh.

'We've got to go,' Perdita exclaimed. 'We're in an awful rush.'

As Gavin was trying to work out what the book was called, Perdita stepped in front of the librarian so that he couldn't see.

'Must dash,' Perdita said but remained standing still. If he didn't move away, he would see that she was the one paying for the book, and then he would know that she'd lied. She turned pleading eyes towards the librarian, who shrugged, sighed and joined the queue at the pay desk.

'You've progressed then,' Gavin commented approvingly. 'You're the last person I expected to see in this place. Well, perhaps the second most unexpected person. First place would go to someone wearing a habit or a cassock. Are you sure that's not Sister Margaret? And my, you have come a long way since you're giving advice to someone so much older than yourself.'

'Mm.'

Gavin squinted at her in the dim light. 'Are you blushing?' He looked towards the pay desk. 'Who is that woman? It's not Sister Margaret, is it?'

'No, it isn't. How could you think such a thing? What would Sister Margaret need with a book from here?'

'No, I guess you're right.' He laughed as his expression became enlightened. 'But from what you said about this Tony guy, that's exactly what you need, isn't it?'

Perdita gazed over his shoulder, pretending not to have heard.

'I'm right. The book *is* for you.' He stepped towards her. 'Do you even know that woman?'

'Of course, I do.'

'How long have you known her?' Gavin asked suspiciously. 'When did you first meet her?'

'Erm, a little while ago.'

'Who is she?' he quizzed with a stern look. 'Come on, give. And not just half the story. I want the lot.'

'She's a librarian,' Perdita admitted reluctantly.

'A librarian?'

'Yes, she knows about books, and so she's helping me.'

'Where on earth did you meet her?'

Shamefaced, Perdita said, 'In the library.' Most Humiliating Experience Number Six...

Gavin burst out laughing. 'And you persuaded her to come here to help you get a book to tell you what to do?'

'That's exactly what she did,' the librarian said and shoved the book towards Perdita. 'You owe me twelve pounds. *Perdita*.' She held out her hand.

Perdita fished in her purse. 'I don't know what your

name is.'

'Barbara. Barbara Roach. Now, I must shoot off.'

'Thank you so much, Barbara. It was a very kind thing you did.'

'Yeah,' agreed Gavin. 'She needs all the help she can get. She was brought up in a convent.'

'We know,' the shop assistant and two other shoppers said who'd been standing close by taking it all in. 'And she's an orphan.'

Chapter 16

end of March

The antenatal waiting room in Bristol's Southmead Hospital was crowded with toddlers, mums with bumps of varying sizes and two dads-to-be. Perdita sat on a sagging two-seater sofa waiting nervously for her turn, cupping her tea, wondering how much she was going to miss Saul. He was leaving tomorrow, for a whole week, to walk in the Lake District with friends from college. She'd been working up to telling him about Setback Number One but still hadn't had the courage to do so. It would have to wait until after he returned, but the delay was making her increasingly skittish. She was also anxious about her coming appointment – considering how disastrous her initial one had been.

The first ever appointment she'd had with the midwife had been lengthy. First, there had been questions regarding her own health – which was fine – and whether she carried any blood-borne infections – which she didn't as she'd been tested after the debacle with Tony. Then there had been questions resurrecting long-dead sad memories...

'Did your mother have any difficulties with her pregnancy?' the midwife asked.

'She had cancer.'

'Did your mother have any other health conditions?'

'I don't know.'

'Any history of diabetes or a heart problem?'

'I don't know.'

'What about your father?'

Perdita felt she should have a card to hold up saying she didn't know. 'All I know is that he was fond of his drink.' He'd been celebrating the news that he was going to become a father when he'd been run over by a truck. 'He died and so did my mum.' It had been Sister Margaret who had given Perdita the lowdown about her parents. No medical documents of any kind had been among the things that had been passed on to her after Maureen Riley's death.

'Do you know if anyone from his family suffered from–?'

'I don't know anything else about either of them,' she said more sharply than she'd intended.

'I do have to ask. It's part of my taking care of you when–'

'I know. I'm sorry.'

'Now I need to ask you about the medical history of the baby's father.'

Perdita began to have that uncomfortable feeling again, and breathing became more strained. To help calm herself, she imagined a beautiful brightly-coloured flower waving in a gentle breeze, on a hillside with lots of grass. 'The only thing I know is that his name is Anthony Crawley.' How stupid did this make her look? Precisely as stupid as she'd been. As the pointless questions – from Perdita's point of view – continued, she shielded her face with her hands, hoping for a fire drill that would bring the interview to an abrupt end.

The midwife put a gentle hand on her arm. 'I can see this is distressing you. I don't mean to upset you. But I am bound to go through the form, and I can't miss anything out. I've finished with the medical questions now. But there is something else that is very important that we discuss. Can you show me that you are listening?'

Perdita sneaked a peek at the midwife through a gap she made in her fingers. She wondered if she was allowed to come to future appointments wearing a handkerchief, highwayman-style. Or a mask. Or, better still, a paper bag over her head.

'Perdita,' the midwife said, 'I would like to see your face. Please lower your hands. The worst is over, I promise. No more awkward questions.'

Slowly, Perdita lowered her guard.

'I see many young women in a similar position to you. I want you to know that I don't judge.'

Perdita folded her hands in her lap.

'Good. Now, we need to talk about your birthing options.'

The flower waving in the wind disintegrated, Perdita's heart began hammering away, and she gripped the arms of her chair. She wondered if she was going to be sick. The room didn't feel real, the woman opposite her didn't seem real, and she, herself, was something different, something indefinable and very strange. The sense of what the midwife was saying managed to filter through her uncomfortable bodily sensations.

The midwife shifted her chair forward so that she was close enough to hold Perdita's hands while she told her about alternative places for... germination... to take place, where there would be minimal medical intervention. Knowing she did not have a high tolerance to pain, Perdita decided to give these a miss and opt for a standard hospital… germination… in case she wanted an epidural. The thought of the whole process filled her with fear. The thought of going through it alone filled her with hysteria.

Perdita's nausea rose and rose until there was screaming in her ears. She was unable to speak, to explain her difficulty and was barely able to stand. That was when she leaned forward and vomited onto the midwife's lap. And mentally wrote up Most Humiliating Experience Number Four.

The appointment Perdita waited for now, having had her scan, was with her consultant. She studied the wall in front until she was brought back to the present by another midwife announcing to the group that one of the consultants, Mr Qureshi, had been called to perform an emergency Caesarean. Perdita resisted an urge to run.

'Poor woman,' murmured the red-haired woman about to sit down beside her.

Perdita turned, surprised, as she'd missed the woman's arrival. 'Yes,' Perdita agreed heartily, 'it's one of my worst fears.' Perhaps she wouldn't need her running shoes just yet.

'Mine too. The other is losing my baby – I've had two miscarriages already.'

'I'm so sorry, how awful for you.' Perdita placed her empty cup on the coffee table, nausea threatening.

'I've given up my job so that I can take things easy,' the other woman said. 'We've tried for a child for so long now that it's the only thing I can think about.'

'How many weeks are you?' Perdita was unfamiliar with bump sizes and shapes and worried she might confuse bump for lump or vice versa and cause offence.

It was a tricky thing.

The red-haired woman touched her bump and told her. She was only three weeks ahead of Perdita. 'It's the farthest I've got.'

'You must be worrying all the time,' Perdita sympathised.

'When's your baby due?'

Perdita gulped at the instant shot of nausea that word gave her. 'August. The 25th,' she croaked.

'Is it going well?' her companion asked.

Perdita cleared her throat. 'Yes. I've been lucky.'

'That's good. And the father – is he pleased?'

Perdita's breathing was becoming more laboured. 'He doesn't know.' It was time she pulled herself together and invoked that beautiful brightly-coloured flower.

'Oh.'

'I'd misread his intentions. I found out later he'd... been to bed with every available woman under the age of fifty,' Perdita explained. Then she added, 'But I might have been misinformed. He might not have had any cut-off point.' Office gossip at the Christmas party had been enlightening, but too late to help her. 'I can't believe how naive and foolish I was.'

'Don't blame yourself. Some men are very clever at getting what they want. How will you manage?' the woman asked kindly.

'I'm staying with friends – for now,' Perdita said.

'Look, take my number.' The woman rummaged in her bag for a scrap of paper and a pen.

'It's all right. Really.'

'No, please – at least you'll have someone to talk to if you're desperate.'

Perdita took the proffered scrap and stowed it in her

bag without looking at it as her name was called. The appointment went well, she was hardly in the room for any time. When she came out, the red-haired woman was nowhere to be seen.

Perdita drove to the town centre, parking in the Cabot Circus multi-storey. A neighbour was looking in on Violet during Perdita's absence. She went to budget clothes shops and bought black Lycra trousers, stretchy leggings and long shirts, a beige and cream pinafore and some T-shirts plus some new underwear. Then she sat at a small round table in a café, ordering chilled lemonade and homemade moussaka. Remembering Saul's comments about a non-existent cookbook, she thought she'd get her lamb 'fix' away from home and cook a Bolognese in the evening. While he was on holiday, she wouldn't have to be so careful. She'd consider it the silver lining to his having to go away.

Chapter 17

mid-April

It was mid-afternoon when Saul arrived home feeling refreshed and healthy from his time tramping up and down mountains in the Lake District. Although he'd badly needed a holiday and had enjoyed the break, especially spending time with his college friends, the last few days away had begun to pall as he'd found himself hankering after home and, to his consternation, Perdita's company.

He'd fought against missing her with valiant enthusiasm, filling his days with exercise to the point of exhaustion. Once he'd found Perdita at the department store, caught her and almost lugged her home, he thought he would stop dreaming about her. But he hadn't. Like before her arrival at Westbridge, Perdita remained forever elusive – but now he chased her with unfettered longing rather than determined revenge.

As for the day-time dreaming – well, that was very different. There he did capture her in his arms. But try as he might to get her into his bed, the imaginary Perdita always managed to foil his attempts at seduction. Usually by stuffing her mouth with food, often strange food – or rather, strange combinations. She'd taken a fancy to tinned fish. As well as the pilchards, crisps and mustard sandwich he'd seen her eat, he'd caught her mashing sardines into potato with mayonnaise and stuffing anchovies into slices of cake.

Glimpsing himself in the hall mirror after setting down his enormous rucksack, Saul saw that he looked travel-worn and tanned from the outdoors. Then voices captured his attention. At first, he thought that perhaps Violet and Perdita had guests, but then he realised it was the strains of Radio 4's afternoon play he could hear. He found Violet and Perdita snoozing in armchairs by the open patio door with Frank stretched out on Perdita's lap.

In relaxed sleep, Perdita's face was angelic and smooth. Her skin was fresh and without blemish. She was the picture of health. Even her body had filled out attractively, and he realised that she couldn't have been looking after herself properly when she'd met him – because she'd given her money away and had not had enough to eat? Surely not?

Studying Perdita, Saul knew he didn't want her to leave them. Turning away, his vision was caught by the profusion of colour on the patio. Easing between the armchairs, he stepped outside into the bright sunlight for a closer inspection and detected a waft of sweet scent. A sparrow fluttered away in fright, seeking shelter on a nearby branch. The pots and troughs brimmed with blooming flowers of yellow, white, blue, pink and purple. The only varieties Saul recognised were the pansies, crocuses and spikes of hyacinths. Perdita not only created beauty, he thought, turning to admire her, but was also enchanting herself.

The sound of his shoe scraping something on the stone slab must have woken her as she started and stood up, making Frank jump down and begin his stretching and yawning routine. Perdita's eyes widened as they met Saul's, and she made towards him. But, as she was stepping out onto the patio, she stumbled, perhaps from lingering sleep, and her body launched towards him. Saul put out his arms to save her, just as he'd done in his study, and found her body pressed securely against him – and her delectable lips brushing his.

There was only one thing for it. He kissed her, unable to resist despite Violet's proximity. Besides, she was asleep, wasn't she?

Perdita's lips were soft, and her kiss tasted of comfort and homeliness. And he didn't want it to end. He pulled back for a moment, and her expression, to his surprise, was of vulnerability. As though to reassure her, he kissed her again. When he broke off the second time, his breathing deep and laboured, Violet coughed, and he immediately released Perdita.

Perdita grabbed one of the chairs on the patio and sank down, her legs refusing to support her. Saul had kissed her more passionately than when he'd kissed her in his study, and she felt he'd ignited something inside her, a flame that, now well and truly lit, would not die. She was in love.

Saul stepped back into the house to greet Violet. Perdita wanted to follow him, but her legs refused to cooperate; they were on strike. Besides, she should show some restraint. She couldn't go chasing after Saul just because he'd evoked strong feelings in her.

Violet stared meaningfully at Perdita when she finally managed to stagger into the dining room. But Perdita couldn't share her secret with Saul yet; she wasn't ready, and it didn't feel right to have Violet as a witness. And it was easier to pretend it didn't exist.

'You've done a great job.' Saul nodded at the patio while addressing Perdita.

'Thank you. Violet helped me choose what to buy. We went to the garden centre together.'

'It's good, really good, what you've achieved out here,' he murmured, his gaze caressing her.

Perdita wondered if there was a punchline that would break the spell she was under. But no, Saul really did seem to like her.

'As a thank you for holding the fort while I was away, how about I treat you to dinner on Friday? And it's time we formally held a truce. New beginnings.'

'I'd like that,' Perdita said. But part of her was filled with misgiving. Would Saul have said that if he'd known what she'd been hiding from him all along?

Chapter 18

While the carer helped Violet prepare for bed that Friday evening, Perdita showered and changed into black trousers and a loose shirt. Then she stabbed silver earrings through her almost closed piercings and watched as the delicate designs dangled prettily through her lengthening bob. The ends of her hair were now touching her shoulders, and she decided to continue letting it grow as she wanted to be able to put it into a ponytail.

She made up her eyes in the same way as she had the evening she'd spent with Tony, hoping Saul would consider her beautiful. Guiltily, she eyed the banana she'd filched from the kitchen. As the acquired book had suggested, she'd performed various exercises on the fruit until it had been squeezed and stroked into a black-spotted length that was, to her mind, no longer fit for consumption. She chucked it into her wastepaper basket.

Then she plucked it out again as something struck her. She examined the shape in her hand and then lightly pressed it against her pelvis, so that it didn't squash. Then she looked towards the wardrobe where she'd hidden the book she'd bought with the assistance of that librarian, Barbara Roach.

What had been in Saul's trousers that day in the office, when she'd fallen onto him, and he'd kissed her? The book had line drawings, but there'd been no mention of scale. And why had he tried to hide... whatever it was? Had it been his bodily reaction he'd been ashamed of? Or could it be that he'd asked his friend for a banana before coming home as she'd failed to replenish stocks – and he hadn't wanted her to view his needing to source a banana from elsewhere as a criticism of her housekeeping?

If it hadn't been the banana she'd felt, that must mean Saul liked her. But did it mean he liked her in the same way Tony had liked her – temporarily – and therefore it was meaningless? Would Saul's body – assuming it had been his body – have reacted in the same way had any female non-relative fallen against him like she had? And could soft tissue ever feel as hard as an unripe banana? She wanted to get to the bottom of it.

Afraid of tripping, she carried her stilettos as she walked down the two flights of stairs. Saul was waiting for her in the hall, wearing navy trousers and a soft-blue shirt. Her heartbeat sped up at the sight of him and there was a sparkly feeling in her stomach, as though butterflies were zapping her with electricity. She wondered if he would kiss her again before the end of the evening.

Smiling, Saul said, 'Are you ready? Shall we go?'

Disappointed that Saul hadn't been more enthusiastic in his greeting by giving her a compliment or three, Perdita said, 'Yes, after I've said goodbye to Violet. Has the carer gone?'

'She has.'

Perdita found Violet in bed, propped up by pillows, watching television. 'We're about to go. If you have any problem at all, press your pendant or use the speed dial on your mobile, okay? We'll come straight back.'

Violet gave her usual lopsided grin as though to say she would be fine and not to worry and then raised a thumb. Then she raised a piece of paper with two words written on it: TELL HIM!

Perdita gulped, quickly proffered a goodnight kiss, waved and went back into the hall, fighting for air.

'Is something wrong?' Saul asked.

'No,' she lied as she inhaled a deep breath. Saul didn't look convinced, and she was suddenly struck with inspiration. Grabbing hold of his arm, she pulled him towards the front door and whispered, 'I think Violet… might have…'

'Farted?' Saul whispered back.

'Mm.' It was a believable scenario. Violet did occasionally have mishaps.

'Was it very bad?' he asked sympathetically. 'Was it one of her silent but deadly ones?'

Feeling treacherous, Perdita nodded.

'Do you think that's why she keeps opening the window in there?'

'Probably.' Had Saul already forgotten that the window was Frank's access point to Violet's room? 'It happens to the best of us,' Perdita said, hoping that Violet hadn't heard any of their exchanges.

In the car, Perdita felt uneasy as neither of them had spoken for several minutes, and Saul's profile appeared set as though he was uncomfortable. About her? 'You seem subdued. We can go straight back if you don't want to go after all. The last thing I want is for you to–'

'Perdita,' he interrupted softly, 'that's not what I want, and you know it.' He shot her a glance filled with a fiery yearning, and a thrill of anticipation shot through her. 'My concern for going out with you, sharing a meal with you, is that I will like it far more than is wise.'

Perdita was not impressed. 'That's not a compliment.'

'For me, it is.'

On reflection, Perdita thought he was probably right. To have reached his thirties looking like he did and not having married, he must have been ducking and side–stepping eligible women on a daily basis. Probably by being short on compliments.

'I thought we'd try out the new Italian restaurant in Clifton – there was a full page spread about it in the local paper. You said you liked Italian food.'

'Yes, I love it.' Italians ate lamb, didn't they?

As they were approaching the suspension bridge that would lead them into Clifton, Saul said, 'You're very quiet.'

Now or never, she decided. 'You know, I won't be offended if you ask a friend for a banana because we've run out at home. Although, I have managed the housekeeping better since.'

'Since when?'

'Since I gave you that box of chocolates in your study.'

'I don't know what you're talking about.'

Perdita squeezed her eyes shut. 'There'd been no need to be so embarrassed about it.'

'Embarrassed about what?' Saul asked. And then the car momentarily veered across the road. 'That hadn't been a banana you'd felt.'

'Oh.' It was good that Saul needed to keep his attention on the road ahead as it meant he couldn't see her goggling eyes. Well, his body liked her – what about his heart?

When they reached the restaurant, Perdita saw that

it had been done out in a rustic style: bare floorboards and plain wooden chairs and tables that had a beaten appearance. Italian paintings were displayed on terracotta walls and there was a trickling of water along a channel fixed to the far wall. She hadn't expected to be going somewhere that was quite so romantic. Had Saul known what to expect? He didn't appear to be at all put out by the ambience helped by candles, single red roses tucked into slender vases and the soundtrack of *The Godfather* being softly played.

The place was already half full, and almost all the tables bore reserved signs. When the waiter showed them to their seats, Perdita chose to sit against the wall, and Saul sat opposite. The waiter took their drink order and left them to peruse the leather-bound menus.

It was then that Perdita spotted two very familiar figures. It was all she needed. When she saw that the boys were destined for the table behind Saul, she coughed loudly to attract their attention. Just as their waitress was asking the boys if the table was all right for them, Luke turned and met Perdita's imploring gaze.

'Great,' Perdita heard Gavin tell the waitress.

'No, it isn't,' Luke said, turning to Gavin. 'I don't like it here. Isn't there some other area we could go to?'

'What do you mean, you don't like it? There's nothing wrong with it,' Gavin protested.

Perdita saw Luke clutch Gavin's hand and nod his head towards her. To her relief, she heard Gavin say, 'Oh... no. This won't do at all. I don't like it here either.'

The waitress regarded Perdita curiously before leading the boys away.

'Are you listening?' Saul asked.

Her eyes widened as they shifted towards Saul's face to show that he had her full attention. The boys had gone. And Saul hadn't recognised their voices. Or had he? Could he have turned around without her noticing? Was that why the corners of his mouth twitched?

'I asked what you fancy having,' Saul said with a grin.

'Oh.' Perdita lowered her head to scan the offerings and soon laid the menu down on the table. 'I think I'll have *Abbacchio alla Cacciatora,* please. What about you?'

'I'll stick to pasta.' Saul shrugged apologetically. 'I'll have a break from lamb. While I can,' he joked.

Perdita picked up her napkin and tried to fan herself with it. Using the Italian name instead of the English translation hadn't sneaked it past Saul. She knew her temporary addiction would have been less noticeable had she chosen something other than lamb, but the pull had been too strong.

'How about a sharing platter for starters? Some calamari and...' Saul read out the selection from the menu.

'Sounds good.'

After the waiter had taken their order, she said, 'It's charming here. Thank you for bringing me.'

'My pleasure.' Saul spoke as though he really meant it. 'Tell me, how did you come to...?' He quickly shut his mouth and then said, 'Tell me about yourself.'

'I suspect you were just about to ask me about F&Z, so let's get that over with. I grabbed the first job I could get on graduating. I needed to pay rent as I had nowhere to live. It was a means to an end, but I honestly did my best for my clients.'

'I believe you. Now let's forget about F&Z... Tell me some more about your family. What happened to your father? I don't recall you mentioning him.'

'He died from a collision with a truck he'd been too

drunk to see coming... He'd been celebrating the fact that he was going to be a dad.'

Saul appeared shocked. He opened his mouth, but it was a little while before he spoke. 'How dreadful for you. For you and your mother... I can't imagine how she'd felt.' He shook his head. 'And because of that brief lack of vigilance, you both lost him when you needed him the most...'

'We did.' Perdita's throat swelled under his sympathy, and she found it hard to swallow.

'About your mother... Did you tell Sister Margaret how you felt? The guilt about her not having had treatment until after you were born?'

'Yes. She said it wasn't my fault. But it had felt like it. Just like with Violet...'

'Is that why you agreed to move in? Because you take the blame for everything?'

'I'd just lost my job too, remember?' Perdita was unable to meet his eyes as she'd left a vital piece of information out.

'Well, I know I've been wrong about you. I hope you forgive me, and I believe it's time you forgave yourself over your mother because, really, it's what any mother would do for her child. It had been her decision; you'd done nothing wrong.'

'I know. Sister Margaret spent a lot of time reassuring me. But when things go wrong for me, it all comes flooding back, and I feel this overwhelming guilt and sorrow. Knowing something logically doesn't necessarily stop you feeling it emotionally.'

'I can understand that. I wish my mum had been around longer, too.' Saul smiled. 'What did you do when you weren't studying or working?'

Perdita played with the corner of her napkin. 'Not

much. I had a part-time job while at university in an old people's home, but that counts as work too. I led quite a boring life, really.'

When the drinks came, Saul waited until they were alone again before asking, 'And boyfriends?'

Perdita shifted in her chair. 'Not really.' What was the definition of a boyfriend? Someone you socialised with more than once, surely? 'Actually, none at all. I was using that loan Sister Margaret mentioned to help fund my degree, and I wanted to do as well as I could so that I'd be able to earn enough to pay it back. And, when I started work, I just concentrated on that. Took as many clients as I could.' That might make him think that it was she who'd avoided the men and not the other way around.

The waiter arrived carrying a large platter, and Saul created space for it. As they filled their plates with tasters of the various dishes provided, Saul observed, 'You're getting on extremely well with Violet, aren't you?'

Perdita wished she had an aunt like Violet. 'I liked her from the start. Most clients treated me with distant politeness, but Violet saw me as an actual person. I enjoyed my visits to see her. She thinks very highly of you. She never stopped talking about "her nephew".'

'Really?' Saul sounded surprised. 'She talked about you too.'

Perdita smiled with pleasure, and then her mood dipped. 'Why did you dislike me on sight then? I know you did.'

At first, she thought he was going to pretend he didn't know what she meant, and then he seemed to think better of it. Taking her hand in his, he said, 'It was self-protection. You posed a kind of threat, standing there so beautiful, looking up at me with those huge brown eyes of yours.'

'Is that meant to be a compliment? Because being called a threat doesn't sound very nice.'

'I'm probably out of practise,' Saul said. 'But I'll try to do better.'

After the waiter had removed the platter things, Perdita's attention was caught by a deep rasping voice that sounded familiar. The burly figure, greying hair and facial profile confirmed the identification of the man as Mike Loader, her ex-boss. As the waitress was making room for Mrs. Loader, Perdita dearly wished that she had let the boys sit there.

But Fate came to the rescue. Mike glanced her way, did a double-take and asked if there was another table available as he felt it was too noisy and busy.

'This is the quietest area of the restaurant, sir,' the waitress replied.

'Then it's not noisy enough. I don't want our conversation overheard.'

'What are you talking about?' Mrs Loader demanded. 'There's nothing wrong with it here.'

'I'll explain later,' Mike Loader hissed, avoiding further eye contact with Perdita. 'Come on.' He put his hand out to help his wife back onto her feet.

Perdita waited until they were gone and the waiter had placed their main course on the table before asking, 'What did you mean the day Fiona came to lunch when you said that she was like your glamorous mother?'

Saul had been gazing over her shoulder, but now he flicked his eyes a fraction and was looking straight into hers. 'Oh. Not a lot. My mother was very glamorous – just like Fiona. That's all.'

Perdita suspected there was more to it. And he seemed distracted. But, if he wanted to keep whatever it was to himself, she decided she would tactfully retreat and pretend that his answer satisfied her. 'What happened to your parents?'

Saul's voice deepened. 'They were killed in a car crash on their way to London to do their Christmas shopping. I had been left with Violet who moved in full time to look after me and stayed ever since.

'I went off the rails for a while until I came to terms with the fact they were never coming home again. Then I became introverted and didn't mix with other kids. Violet fixed up my friendship with Fiona as her parents had been friends of the family. So we spent our holidays in each other's pockets and became quite close for a time.'

Perdita studied Saul's expression. 'How did you feel? After your parents died? Did having Violet make you feel you belonged?' She guessed it might. He'd had a real home, unlike her.

Saul considered. 'I'm not sure what I felt. My emotions were too much of a jumble. It was such a shock – trauma – to lose both at the same time. I can't imagine what it must have been like for you – to have no family. What about friends of family?'

Perdita shook her head. 'Not that I know of. Perhaps in Ireland. But no one ever came looking for me. I didn't know who I was. What kind of person I should be. Anchorless. I had a letter my mum wrote to me before she died. That's something.' She felt tears pricking at her eyes.

Saul regarded her with crinkled eyes. 'So, it's true what Sister Margaret said? You do feel lost?'

Clearing her throat, Perdita nodded. 'My mother and I – we lost each other, and I don't really know where I'm headed. I seem to go where the waves in this big ocean of life take me. I shouldn't have taken that finance job in the first place, but I thought of the money and how I could repay the kindness shown to me more quickly.'

Saul reached across the table and squeezed her hand. His eyes burned with something that Perdita could not identify. It was intense but not with the lust she'd suspected him of when they'd been on the back seat of the car, the day he'd abducted her. Something else. More protective perhaps? Her heart missed a beat.

'How come you haven't married?' Perdita's hand shot to her mouth. Should she have asked that?

But Saul didn't seem fazed by it. 'I had toyed with the idea with my last girlfriend. To my mind, we were in a serious relationship. But then I discovered she was cheating on me, and I haven't had another girlfriend since.'

Perdita's mouth formed an 'O'. Perhaps that explained his mistrust of her. 'I don't know how she could; you're absolutely gorgeous,' she whispered, noticing him blush. 'I could never do anything like that...'

'Well, she did. And I just concentrated on my work and going out with friends. And spending time with Violet, of course. Until I met you...'

Until he'd met her...? Did that mean he'd been developing feelings for her while she'd been developing them for him? Before she could ask him to elaborate, the waiter came to clear their plates, and Saul asked for the dessert menu. And then the moment was lost as Perdita was suddenly overcome by an urge to dive under the table.

'Are you all right?' Saul asked with concern.

'Quite all right, thank you,' Perdita replied sweetly while on all fours. 'Dropped my napkin.'

'It's on the table.'

'Oh, is it? That would be why I had trouble finding it.'

Saul chuckled. 'Perdita, what is going on?'

Her heart sank. Why had Saul said her name so loudly? As she inched back up onto her chair, she raised her gaze to the figure in brogues that she'd spied earlier. And that figure was staring back at her in utter dismay.

Then Perdita heard the librarian address the waitress. 'I'm afraid this table isn't suitable after all.'

The waitress's lips parted in disbelief before aiming an accusing stare at Perdita. Hastily, she took a sip then studied her glass and the bubbles inside it. She didn't dare look up in case Saul suspected something was going on.

'It's too draughty here,' Perdita heard Barbara Roach say.

'The only other table available, madam, is close to the entrance and it will be very draughty there.'

Perdita risked a glance over to the librarian and saw Barbara Roach straighten, pushing out her ample bosom, and the bewildered expression on the face of the man Perdita took to be her husband.

'Some fresh air would be welcome,' the librarian said. She traced a finger along the inside of the collar of her blouse. 'I find it stultifying. Not enough draught.' She then grabbed her husband's arm and led him away, and the waitress followed.

As Perdita began to breathe again, their waiter returned bearing a small blackboard. Now that the danger had passed, Perdita said, feeling distinctly peckish, 'I'll have the profiteroles, please.' A vision of an over-sized orange space hopper floated across her mind's eye, but Perdita firmly batted it away. She was still avoiding Saul's gaze.

'And I'll go for the tiramisu.' Saul looked at Perdita. 'Then coffee?'

'Okay. Thanks.'

The waiter nodded and left.

Saul leaned in. 'Perdita, before there is any more drama, please could you explain why people don't like to sit near you?'

Perdita looked around as though for inspiration but quickly changed tack; other people were glancing her way. 'I don't know what you mean.' But she felt the heat in her face.

Saul grinned. 'Look behind you.'

Slowly, Perdita turned. There was a massive mirror along the wall behind her. He would have seen everything. Feigning ignorance was not going to work.

'Is it always going to be this entertaining when we go out together?' He was laughing openly now, as though he'd been suppressing his mirth for too long.

Could she distract him from the question? 'Would you like it to be?'

Saul pursed his lips in mock consideration. 'Not sure.'

Change of subject called for. 'Why didn't you and Fiona become a couple?'

Saul was silent, appearing deep in thought, and then the waiter brought the desserts.

When Perdita began to tuck in, she assumed the Fiona line of conversation would be closed but then, to her surprise, Saul said, 'I just didn't want to. I thought about it but something held me back, and I believe now I know why. Since that day I saw her with you. The things I heard her say and what she did. It was... malicious.'

Perdita nodded her agreement. At least Fiona's letter

had been an artful creation of contrition that would make it easier for Perdita to face Fiona in the future: *I'm sorry I had been careless of your feelings; had I realised how sensitive you were, I would never have played a practical joke by placing a piece of chicken on your plate; you have a very important role in looking after Violet, and I should not have undermined that* and, finally, *I hope, when we meet again, we can start anew and pretend none of this ever happened*. But Fiona probably hadn't meant the words she'd put to paper.

'She was so different to me when we were in our teens and twenties,' Saul said. 'A wild child. I was more serious; Violet's influence had calmed me down.'

'Fiona wasn't the stereotypical librarian then?'

Saul's laugh was low. 'No. Anyway, we were separated as I took my degree in London – LSE – and then got my first job up there, so I didn't see much of her. Now that I've taken over the practice with Bruce in Bristol, I'm home again. You must meet him, I'm sure you'll like him.'

Perdita smiled noncommittally. 'I went to King's. So, we were both in London.' But she hadn't liked it there. London was too busy, too noisy and too scary.

'But not at the same time. What are you, twenty-eight? I'm thirty-five.'

Perdita thought that was a very good age for a man to want to settle down and have a family.

The waiter cleared the dessert plates and brought the coffee.

Saul said, 'You seem too good to be true. Don't you have any vices? I already know you don't drink or smoke, I can't conceive you've been on drugs, and you said that boyfriends passed you by.'

Perdita played with her hair. Saul putting her on a pedestal made her feel uncomfortable.

'Well, do you have any hidden vices?'

'No. But...'

'Yes?'

Say it, she told herself. Say it and be done with it. But she couldn't, not here, not in front of so many people, where she would undoubtedly cry, and he would walk out. Fear gripped her, and Perdita chose the safest course. Her voice trembled. 'I don't have vices, but I'm no Virgin Mary either. And someday soon – but not now,' she added hastily, 'there's something I need to tell you.'

Saul raised his brows. 'No Virgin Mary or no virgin?'

Hiding behind a napkin, her cheeks so hot she might set it on fire, she whispered, 'Neither.'

Saul pressed the top edge of the napkin down with his finger, and he scrutinised her.

'I just don't want you to put me on a pedestal when there shouldn't be one. I have faults and make mistakes like everyone else. Big mistakes. Mistakes… that can't be undone.'

She could see that he didn't understand. She'd told him she hadn't had time for boyfriends yet she was admitting to having... been intimate. What was he thinking? That she went in for one-night stands, so that men were never around long enough to be described as a boyfriend? Or that she'd been... attacked?

'I see,' he said, frowning. 'Have these mistakes got anything to do with the people who didn't want to sit by you? I recognised Gavin and Luke – but the other two?'

Avoiding the appraising stare she knew must be there, Perdita replaced her napkin on the table and concentrated on watching a couple leave. 'No, the mistakes have nothing to do with the people here tonight. The man who came after Luke and Gavin was my ex-boss and the woman who arrived after him is... is... someone.' Her face burned with shame, and she covered her cheeks with her hands. 'I can't explain about her as I might spontaneously combust from mortification, and that won't be fun for anyone here.' As an afterthought, she added, 'And if I weren't to spontaneously combust, I'd have to go into deep hibernation, and no one would see me ever again.'

'I won't ask any more about it,' Saul said. 'There's no need to hide anymore; you're safe to show your face – although you must have made quite an impression for her to have behaved like that... But then... it seems that's just what you do... Shall we leave past embarrassing situations in the past?'

Perdita smiled with relief. 'Yes. That's a good idea.' Did that let her off the embarrassing Tony situation? Perhaps, for now, Perdita thought.

Chapter 19

When they arrived back, having had an almost silent ride home, Saul suggested, 'More coffee?'

'I'll make some for you while you check on Violet; I'll have some juice.'

By the time Saul returned, reporting that Violet had fallen asleep, Perdita was pouring from the cafetière. She placed his mug on the table with her glass of apple juice.

He came closer and murmured, 'I don't know what it is, but the more I see of you, the more I want you.' He took her hand and held it for a moment before passing it to his lips, lightly touching her skin with his. The trail of sensation remained even after Saul straightened and lowered her hand.

But he didn't let go, and her pulse quickened. Scraping a chair back, he sat down, guiding her onto his knees. It felt awkward; she'd never sat on a man's lap before. Sister Margaret used to bounce her up and down, but she thought she was too heavy for Saul to do that. As her thighs spread out across his legs she wondered if Saul could feel the expansion too and would consider her fat.

'That awful day in the store, I didn't mean the things I said – I just had to take it out on someone. Every time I think about it, and how I manhandled you, I cringe. I'm ashamed of how I behaved.'

'You did behave badly...' Perdita cleared her throat

as it sounded like she was talking through a glass of water. 'But you know... ahem... no one's ever stood up for me like you battled for Violet.'

'Violet means the world to me.'

Could she mean the world to him, too? Saul had one hand on her waist and another on her thigh. The one on her thigh moved slightly, and Perdita wondered whether she was old enough to suffer a heart attack. Her heart was hammering away like a room full of frenzied elves nailing soles onto shoes for customers. And because her postural muscles were melting, she leaned against Saul for support. Then he lifted her chin and kissed her. And she thought she was about to die.

'Are you okay?' Saul asked with concern.

She wasn't sure. Should she tell him she might not be long for this world?

'Do you have asthma? Have you got your inhaler with you?'

'Sorry?'

'Your breathing. You're having difficulty.'

'I... I'm not used to this kind of activity.' She tried to even out her inhalations with her exhalations so that they became smoother and less ragged.

'Do you want this to stop?' He stroked her cheek.

'No,' Perdita said softly. 'I like kissing you. Do you like kissing me?'

'I adore kissing you.'

'Perhaps you should do it more often, then. Think of it as a new hobby; one we could share.' But such a hobby and Setback Number One were definitely incompatible, and really, she ought to let Saul know.

'I'd like to do more than kiss you,' he said with a gentle groan.

Perdita clutched her chest. She had to make sure that

her heart didn't leap out into Saul's face. Did this mean he cared about her? She certainly cared about him.

'Please say no if you have the slightest qualm. It's just that here, in the kitchen, I can't do with you what I'd love to do...'

'And that is?'

'Carry you off to my room... or your room, if you prefer.'

His words hung between them, and she gulped. 'You mean...? Are you sure you want to?' Had Saul asked her to sleep with him tonight because he'd discovered she wasn't a virgin? Did he, like Tony, dislike them? Years ago, they were highly prized, and there would be trouble if the woman wasn't a virgin. Did virgins now have to hide the fact that they were virgins in order to lure a man into bed with them? And, only once over that first hurdle, were men happy to sleep with them?

Saul laughed. 'What do you mean, am I sure I want to carry you off to my or your room? Of course, I'm sure.'

Perdita yearned to have him carry her off to any room and to make love to her, even if it was for just the one night. Before she told him. The temptation to experience further exquisite sensations was too great to turn down.

It was wrong, dreadfully wrong of her, but she felt that if she had this night to remember for the rest of her life, at least she would have known what... doing it... with a man she'd fallen in love with could be like. As for the morning after... well, Saul might do a runner like Tony had. She felt this might be her last chance saloon.

'Spend the night with me.' He caressed her cheek as he spoke, and Perdita felt like grabbing his hand, saying, well what are we waiting for then?

The angel on her right shoulder said, 'Don't do it!' but the devil on her left shoulder said, 'Go for it!' The devil reasoned with her. Surely, she could, just once in her life, do a selfish act? After all, Saul had not categorically declared any love for her. While chatting to the devil, the angel's voice became more distant. Perdita could just make out, 'Promise you will tell him in the morning.'

Of course, she would. Definitely. Mentally, Perdita flicked the angel from her shoulder. She wanted tonight, and she wanted Saul.

'Whose room?' Saul asked.

'Yours.' She wanted to see his room, to be in his bed, to smell his sheets. And then Perdita wouldn't have to suffer his absence from her bed if it went wrong.

They tiptoed up the stairs like naughty children, not wanting to disturb Violet. Saul put on his bedside lamp, and it emitted an orange glow through the tangerine lampshade. Perdita noted old oak furniture, large black and white architectural prints on cream walls, and a sandy carpet. There was a small bookcase, and now she knew why his study had lacked fiction. It was all up here, predominantly crime and thrillers. There was a neat section of PD James novels and Perdita recalled the scene in the store when Saul had mentioned the name Dalgliesh.

Saul fumbled in the bedside drawer and then took out a small and shiny square packet. She guessed what that was. What would it feel like? Then she felt afraid. The book she'd bought with the help of Barbara Roach had mentioned that it was a good thing for the lover to put it on the man. The moment Perdita realised she would have to buy a box of the things to dress the bananas, she'd balked and had closed the book near to panic.

Saul stood in front of Perdita, looking her over with open admiration. 'You're beautiful. I've always thought so, but you're even more beautiful than when you first arrived.' Then Saul bent his head low to kiss her.

'I'd like you to last all night,' he murmured seductively. 'But,' he added regretfully, 'I don't think I could manage it.'

This seemed like an appropriate time as any. 'One,' Perdita whispered in his ear.

'One what?' Saul murmured, nuzzling her neck.

'You know,' Perdita answered. 'Number one.'

'You're telling me I'm number one for you?' Saul mumbled in her ear.

'No,' she said, confused by his inability to understand. And she was meant to be the inexperienced one! 'You'll be number two.'

Saul pulled away. 'Are you telling me you *count* your lovers?'

'Isn't that what you're supposed to do? I give you my number and then you give me yours?'

'No. At least, not right now. And not like this. Perdita, your timing is very off.' Saul gazed at her disapprovingly.

'Oh,' Perdita said, the light dawning on her, 'you say it afterwards, do you?'

'Why say it at all? Does it matter?'

'Oh.' She'd so wanted to get it right.

'We might have that conversation further down the line, but this is too soon.' He kissed the corner of her mouth. 'Don't let's spoil the moment.'

She kissed him back, eager to erase her folly.

'I can't wait much longer,' Saul groaned.

Determined to get something right, Perdita shut her eyes and aimed her hand in the region of his flies.

'I guess you can't either,' he murmured happily and whisked her off to his bed.

When he began to undress her, Perdita felt it was best to copy. However, the belt buckle was more than she could dare, but it didn't matter. Saul did it for her. And soon they were both in their underwear on his bed.

'Do you mind,' Perdita ventured in a little, timorous voice, 'if we get under the duvet now?'

'Cold?' Saul asked, sounding concerned.

It was easier to nod than admit she felt exposed, vulnerable and uncomfortable under Saul's roving eyes.

'Come on then.' Saul pulled the duvet out from under them and drew it over their bodies. 'Better?'

'Much. But it's a bit too bright.'

'You'd like the lamp off?'

Perdita nodded.

Saul switched off the lamp, and the room turned black. Perdita slipped her arms around his neck and drew him closer. Saul's lips met hers while he removed her underwear. Was she supposed to remove his underpants? She'd have thought she ought to seek his permission if she were going to attempt the task, but he hadn't asked her when he'd fiddled with the clasp of her bra. Or when he'd stuck his hand between her buttocks and her knickers before easing the material down and away. Was there some kind of etiquette book she should have read? But the dilemma became irrelevant when Saul twisted his body next to her and then she felt... something different pressing against her.

Later, caressing her hair and face, Saul asked,

'Whatever's the matter? Did I hurt you?'

'No,' she sniffed. 'I hadn't realised… how wonderful it could be.' And now she knew. She definitely, absolutely, loved him. But this was not what she'd expected. With this love came deep insecurity and defencelessness. With this love came pain and a deep need for Saul, and there was no certainty she would get him. Would he be another Tony?

He laughed softly. 'The first time is rarely pleasing.'

'Was it bad for you as well?'

Saul chuckled. 'No. It's different for men. It's far easier to have a good time.'

'Was it a good time for you, then?'

'Fantastic.' He kissed her tenderly before becoming quiet and still.

She lay awake long after she heard his snoring, savouring the weight of his arm around her waist and the afterglow of the experience they'd just shared. It wasn't until after the dawn sun began to illuminate the room through the fabric of the curtains that Perdita finally fell asleep.

Chapter 20

The loud rap at the front door roused Perdita. For a moment, she was confused by being in another bed, another room, but then, in a rush, the memory of the night before swamped her. She smiled as she imagined Frank grinning when presented with a freshly opened tin of pilchards. In tomato sauce.

Perdita could easily make out that Saul was not beside her, and she stretched lazily. She listened for sounds of Saul opening the front door, but when the rap was repeated, she realised she'd have to go down. Perhaps he was having a shower in the family bathroom so as not to disturb her or was in the garden.

Springing out of bed, she pulled on her long over-shirt from last night and stepped into her knickers. As she ran down the stairs, the person knocked again. Opening the door, Perdita poked her head around the gap enquiringly, keeping her body out of sight. She expected to see the postman or a neighbour. But it wasn't either of them.

Her whole world seemed to crash around her. Razed to the ground in a second. Unthinking, she stepped full into view, ignoring the impulse to shut the door on him. She watched as he took in her appearance. She took in his height, his blond wavy hair and his piercing topaz eyes.

'Tony!' Perdita exclaimed. 'How…? What…?' How had he found her, and what was he doing here? 'I don't want to do it again. It hadn't been nice.' She tried to close the door, but Tony stuck his foot out.

Perdita glanced behind her to check if Saul had come to see who was at the door. What would he make of Tony's presence? There was no one behind her. 'W... what are you doing here?' The end of her sentence rose in pitch. Saul would think she'd lied over never having had a boyfriend or think that she'd gone to his bed on the rebound.

'I'm running seminars in Bristol – this last week and next. I'm staying in Clifton. I was also asked to run a workshop at your office yesterday. I was hoping you wouldn't be there, but then I worried because you weren't. We need to have a chat.'

'I'm working. I can't see you.'

His brows shot up as he scanned her bare legs and long shirt. 'Is that what you wear to work?'

'I start late this morning, but I shall have to go as I need to get ready.' She felt as though someone had tied a cord around her neck.

'When can I see you then?' Tony's voice had developed an edge that Perdita didn't understand.

'I don't think we've got anything more to say to each other,' she told him, her palms sweating and her ears listening out for Saul's approach. 'Please, I've got to go.'

His foot was still in the way of the door. 'You don't understand. I mean to see you. There's a small matter to discuss. I can see you've put on weight, and I have it on good authority that you are having a baby.'

'Ha,' she gasped. Feeling faint, Perdita gripped the door, desperately invoking the beautiful brightly-coloured flower. How did he know? What did he know? Could she bluff her way out of it? A horrible creeping fear stole over her with a premonition of disaster. Saul must not find out like this.

The angel returned and said, 'I told you so,' and the devil on her other shoulder just chuckled gleefully.

If only she'd been prepared, had time to *think*. If only she'd told Saul. 'How did you know where to come?' It was important she knew exactly what Tony knew and how he knew it.

'Someone called Lucy wanted to know if I was a friend when she heard me asking someone if you were in. She looked at me strangely, so I asked her what was wrong. She said she was worried about you.'

Was that true? Did Lucy, or any of them, spare her a moment's thought in their hectic lives?

'Then I asked her to tell Uncle Tony all about it, and we sat down for a cosy chat.'

I bet, Perdita thought. Had Lucy had dinner with him last night?

'Lucy said she'd tried to call your landline to see how you were, but the person who'd eventually answered had never heard of you. When I asked why she was worried, she told me that you might be pregnant.'

Perdita almost gagged and conjured up the image of the flower as an antidote.

Tony peered more closely at her. 'She said that, although you'd never mentioned anyone, you might have a secret boyfriend. Well, you and I know that you never had a boyfriend, had you Perdita? You'd waited all those years to have–'

'Please... I get the picture.'

'And I don't think it was an earth-shattering experience for you, was it? You've admitted as much.'

'I have period pains,' Perdita said weakly. 'My doctor said the pill would help, and it didn't agree with me. It made me sick.'

'And do your period pains also give you a bigger belly and boobs?'

Perdita nodded. 'Absolutely. Trapped wind. I'm often bloated. I'm surprised you hadn't noticed. And water – water retention.'

'Oh, I notice women's bodies, Perdita, and yours was a lot slimmer then. Although, I must say it suits you; you are looking very good on it. You're a fertile little thing, aren't you? Once was all it took.'

'You are mistaken.'

'No, Perdita. I'm not mistaken. As soon as Lucy started to talk about it, my suspicions were confirmed. It didn't take much to get your address from her. I went to your flat late last night, but Lucy was right, you'd moved out. A neighbour gave me directions – but only after much persuasion. Luke?'

Perdita was outraged. How could Luke have led Tony to her? Why had he stuck his nose in? And why on earth hadn't he warned her? Then she remembered that she'd left her phone in her bag, and her bag had been left in the kitchen. Luke had probably tried to warn her. And he'd always been concerned that the father didn't know her news.

'You should have told me, Perdita. You had no right to keep it to yourself. I should have been consulted about what I wanted.'

'What happened to Marcia's bump, Tony? Where is it now?' Tears welled up as she pictured a defenceless being and a defenceless mother. From what she'd found out from Lucy, Tony's former conquest, Marcia, would have been happy to keep the growing bump if she'd had Tony's support.

Tony's darkened expression informed Perdita that the conversation she'd overheard at the staff Christmas party had been accurate. Tony had persuaded poor Marcia to have… an uprooting.

Tony stared at her. 'How do you know about Marcia?' Suddenly, he leaned forward and pointed a finger at her. 'You have no right to bring that up,' he growled. 'How did you find out about her?'

'At the Christmas party. Two of the women I was sitting with at dinner had rather too much to drink, and they came out with all kinds of things. But the only part of their conversation that interested me was about a friend of theirs who had been taken in by you. Just like I had. It's a shame that Christmas party hadn't been a year earlier. Because then I wouldn't have let you near me.'

'Can I come in? We shouldn't be having this conversation on the doorstep.'

'No.' Perdita glanced over her shoulder.

'What are you worried about?'

'They don't know. I'll get the sack if they find out.'

'When can we talk about it?'

Perdita wanted to get him away from the house as quickly as possible. But if she were away any time this weekend it would arouse curiosity and even suspicion, after her intimacy with Saul. He might expect to know all about her life from now on, where she was going and who with. 'What about in the week – during your lunch break?' Saul wouldn't be home then.

Tony shook his head. 'You know what these seminars are like; I can't just disappear at lunchtime. I'm running the show, and it wouldn't give us long enough. Tonight. At The Berkeley Square Hotel.'

It was a boutique hotel that she'd heard of but had never been to.

'Well?'

Perdita didn't think he'd given her much choice. 'I'll

be there.'

'Six o'clock. And if you're late, I'll come to get you.'

Shivers ran down Perdita's legs. 'Can I have your number? In case something turns up?'

'We can swap numbers but, as I said, I'll come to get you if you don't show up; this needs to be sorted tonight.'

'Text me so that I have your number. I don't have anything to hand to write with.'

Tony tapped the numbers she spoke into his phone and showed her the screen as his text message to her was sending. As soon as he left, Perdita charged upstairs to shower and change into fresh clothes. Then she rushed down to find Violet.

She was in her room, sitting by the open window. She must have seen everything. Had she also heard? Stricken, Perdita looked at Violet's face. But Violet turned away.

'I'm sorry,' Perdita wailed. 'The longer I kept it to myself, the harder it became to say anything. I know you wanted me to tell Saul before now. I will tell him at the first opportunity. I'll look for him this instant.' She must tell Saul immediately otherwise things would go pear-shaped as well as bump-shaped. Perhaps Saul, like Violet, had already heard? Her heart thudded painfully, and she felt panic rise. She didn't want to lose him.

On the kitchen table, Perdita found a note.

Perdita,

I've gone shopping. I'm cooking tonight. See you later, Saul.

Chapter 21

Saul placed the peppers, onions, garlic and tomatoes carefully into his large shopping bag at the greengrocer's till, ensuring not to squash the bloomer he'd bought from the baker's. Next, he needed to cross the road to reach D. Murphy Family Butcher, his last port of call.

When Saul entered the familiar shop, David Murphy, a man Saul had known as far back as his school days, was behind the counter.

David greeted him warmly. 'And what can I do for you, Saul? I've got some lovely spring lamb.' David half turned in the direction of the cold store at the rear of the shop.

Saul laughed. 'That's exactly what I want. I'd like a leg, please. Big enough to feed five people.' Saul imagined Perdita tucking in and decided to amend his order. 'No, make it six people.'

David disappeared into the back and re-emerged carrying a large leg of lamb. He put on his Kevlar gloves and cut the joint into a smaller size. 'Perdita not well? She usually does your shopping now.'

'She's fine. I thought she could do with a lie-in.'

'Yes,' agreed David, 'she probably could.' He checked the weight of the larger joint of meat using the electronic scales. Now, with an edge to his voice, David added, 'I expect you're thinking of wedding bells soon.' He gave Saul a meaningful stare.

'Wedding bells?' What did David mean? Or was it so obvious that he'd fallen in love with Perdita? Had last night's passion left a visible imprint on his face, advertising what he and Perdita had got up to? 'Well... er, it's a bit premature to be discussing anything like that.' He was not that friendly with David. And what business was it of his? Then Saul considered that David might not be thinking of Perdita at all. 'Who exactly are you referring to?' David's incredulous expression made Saul feel uncomfortable.

'Well, Perdita, of course. Who else? You can't keep the woman waiting. She needs to be married. To have a proper family.'

Saul thought David was taking his well-meaning attitude towards Perdita a tad far. 'Look, I hardly know the woman. Perhaps, in time–'

David snorted in disgust. 'You know her well enough in the biblical sense. It's the only proper thing to do. I must say, I didn't expect you to shirk your duty – bringing her here to live with you and not marrying her.'

Saul flushed. How did David know he'd slept with Perdita? 'I don't know what business it is of yours, David, but Perdita came to look after Violet. Not because I'd been fornicating with her.'

'Whether you are now or not, you can't tell me you haven't done it at least once, because I shan't believe you.' David stood firmly in front of him as he handed Saul his bagged meat. 'And although you no doubt want it kept a secret, some things just don't stay that way for long. People are already talking. There'll be no use denying it later. The whole town will side with Perdita. You could do a lot worse but not much better, I reckon. So why don't you have a word with Father

O'Connor? He's very understanding. You'll like him.'

In a daze, Saul turned to the cashier counter and handed Catherine a banknote.

'I trust you,' she said when she handed over his change, 'to do what's right.'

Saul said, 'I have no plans to marry Perdita – whether or not I do in the future is none of your business, and I'll thank you not to spread gossip.' He then headed for the open door, brushing past a young mother with a pushchair.

Thinking David and Catherine had a rather Victorian attitude to relationships, Saul was happy to make a fast retreat. He decided to leave the meat-buying to Perdita in future. They must be touched to talk to him like that, trying to coerce him into marriage. Bloody Catholics.

Then he remembered that Perdita was Catholic too. Well, it hadn't stopped her last night. And she certainly hadn't informed him that the price was marriage. Saul wondered who Perdita's first lover had been, and he experienced a sharp twang of jealousy. Why hadn't it worked out? Had the other guy refused to marry her? Saul had suspected one of those hunks who'd helped her move in of being her boyfriend, or an ex perhaps, but it had been clear when he'd seen them at the restaurant that Luke and Gavin were a couple. So it was doubtful that Perdita had slept with either of them.

Saul was beginning to suspect that Perdita might have misled David and Catherine. It was conceivable that she'd spread a tale of being engaged, or almost engaged, to Saul to cover up the real reason for her being at his house. That would have given David the idea that Saul was forestalling marriage. He would have to ask Perdita.

Disappointed that his shopping had marred his morning's pleasure over having a possible partner again, Saul's tread was far heavier than when he'd left the house that morning.

He found Perdita alone in the kitchen, drinking coffee. Her greeting was not as bright as he might have expected – was that because she'd guessed he might have gone to the butcher? 'You found the note?'

'Yes,' Perdita said as she fiddled with the spoon that lay next to her mug. 'Saul, there's something I've got to tell you; it won't be easy, and I don't know how to start.'

'I think I already know,' he said grimly, convinced that his suspicions were well-founded, 'and I can't think why you did it.'

'Did it?' Perdita whispered.

'David Murphy. You know; the butcher. He thinks we should get married. He knows we've slept together, and I am to make an honest woman of you. Since he couldn't possibly have known about last night, the only conceivable explanation is that you've been telling stories. And now you've been found out.'

Perdita's eyes bulged. 'Saul, I didn't tell him anything about us – there was no 'us' until last night and, unless I rang him first thing this morning, how could I have told him? And why would I do such a thing?'

'I thought perhaps you'd told him you'd come here as my girlfriend. To avoid embarrassment over being dragged here.'

'I said no such thing,' Perdita spluttered. 'Nor did I suggest we were on intimate terms. How could I since the truth, from your behaviour, is obviously far from it? I can't talk to you when you have just unfairly accused me of this. Please remember that I'd wanted to tell you something when you came in. But I can't now. Not when you're in this mood.'

But he just glared at her. 'What have you done? Tell me what you have done.'

She aimed pleading eyes at him. 'Not right now. I will, I promise. Just not right now. And... I hope you'll be able to forgive me.' Then she left the kitchen, and he heard the pounding of feet as she ran upstairs to her room.

Perdita found lunch quiet and awkward, and the kitchen seemed to have shrunk in size, its walls and units closing in on her. Violet looked questioningly at Perdita, and she shook her head almost imperceptibly. Violet's gaze scolded her. Perdita didn't know how to explain why she'd been unable to confess about being pollinated to Saul using just body language. Violet indicated sharply towards Saul with her head. Surely she didn't expect Perdita to tell Saul now? With Violet listening in?

'Are either of you going to enlighten me as to what is going on?' Saul asked. Although he'd addressed them both, he was looking directly at Perdita.

Perdita glanced at Violet and felt the kick of Violet's shoe. 'I think there's been a misunderstanding with David Murphy,' she said.

'I'd love to hear it,' Saul said dryly. 'I don't know if Perdita told you, Violet, that when I was out buying food for dinner tonight, David and Catherine told me in no uncertain terms that I should marry Perdita.'

Violet's eyes lit up, and she nodded vigorously.

Saul's laugh was forced. 'You're telling me that you think I should too?'

'Es...' Struggling to form the word more clearly,

Violet tried again. 'Yes.' She put her hand on his.

'At the moment, that's beside the point.' Saul pulled his hand away. 'Perdita, please would you explain how David got the idea that I should marry you? That he should think there was anything at all between us?'

Cornered, Perdita sat mute. She knew David had been acting in what he'd thought was her best interests when he'd had that talk with Saul, but she wished he hadn't had that talk today. Or tomorrow. In a few weeks, maybe, when Saul had got used to the idea of an unexpected addition to his household. But she had to tell him now. She *must*. 'Well,' she began, licking her lips to help lubricate her way to telling the truth, the whole truth and nothing but the truth. 'It all started in November. The day I first met you, Saul.'

Violet started, a hand flicking briefly to her cheek.

Fiddling with her fingers, Perdita went on. 'During that last visit, it wasn't just me who'd been giving advice–'

'You?' He looked astonished. 'What did you need advice about?'

What hadn't she needed advice about? A shame Violet hadn't given her warnings about predatory men and how to tell a good egg from a bad egg. 'Violet asked if I was single, and I said I was, and she said it was the brightly-coloured flowers that attracted the bees. I noticed what I was wearing, and, although it was smart, it was not very colourful. A bit boring.'

Violet's expression cleared, and her eyes widened questioningly.

So, Violet had already guessed the rest of the tale. Perdita gave a tiny nod.

'You're doing it again,' Saul grumbled. 'You're sending secret messages to each other, and I don't know what the hell is going on. It's like the two of you are in collusion about something.'

'No, not at all,' Perdita denied hotly, and this was confirmed by Violet's sharp shake of the head.

'That makes it look even more suspicious,' Saul griped. 'So, what's the big deal about wearing boring clothes?'

Perdita hesitated. How could she admit to wanting Tony to notice her?

'I wish you'd get on with it,' Saul said. 'I don't want to be sitting here until it's time to be off to work again Monday morning.'

Taking a deep breath, Perdita looked Saul squarely in the eye. 'I thought about what Violet said and knew she was right, and I thought that perhaps that's why I didn't have a boyfriend. Because of how I dressed. I wasn't attracting the bees.'

'Bees? On second thoughts, don't bother explaining. So, you went out and bought some new clothes? What of it?'

'I bought them in time for the next conference I was going to because there was a particular bee I was interested in attracting.' Perdita felt the blush under his scrutinising gaze. He was beginning to get the idea now. 'And that bee noticed me straight away, so Violet's advice worked.'

'Are you telling me,' Saul asked harshly, 'that you've got yourself a boyfriend?'

'No. And I don't have a boyfriend.'

'Or bee-friend?' he added sarcastically.

'No, I don't have a bee-friend either.'

Saul raised his gaze to the ceiling. 'Then what, in heaven, are we talking about? Where is this conversation going?'

Just then, the landline began to trill. Perdita expected Saul to jump up to answer it, but it wasn't until the eighth ring that he got to his feet and grabbed the cordless handset that was in the kitchen.

'Hello?... Yes, that's right... About seven o'clock?... We can make it later if that's a problem... Okay, great. And how's Gerry? Good, good. Okay, see you both then. Bye.' As he replaced the handset on the charging station, Saul said, 'I've invited my partner, Bruce, and his wife, Gerry, to dinner tonight. I arranged it this morning, but Bruce had already gone out when I called. I bought all the food anyway as Gerry seemed to think there would be no problem about being free. Violet knows them both well, and I'm sure you'll like them too.'

'Oh,' Perdita cried out in dismay, 'I've arranged to go out tonight.'

'Go out?'

There was a stunned silence.

'Yes,' she said in a small voice. 'I'm going out.'

'Can't you un-arrange whatever it is that you planned to do?'

'No, I can't. I'm ever so sorry. But I'll be back later.'

'I would damn well think that you'll be back later.'

Perdita blushed at the imputation. 'I meant,' she said in clipped tones, 'that I don't expect to be late, and that I will probably be back before your guests leave.'

'I certainly hope so since I mentioned that you would be here.'

'Well,' she said acidly, 'it would have been sensible to check with me first whether I would be here. You can't make an arrangement and expect me to fall in with it if you haven't discussed it with me. It seems even Gerry has to check with her husband before she can accept an invitation to dinner. It's a shame you didn't allow me the same respect.'

Saul's gaze was so penetrating it could have been a proton beam aimed at her. 'I have never known you go out on a Saturday evening since you came. You always eat with us, and I wanted it to be a surprise. I wanted to cook for you, for a change. I bought the lamb especially for you.'

Perdita's angry bubble burst. She'd messed up again. 'I'm sorry. I'm sorry I spoilt the surprise. It's a lovely thing to do, and if it weren't for the fact that I'd arranged to go out it would have been great.'

'Who is it you're meeting?'

Unsure whether Saul's attention switching from the David Murphy episode to tonight was a good thing, Perdita murmured, 'Someone from work. There's a bit of unfinished business to clear up.'

'Work? On a Saturday evening?'

She found it impossible to meet Saul's eyes. Perdita wished she could cancel her rendezvous with Tony, but she knew he'd come to the house if she didn't show.

'Can't you cancel and go out another night?'

Perdita shook her head miserably. 'I'm so sorry, but I've got to go. This was the only time that could be arranged.' She'd carefully chosen her words so that the use of gender terms was unnecessary. And she didn't dare glance Violet's way.

'Can't she come here? There'll be enough food to go around,' Saul suggested.

Perdita flinched at the use of 'she'. Her silent acceptance of it being a woman she was to meet made the subterfuge worse. Perdita could feel Violet's gaze boring into her, willing her to come clean. But she couldn't, not now. 'That's very kind of you, but my ex-colleague has got some problems to discuss – they're very pressing, and I said I'd try to help out.'

'I see.' His tone made her shiver. How quickly he'd reverted to type and become a Neanderthal caveman again.

Slowly, she pushed her chair back and retreated with Violet to Violet's makeshift bedroom as Saul began to clear away the detritus of lunch. Perdita promised Violet she'd explain to Saul tonight, after his guests had gone as telling him before would completely ruin his dinner party. Violet shrugged as if to say it would have to do.

Later that afternoon, Perdita found Saul in the kitchen, cutting up the lamb into cubes.

'Saul?'

'Yes?' He didn't look up, too intent on the meat.

'Can we have a chat tonight? After your guests have gone? There's something I must tell you, and it has to be told today.'

'Why not now?'

'Now's not a good time.'

'Why not?'

'Because you're angry with me. You have every right to be. I just think it's best done later. It's about my past and the mess I've got myself in.'

'Oh? Didn't you tell me last night all there is to know? That's of any consequence?'

'I left a bit out,' she said meekly. 'A big bit.'

'And now you want to tell me?'

'Yes. Tonight.'

'Confessions of past associations? I'm not in the mood to listen about past boyfriends.'

She sighed. And now she would have to work out how to deal with Tony.

Chapter 22

Once out of sight of Westbridge, Perdita stopped her car to secure a pillowcase, lightly-filled with kapok, around her middle to accentuate her bump. She'd bought the stuffing to make a soft toy but hadn't got around to starting the project. Continuing her journey to Bristol, she hoped that the added layer would make it obvious to Tony that there needn't be any attempt to try to bulldoze her into having an uprooting like he had with Marcia.

If there was another reason he'd come, she would have to get to the bottom of it... without him getting ideas about getting to the bottom of her. She remembered his comment about her looking good with the extra weight. She would have to scare him off so that he didn't get any ideas about her being part of any package he had in mind. And she'd concocted a plan to do it thanks to the three failed dates with Burglary, Anaphylactic Shock and Meteorite.

She'd discussed the dates with Luke and Gavin over Skype last week and how she'd asked questions such as: Are you ready to get married? Would you like children? How do you visualise sharing household chores? It had been then that the men had retreated to the gents' toilets – presumably to arrange a fake call – and then they'd scarpered with the rapidity of a jet engine on take-off. If she used similar tactics with Tony, any hopes he might be harbouring in terms of gratifying his intimate needs with her would disappear.

'You are mad,' Luke had said, 'asking questions like that on a first date. No wonder the blokes lied to you to get away.'

'I suspected as much when Tony said there'd been an alien invasion. That wasn't even remotely believable, even for science fiction lovers.'

Gavin's face approached the webcam. 'How could you have believed, even for a second, that those excuses were for real? If you'd told us at the time, we would have set you straight.'

'I wanted to believe that my first date had been burgled, that my second date's babysitter had been rushed to hospital and that my third date had had a meteorite land on his roof because, if these things weren't true, it meant my dates were running away from me. That there was something wrong with me.'

Gavin opened his mouth but, on receiving a sharp elbow from Luke, shut it again.

Having now parked her car close to the hotel, she muttered a quick prayer to her Guardian Angel, who Perdita hoped hadn't abandoned her after yesterday evening's activity. She went through to The Berkeley Square Hotel reception. 'I'm meeting a guest here,' Perdita explained, admiring the display of fresh flowers. Glancing around, she had to admit it was different from anywhere she'd been before. Chic. Elegant. Arty. When the receptionist verified details, Perdita was invited to sign the guest register before being let through the 'Members Only' door.

Once in The Square Lounge, Perdita spotted Tony, turned out in a crisp jacket and open-necked shirt. He was sitting on a mauve sofa, one ankle resting on its neighbour's knee, perusing a newspaper.

'Hi, Tony, am I late?' She stroked her bump. She thought she saw a flicker of… disgust? She placed her shopper bag on the floor. Recently, she'd been using it in preference to her strappy bag because it held so much; it meant she didn't have to huff and puff up the two flights of stairs at home if she forgot something. Easing herself onto the blue armchair by Tony, she noticed there were only two other guests in the room: young, male, slickly dressed and probably still single since they wore no wedding bands. They'd broken off their conversation to watch her and Tony. 'You were right, Tony, I admit it. There is a seed in there.'

'Why the fuck are you calling it a seed? This isn't botany.' The other men sniggered, one spluttering into his wine glass as he'd just taken a sip. Tony folded his paper. 'Shall we go into the restaurant? We can order your drink there.'

Was this the first time in his life that Tony hadn't felt like he was a cool dude? Perdita tried to imagine him pushing a pram, but it was impossible.

The waiter took them to a table in the far corner of The Square Kitchen and made extra room for Perdita. He was about to offer her a drinks menu when she smiled and just asked for an apple juice.

'And I'd like a half bottle of house red,' Tony said.

Another waiter came and passed them each a food menu. After a few minutes of silence, Tony asked, 'What would you like to eat?'

'No starters, just the lamb, please.' She wasn't actually hungry. A lot hung on this evening.

When the waiter returned, Tony ordered a main course for them both.

'Why did you look me up, Tony, when you've not shown a shred of interest since that night? Do you want to play Happy Families? Because, from what I remember of that card game, the aim is to make a complete family, with no one missing.' She decided to press further. 'Shall we be a "Happy Family"?'

'That's not what I'm here for,' Tony said. 'I needed to know whether you were pregnant or not.'

'You don't strike me as the daddy type,' Perdita said.

'I'm not.'

Was he as self-seeking and narcissistic as he seemed? 'Well, I'm single with no job and no home.'

Tony's brows knitted together. 'What do you mean no home? You had somewhere to live when I found you.'

'Uh-uh. Once they know about what's inside me, my guess is I'll be asked to leave. And, by the size of me, they will soon guess that I'm not just getting fat. I need a home, and someone needs a father. Do you live in a good area?'

Tony flinched. 'I'm based in London. I've got a flat, but it's not big enough for three. You can't move in with me.'

'We'll have to find somewhere else then.'

The waiter brought their food, but she wasn't sure she'd be able to eat it. A second waiter showed two men in suits that had seen better days to the table next to theirs. Perdita pulled her shopper bag further in so that they didn't trip up on one of its chunky straps.

'Look,' Tony said, 'we are not living together. You made the decision not to terminate the pregnancy, so it's your responsibility. That's what I came to tell you.'

Gripping her cutlery tightly, Perdita focused on that beautiful brightly-coloured flower she kept imagining. 'Seedlings need both parents when they're growing up. People they can rely on. I agree I should have told you but I thought you'd suggest I should... do something about it.'

'From the look of you, that boat has sailed.'

The waiter took the orders from the table next to theirs. She did her best to eat every morsel of the only meal Tony was ever likely to buy her.

'I can't help you find a place...' He broke off, picking up his knife and fork, waving them helplessly. He'd chosen the rib-eye steak with triple cooked chips.

'You mean you won't,' Perdita corrected, cutting boldly into the centre of a lamb noisette smothered in rosemary and lemon jus. 'You got me into this predicament; you must help me.' It sounded like a pleading whine.

'I'll have to think about it.' His finger traced a line back and forth over his upper lip.

'It's cheaper if we live in the same place. And nannies are very expensive. Then there are the clothes, the cot, the pram, the nappies. It'll cost thousands each year.'

Tony made a feeble attempt to cut his steak. 'What about your mum, can't you live with her?'

'I was orphaned. I have no family.' Didn't he remember anything about their evening together?

Under his lashes, Tony's eyes flicked rapidly from side to side, as though his mind was working furiously to get himself out of the muddle.

'If we can't afford a nanny, perhaps we'd be able to find a job we could share – of course, that would mean you working close to home, so there wouldn't be any need for you to spend hours at the wheel of your car. You said how much you hated it. Life would be less hectic.'

Tony's jaw hung loose as though the strings holding his mouth together had just been snipped.

Perdita saved the final thrust until last. 'I thought we'd get married.' She tucked into her food with a bit more enthusiasm. She was probably home and dry.

'I don't want to marry you.' He threw down his cutlery and took a big gulp of wine.

Goal to Perdita. 'Perhaps when you're used to the idea.'

'No. Never.'

'I'll need to know your address for registration purposes.' He nodded glumly. 'And we need to talk about child maintenance and how often you intend visiting.'

Pushing his barely touched plate away, Tony grimaced. 'I'm not paying child maintenance – I would have told you that right away if you'd consulted me before letting it get this far.' He refilled his glass and gulped down half of it. 'And I won't be visiting.'

'I think the law will say you have to pay child maintenance.' Although Perdita balked at the idea of asking Tony for any money, ever, she doubted that she would manage without it. It was highly likely Saul would ask her to leave, and she would end up homeless with no income. As for visiting, surely Tony would become curious when the time came?

'I won't do it,' he told her, downing the rest of his wine.

'You'll have no choice.'

Tony signalled the waiter by waving the empty bottle.

It was not the best time, but lately visits to the bathroom had been getting more urgent and more frequent. 'Excuse me, I must pop to the loo.' She'd seen the sign for it when she'd been in the lounge so knew where to go.

Tony had not asked a single question about how Setback Number One was going and seemed to have no compassion at all for the seedling inside her. Her three dates' lack of interest, she'd concluded, had been due to the fact that they hadn't yet matured adequately;

like grapes, Burglary, Anaphylactic Shock and Meteorite needed to ripen before they were of any use in starting a family. Tony was also shaping up as unripe. Would he ripen sufficiently in the future to become a safe person to introduce as a daddy should he change his mind about visiting? A fair-weather father, as she suspected Tony could only possibly ever be, was not something she wished for the little life inside her. She worried about the kind of damage that could inflict. If Tony was going to be in their seedling's life, Perdita wanted him to be in it for the long haul. From how this evening was going, that seemed as likely as Tony opting for celibacy.

On her way back to the table, Perdita saw that the waiter had cleared their plates. When she sat down, she found she'd regained her appetite. 'What's for dessert?' she asked.

For some reason, Tony kept looking across at the men sitting at the table next to them. Had they said something to him when she'd gone to the loo? Bravo if they had.

'Dessert?' Tony gave another furtive glance to his left. 'Or we could just leave. Now.' He raised his eyebrows meaningfully, but the meaning escaped Perdita.

'I'd like some cake.' She noticed that Tony was gripping the edge of the table. Glancing at the men at the next table, she saw the smaller of the men nudging the larger man, whispering.

Then, to Perdita's surprise, she saw the bigger man turn towards Tony who immediately said, 'Let's get out of here,' and made to stand up.

Not understanding what was going on, Perdita said loudly, 'But I want cake.' She really fancied something sweet now, and there had to be exceptionally yummy desserts in a place like this. She hadn't noticed that Saul had bought any for his guests.

A growly voice said, 'You heard what the lady said. She wants her cake.' The man leaned right over, crossing the gap between his table and theirs, thrusting his face close to Tony's, and Tony gave up his attempt to stand.

Perdita froze. The voice had a familiar ring to it. And as the larger man swivelled around, recognition was instantaneous. And mutual. Of all the restaurants and of all the days...

Muscle Man, aka Elliott Bletch, the man who'd seen Saul abduct her from the store, gawped at her face, then at her bump, then at Tony. 'Is that yours?' He pointed at Perdita's bump.

Tony glanced at Perdita before nodding.

'And what does her old man have to say about that?'

Perdita broke out in a sweat, surreptitiously searching her bag for her car keys; this called for a quick get-away. Perhaps she should have had an accomplice waiting in her car ready to fire the engine at a moment's notice.

Frowning, Tony said, 'She hasn't got a husband. She hasn't even got a boyfriend. Never has.'

Perdita's hand trembled as it fumbled in her bag.

'I suppose she hasn't got three kids either,' Muscle Man continued contemptuously, ending in a harsh laugh.

Perdita wanted to tell him to shut up, but she saw that Tony was focused on Muscle Man.

'As a matter of fact, she hasn't.' Tony straightened to his full sitting height. 'And who are you? And why do you think this bump is any business of yours?'

Muscle Man's face went purple. 'Are you telling me...' he paused briefly as though trying very hard to remember something. 'Are you telling me that... Perdita here has no husband and no kids?'

Perdita bowed her head low over her bag again.

'Do you know this man?' Tony asked. 'You've become very quiet all of a sudden.'

Perdita's head shot up, and, without meeting Muscle Man's gaze, she admitted, 'I've seen him before.'

'Why does he think you're married with three kids?' Tony's gaze burned into her. 'Why,' Tony repeated, 'does he think you're married with three kids?'

'Because someone told him I was.'

'Why would anyone do that?' Tony quizzed.

'A bad joke.' Frantically, Perdita's fingers emptied half her bag out onto her lap, rifling through the remains at the bottom. The keys weren't there.

Muscle Man looked furious. 'Has someone been taking the mick?'

It was no use. She couldn't find the keys. She'd have to try to defuse the situation. Meeting Muscle Man's gaze, Perdita said, 'That day in the shop, I was telling the truth about being kidnapped. I did know the man but didn't recognise him at the time.'

'That man lied to me?'

'Yes.'

'Who's this then?' Muscle Man asked, pointing at Tony.

'I think we should go,' Tony said.

'Great idea,' Perdita agreed.

'Look, mate,' Muscle Man said, in a steely, no-nonsense voice, 'there's some mystery here, and I mean to clear it up.' He turned to Perdita and repeated his last question, pointing rudely again at Tony. 'Who's this?'

'The man who...' She pointed to her belly.

'But he's not your boyfriend?'

'No.'

'Do you have a boyfriend?'

'No.'

'And the man that was in the shop? Where's he?'

'At home,' Perdita admitted.

'Your home?'

Rocking her hand to introduce an element of uncertainty, Perdita whispered, 'Our home.'

A deep crease formed between Muscle Man's brows, and his lips turned down derisively. 'You live together?'

'Mm...' Perdita rocked her hand from side to side again, '...kind of. Separate bedrooms. But same building.'

'You're living with someone who kidnapped you, and he doesn't mind you having an affair with someone else?'

'He gave me a job. That's all.'

'He's not your boyfriend?'

Tony's gaze was spiked with interest, and Perdita knew that she had to be very careful that there wasn't the slightest inkling that Saul was more to her than a boss. Her fingers finally found her keys wedged in the outer pocket of her bag. But there was no way out now. Tony, Muscle Man and Muscle Man's friend were hanging on to every word of this mini drama. There was no harm in trying though. 'I just need to go to the...'

As she stood up, two pairs of hands pushed her back down. Tony and Muscle Man had sided together.

'The baby's not mine?' Tony asked hopefully.

A beautiful brightly-coloured flower waving in a gentle breeze, on a hillside with lots of grass... And a deep, relaxing breath. 'It's yours, Tony. I really am living in the attic room of the house as an unpaid companion to Saul's sick aunt. When she can cope again, I'm out.'

'And you agreed? To work unpaid?'

'Remember the woman I was concerned about the night we... talked? Well, her portfolio was annihilated with the crash in the Far East. My helping out was agreed in lieu of compensation. And I needed somewhere to live. A woman in my condition is not an asset in the eyes of an employer. And you,' she pointed a finger at Tony, 'got me into this mess. What are you going to do about it?'

'How much did his aunt lose?' Tony asked.

'Twenty-five thousand. If he knew I was... ' she gestured towards her bump, 'he'd probably chuck me out, then where would I be?'

Tony's brows knitted together. 'How come he doesn't already know? He must be blind...'

'He's been away. I'm careful how I dress when I'm there. And, as I said, they just think I'm getting fat.'

'You should have denied liability. You still can,' Tony advised.

'I have nowhere to go, and he got me to sign something,' Perdita said, deciding it was too complicated to explain that Saul had since ripped up his copy of the Agreement. She began to cry. Tomorrow, she might be truly homeless.

Muscle Man asked Perdita, 'What was your job?'

'Financial adviser.'

'And his?' He pointed to Tony.

'He trains us.'

'I'm surprised you two can sleep at nights, causing misery, robbing people. You deserve each other. Is that how you met?'

Perdita nodded.

'And when did he break it off? When you told him you were pregnant?'

A beautiful brightly-coloured flower… 'I think it was straight after we… It hadn't gone well.'

'What a pair.' As they stood up to leave, Muscle Man's parting shot rang out. 'I prefer your husband to him.'

So do I, Perdita thought sadly. So do I.

Chapter 23

As Perdita removed the pillowcase accessory in the same spot she'd put it on, she saw that it was not yet eight o'clock. She would be in time to meet Saul's friends.

One big hurdle was over, another to go.

As she entered the house, Saul came grinning towards her. 'I missed you.'

'Does this mean we're friends again?' she whispered.

'We'll talk about it later.'

'Me first this time? I can't hold off telling you any longer. My secret. I don't think you'll like it. Then you will understand what happened at the butcher's this morning. It's connected.'

Saul's grin dissolved into a flat line. 'Later. My guests are still here. Come and meet them.'

As Saul ushered her into the dining room, Perdita saw dirty plates, wine glasses and empty coffee cups strewn over the tablecloth. She would help Saul clear it up after his guests had gone.

'This is Perdita. Perdita meet my partner, Bruce...'

'Hello.' Perdita took Bruce's outstretched hand across the table as he stood to greet her.

'Pleased to meet you. We've heard rather a lot about you this evening,' Bruce said.

'Oh?' Perdita said, mustering a smile. 'All good, I hope.'

Bruce inclined his head to mean but of course, and

released her hand.

'...and his wife, Gerry,' Saul said.

As Gerry struggled to her feet, Perdita noticed her flame-coloured hair and felt the room spin. Short of throwing a non-existent jug of water into Gerry's face, Perdita didn't know how to stop the looming catastrophe.

'Why, hello again! I had no idea *you* were Perdita. How well you look. And you don't show a bit. I'd never have known.' Gerry turned to Bruce. 'This is the woman I met at the antenatal clinic.'

Perdita wondered if perhaps she could drag Gerry from the room and ask her to refrain from saying another word? But Gerry was on the far side of the dining table, and Saul was blocking the exit. The patio door was shut, and Violet was in the way.

Perdita felt her skin crawling with the heat of her blush as she slowly turned to face Saul.

Slate grey eyes regarded her starkly. 'You're pregnant.'

Although she tried, the beautiful brightly-coloured flower did not appear. Most Humiliating Experience Number Seven. She had messed up. Big time. 'Yes.'

In a distressed tone, Gerry said, 'I didn't know it was a secret. I'm so sorry.'

Still looking at Saul, Perdita replied, 'It doesn't matter,' although it plainly did. 'It's the sort of secret that grows too big to keep.' Perdita gave a feeble smile. She didn't want Gerry to be upset.

Then Perdita caught Violet glaring at her.

'I think we should go,' Gerry said softly, her hand a gentle hint on Bruce's arm.

'Oh, yes. Of course.' Bruce moved behind his chair to tuck it under the table giving room for Gerry to pass.

'It was a great meal, Saul. Thanks.'

'It was lovely,' Gerry agreed.

Saul's smile of acknowledgement did not reach his eyes, and then he and Violet left the room to follow Bruce.

'Please phone me so that we can meet sometime,' Gerry urged Perdita from the doorway. 'I'd really like to get to know you better.'

Perdita felt glad that someone did as she was obviously not a favourite of either Saul or Violet at the moment. 'I'd love to. I did keep your number. I didn't ring because I wasn't sure if you really meant me to.' She stepped closer.

'Of course, I did. Promise?' Gerry squeezed her arm affectionately.

'Promise,' Perdita said, thinking of the impending storm of Saul's rage, made all the fiercer because it would be justified.

When Gerry disappeared from view, Perdita, unable to face anyone, slipped down and crawled under the table. She heard the swift goodbyes and then the closing of the front door. Frank must have run in as he was sidling up to her. She edged to the far end of the table and sat with her legs crossed, shielded by the deep drop of the tablecloth. Burying her fingers in Frank's fur, she stroked him, creating tracks radiating from his head. He edged forward putting his front half on her thigh. It was a half-commitment posture he often adopted as though keeping his options open.

There were sounds of Saul assisting Violet to bed and then the clattering of things in the kitchen. Perdita wondered whether she dare venture out to help. But she didn't consider it safe. Saul might tell her to leave, and she wasn't ready to. If he couldn't find her, he couldn't tell her to go.

Suddenly, Saul's feet were in the room and they were approaching the table.

'Meeeeooow.'

Frank moved to full commitment, tucking his tail in tightly, and Perdita realised that Saul must have trodden on it. She soothed Frank with vigorous strokes expecting Saul's face to appear to check if Frank was all right. But instead there was the clatter of crockery being stacked. Then she saw Saul's feet walk back out again, the crockery tinkling as he left.

When his feet returned, they approached an armchair. Perdita heard the give of the seat and then, to her astonishment, the rustle of a newspaper being unfolded. What was Saul up to? It seemed odd to be catching up with the news at a time like this. And could he actually concentrate? It was perturbing to witness such calm behaviour in someone who had just been dealt a massive blow.

Perdita needed the toilet. Saul was here and Violet was in bed so the downstairs loo was free. But how was she to sneak past Saul? And did he know she was there? Was he playing jailer?

'Are you planning to spend the night under the table? Shall I bring your pillow and duvet?'

Perdita squeezed her eyes shut. 'How long have you known I was here?'

'I watched you crawl under. I came back briefly because I wanted to check that my guests had not left anything. And I knew you were still here because of Frank's determination to stay under the table when I stepped on his tail – by mistake – and, of course, I can hear him purring – which he doesn't do when he's all by himself.'

'Oh.'

'Are you going to come out?'

'I'd much prefer it if you joined me here. The lighting's not nearly so harsh. It's quite cosy really.'

'More comfortable here,' Saul said.

'I need the loo.'

'I'm not stopping you.'

Perdita sighed. It was a wrench to leave her refuge, but the call of nature could not be postponed any longer. She began to crawl out from under the table and then decided that she quite liked the view of the floor and crawled out of the room, across the hall and into the cloakroom. And, when she was done, Perdita crawled all the way back into the same space that she'd vacated a few minutes previously. But this time she didn't have Frank to comfort her. He'd scarpered.

The lump in her throat that had formed earlier suggested that she might need tissue whilst under the table and she'd brought a handful of toilet paper back, stuffing it into her bra as she didn't have a pocket.

'You wanted to talk to me,' Saul said, 'so now talk. I'm all ears.'

'I'm very sorry,' Perdita said contritely. 'I was going to tell you… my news… as soon as your guests had left.'

'Isn't it news when you have newly acquired information or something new has just happened? It doesn't sound like you only just found out "your news" considering you've been visiting the antenatal clinic.'

Perdita put her hands over her face. He was right, of course.

'I asked Violet if she knew "your news", and she did. I presume Gavin and Luke know too. And Sister Margaret. Do David and Catherine Murphy also know "your news"? Is that why they thought I should marry you? Is the whole town buzzing with gossip about me, under a misapprehension that I am the father? Am I the last person to know?'

Perdita picked at the skin around her thumb. 'David and Catherine guessed and promised to keep my secret. I don't think there is any gossip in the town. I've not told anyone, nor have I implied that you are the father. And I'm sure there are many people who don't yet know.'

'But I'm the last person in your social circle to find out?'

The lump in Perdita's throat grew bigger. 'Yes,' she croaked.

'You should have declared your news before you agreed to come.'

'You bulldozed me into coming. You threatened me. My situation would have been even worse if you'd sued me. I couldn't risk that. And I wanted to help Violet. As I pointed out to you when I arrived with my things, I might have had a husband. I might have also been an aunt batterer or an arsonist. You didn't care about anything except getting your own way. I made use of that so I would have a roof over my head for when the seedling comes.'

'Seedling?'

'Yes, seedling. I don't like that other name. It makes me feel unwell.' Perdita sighed raggedly. 'Did you really expect a perfect ministering angel to metamorphose from someone you kidnapped and threatened with legal action? Not to mention about the threat with the local paper? I've wanted to tell you loads of times, but I thought you'd ask me to leave when I have nowhere to go. I didn't trust you to let me stay.'

'You let me take you to bed knowing you were pregnant,' Saul bit.

Nausea spiked. 'Pollinated,' Perdita corrected. 'I

don't like that other name. It–'

'Makes you feel ill?'

'Yes. I'm sorry. So, so sorry. I tried to tell you this morning. I just couldn't get you to listen. And it was something I needed you to listen to. I tried to tell you more than once today. I really did. But each time something happened to make you unreceptive.' Perdita traced patterns on the carpet with her finger.

'Why didn't you tell me the night before?'

'I know I should have done. It was selfish of me. I'm sorry.' Silence. 'I've slept with one man besides you. *Once*.'

'And that's all it took? Did you think you could pass it off as mine? Make yourself a new home here – permanently?'

'Of course I had no intention of trying to pass it off as yours; I was pollinated in December. I went to bed with you because I wanted to. Not because I had designs on you.'

'I don't believe you. I don't think I'll ever believe you again. Don't forget, it was you who later wanted to hold me to that contract – I was willing to wipe your slate clean.'

'And in your eyes that damns me further? Where was I to go with no money and no job? And I had little prospect of finding one. What would *you* have done?'

'I don't know,' Saul said in a bemused voice. 'But I wish I'd never seen you in the shop that day. I wish that big bloke had stopped me…'

A distinct picture of Muscle Man came to her mind.

'Who's the father?' His words were strangled.

'A training adviser. He runs courses and conferences.'

'How long had you known him?'

Perdita pulled her lips to one side as she considered. 'You mean, since I first saw him? A couple of years.'

'No. From the time you had your first proper conversation with him.'

'Oh.'

'How long is "oh"?'

'Does it matter?'

'It does to me.'

'I thought, from what he said and did that he really liked me, was growing to care for me.'

'How long?'

'Just that evening and night.'

'One night? And you kept his child?'

'I mistook my long-standing infatuation for love – and his lust for love. I didn't know the kind of man he really was.' She scrabbled inside her bra to retrieve the bundle of tissue. Separating a section, Perdita dabbed at her eyes and nose. She didn't want to give Saul the satisfaction of hearing her blow it. Then she sniffed and swallowed hard. 'I had dinner with Tony this evening. He called on me this morning when you were out. The reason I couldn't cancel, so that I could be with your guests, was because he said he would come and get me if I didn't go. Someone from work told him she thought I was pollinated. So, he tracked me down. He knew he had to be the father because I was a virgin when he... slept with me.'

'What did he want?' Saul asked.

Perdita detected a slight altering of Saul's tone as though he was feeling under threat. 'He wanted to tell me he wants no part of the situation,' Perdita said distantly, as she recalled sitting opposite Tony while they discussed the matter. 'He said it wasn't his choice that I decided... not go to a clinic. I thought, when he came this morning, that he might have ideas about visiting us both after the… germination… That he had some interest in me because he said I looked good with the extra weight. I think I did a good job of putting him off. But it seems like he doesn't want anything to do with the seedling either.'

Saul didn't say anything, and Perdita felt a sudden anger. 'It would have made things so much simpler for you, wouldn't it, if the business with Tony had never happened? But then, I would have returned Violet's calls straight away as I wouldn't have been in a blind panic wondering what to do. Then I wouldn't have kind of resigned because I'd have come to see her and discussed her investment with her rather than let it fester. And then, I wouldn't have been in that shop at lunchtime, and then you wouldn't have seen me. None of this would have ever happened. Is that what you'd have preferred?'

Saul's newspaper crackled as though he were folding it up, and then it landed smartly on the floor in front of her. She assumed Saul hadn't flung it her way in order for her to scan the headlines.

'I've made two mistakes,' Perdita said forlornly. 'The first was to sleep with a man who doesn't like virgins, the second to sleep with a man who does – after I'd slept with the man who doesn't. I think I'll go to bed now.' And with that, Perdita crawled out of the room without looking Saul's way once; she couldn't bear to see his censure or for him to see what was probably swollen red eyes and a wet blotchy face.

Chapter 24

early August

The time since Saul had discovered that Perdita was pregnant had dragged by. The more her belly swelled, the harder it was for him to contemplate the weeks and months ahead. He couldn't forgive her for keeping that secret hidden, especially since she'd allowed him to make delightful love to her in ignorance of her condition. His world had come crashing down as Perdita's betrayal of his trust had been revealed, leaving an indelible scar on his heart. And now, he had an additional gripe.

Not only had she been a Trojan horse, smuggling in a foetus that he felt he had no option but to shelter, she'd also infiltrated the home of his best friend where Saul had once been welcome to drop by at any time. The mutual awkwardness he and Perdita had obviously experienced when they'd been invited in, by happenstance, minutes apart, to Bruce and Gerry's living room, had made the prospect of future shared calls untenable. For all of them. Which was why Saul had to check if there was any danger of running into Perdita before turning up to see Bruce, and Saul suspected Perdita always checked with Gerry if she wanted to pop in outside office hours.

Gerry had given birth to a baby boy on Monday, and Saul, having taken up the slack at the office due to Bruce's long absences at the hospital, had put aside

Saturday afternoon to pay them a visit. But when Saul had phoned to check whether his calling round was convenient for Gerry and baby Jack, he'd been told Perdita was there. Miffed that Perdita had been introduced to his best friend's baby first, Saul had needed some solitude while he waited for the coast to be clear. If he was careful enough, there was no reason why he would see Perdita before tomorrow morning. Going by her usual pattern of behaviour, she was likely to be home soon; she couldn't be away from the trough for long. And that was why he was headed for The Dick Whittington.

It hadn't been an easy visit. Perdita had had to psych herself up before going to see Gerry. Seeing Jack made it harder to picture that beautiful brightly-coloured flower and gave more substance to what was really inside her and what was actually soon going to emerge.

Dutifully, Perdita kept a grin plastered on her face while she struggled to get the key into the ignition. Her hands didn't feel like her hands, and her fingers seemed more akin to jelly than flesh and bone. But eventually the key fitted into the slot. She fired the engine, and then she waved goodbye to Gerry.

Despite an impulse to drive far away, in a fruitless attempt to escape her pending fate, Perdita would probably spend the evening watching TV with Violet, especially if Saul was out. Violet's speech and mobility were progressing well now, and their relationship was mostly healed following Perdita's suggestion that she contact the council to seek emergency accommodation. Violet had said she wanted Perdita to stay on and that it would be sure to ruin everything if she were to abandon ship now; she must work things out with Saul.

How she was meant to achieve this feat, Perdita hadn't a clue, and Violet hadn't given her any tips. And Saul's brooding manner sometimes made her wonder if it would be worth the trouble to try. She'd been having to tiptoe around him, trying not to upset him further, by stashing Catherine Murphy's donations of pram with carrycot in the garage and the smaller lent items in the cupboard in her room so that Saul wouldn't see. Perdita had taken the tiny clothes out, washed them and hung them on the line to dry – bringing them back in again before Saul was due home.

By way of revenge for the exposé, Perdita suspected Saul had amended Jim The Gardener's job description to make life more difficult for her: Mow lawn weekly during the summer months. Weed garden. Plant perennials. Prune. And scowl at Perdita whenever the opportunity arises. And that opportunity arose whenever Jim was present and she had occasion to sit in the garden or attend to washing on the line.

When Perdita was approaching Westbrook Lane, she recalled Gerry asking her who was going to support her during the germination. The question, or rather her answer to it, made Perdita feel sick: no one. On impulse, she signalled left and drove into the car park of The Dick Whittington. Violet would be all right if Perdita didn't go straight home as Saul would be there to keep her company. Hopefully, by the time Perdita left the pub, Saul would have gone out for the evening as she couldn't face him right now. She didn't want to risk him seeing her unwell and jittery as he might ask what was wrong, and she wouldn't be able to tell him.

The thought of going it alone was making it difficult to breathe. Sitting with strangers at the bar might help distract her. It was good she was wearing flat strappy sandals with her maternity dress as she was a little wobbly on her feet. Feeling as though a draught could knock her over, she straightened, took a deep breath and concentrated on walking in a straight line. If she appeared composed, she might feel composed.

The considerable lounge area was quiet with only a few tables occupied and a couple of people sitting at the bar. There was a garden which would probably be packed on a day like this judging by how it had been when she'd come here with Luke and Gavin. Perdita was about to place her order when the image of little Jack flashed up in her mind, and she quickly veered towards the ladies' loos. Soon she was heaving over the toilet bowl.

When she was rinsing her mouth, she caught her reflection in the huge mirror. She saw enormous frightened eyes in a white face and the upper part of a big space hopper belly.

She'd messed up and wondered if her mother could know from wherever her soul, or spirit, had ended up. Until last November, Perdita had thought she'd been doing pretty well. The uncomfortable school days were behind her, she'd thankfully lost touch with her fellow orphans at the orphanage and had managed to have a successful career. But now that things had gone so very wrong, she found herself being sucked into her unhappy past. Memories of not fitting in, of being the odd one out and alone, were rushing back to torture her. How was she going to cope with any of what was to come? Sinking to the floor, with her knees up, Perdita put her head in her hands and started to bawl.

It wasn't long before another woman burst into the toilets and stopped at the sight of her. 'Are you all right, love?' It was a kindly, middle-aged-sounding voice.

'Fine.'

'You don't look fine. What's the matter?' The woman was by her side now and put her arm around Perdita, handing her a tissue.

'I'm not having a... *baby*,' she whispered.

'Oh, I'm sorry, love. Have you just lost it? Do you need an ambulance?'

The word 'ambulance' gave Perdita a jolt. She pulled herself together and hauled herself up using the edge of the sink and then blew her nose. The woman, who was a wiry forty or so year-old with short bleached hair, was staring at her huge bump.

'I'm fine,' Perdita said, 'really, I am. And it's still in there.' Then she left. But once outside the loos, she realised she would have an over-ripe tomato attack face. She turned to go back inside to repair the damage but found her path blocked by the middle-aged lady who seemed to have changed her mind about needing to relieve herself.

'Would you like me to take you 'ome?'

'No, thank you. I can make my own way. Besides, I can't go just yet.' Perdita attempted to get past the woman.

'I want to 'elp.' The woman blocked her path. 'You were in quite a state when I found you. Why can't you go 'ome?'

'Because I'm hiding from someone,' Perdita said.

'Who?' the woman asked.

'That would be me,' a deep voice said from behind Perdita. And she recognised it.

As Perdita spun around, Saul was shocked by her tear-ravaged face. He'd just come from the gents' loos as the beer he'd ordered had over-spilled onto his hand, and he'd needed to wash it. 'I'll look after her,' he said firmly. 'And I'll make sure she gets home safely.'

'But if she was 'iding from you…' the woman said uncertainly.

'It's okay,' Saul said. 'It's a game we play. Hiding from each other. Luckily today we chose the same place to hide. Eh, Perdita?'

'Mm.'

'Is this a domestic?' the woman asked. 'Shall I get the landlord? Or the police?'

Saul expected Perdita to tell the woman that neither option would be necessary, but Perdita was taking her time, gawking at him through wet lashes as though in a daze. Then she came to and said, 'Oh no, I'm perfectly safe with Saul.' And she gave the woman one of her dazzling smiles. The woman went back into the loos.

'Why don't you wash your face and then join me? I have a table at the back of the lounge. Let me buy you dinner.' As Perdita was about to protest, he added, 'And don't worry about Violet. I'll let her know, and she can heat up the leftovers in the microwave.' He'd call Bruce while he was at it to postpone his visit. Helping Perdita in distress was more important right now despite it churning up all kinds of emotions.

While he waited for Perdita to join him, Saul perused the menu. There was just the meal for her. He wondered whether her predilection for lamb and strange food combinations would continue once she was no longer pregnant. He hoped not as he was sick of lamb and found it difficult to watch Perdita eat some of her other meals.

When she lowered herself onto the seat opposite, her face and eyes almost back to her usual colour, she said, 'Is this a second truce?'

He shrugged. 'I guess so.' He wondered what had upset her and whether it was anything to do with seeing baby Jack. He suspected it must be. 'They do a lamb hot pot. Fancy it?'

Perdita gave a shy smile. 'I rather think I do. And could I have an apple juice as well, please?'

When they were half-way through their meal, Saul asked, 'Do you want to talk about earlier?' The sight of her stricken face had tugged so forcefully at his heartstrings he'd just wanted to put his arms around her and hold her close, tell her that whatever was wrong they would deal with together. But he'd been unable to do that, and now he just hoped that she would let him get close enough to help while allowing him to keep a protective emotional distance.

'It's better that I don't,' Perdita said softly.

'I want to help.'

Then her gaze met his, and she seemed to search for something deep within him. 'Thank you, but no thank you.'

He was acutely disappointed.

'Do you often hide?' she asked.

He was surprised by the question and by the way she'd asked it, as though she hoped he did. 'No.' He was going to add only since he'd met her, but didn't think that was very kind so didn't.

She looked crestfallen. 'I think I do it a lot.'

He'd noticed. 'Want to talk about it?'

'I'm not sure.'

'When I came to your office at F & Z to see you, they couldn't find you. Were you hiding then?'

'In the loos. Sorry, I just couldn't face you. I'd recently had some unsettling news…' She pointed to her belly. 'It was all I could deal with.'

He could understand that. 'I also noticed in the Italian restaurant, when there was someone you didn't want to see, that you dived under the table. You crawled under the table the evening Bruce and Gerry came around. And again here, this evening, you were hiding from me...' He imagined her inner demons being held in check as Perdita's expression underwent numerous changes.

'I know it's weird…'

He aimed a bland but interested expression her way to encourage her to reveal more about herself. 'When did you start hiding?' She reminded him of the goldfish he'd had as a child, that would constantly open and close its mouth when stressed. He suspected no one had ever asked her that question before, and she was rooting around in her mind trying to find the right words to explain her behaviour.

'I knew I wasn't like the other orphans when they teased me about my name. Theirs were solid Catholic names like Mary, Elizabeth and Anne. Mine was nothing to do with a saint – it was Shakespeare's creation. In fact, the other kids associated me with a dog who'd had ninety-nine puppies thanks to the author, Dodie Smith – you know, *101 Dalmatians*. I dreaded that film being shown.'

Saul remembered the book but had forgotten that the dog who'd had all those puppies had been called Perdita.

'It wasn't nice being called a bitch or being barked at. So I sneaked to the chapel attached to the orphanage – my mother used to sit there after she got the news… about her cancer. Sister Margaret told me.'

'Did that help?'

'Mm. I felt close to my mum... Then, in my teens, I

agreed to be Angela's study buddy. But as our GCSEs approached, I became more and more anxious until I felt like screaming. A week before they started, I just couldn't revise any more. So I hid in the confessional – with a book and torch so that Angela couldn't find me and ask me to work.'

Saul supposed Perdita was too embarrassed to meet his eyes as she kept her head bowed. In a tiny voice, she added, 'The same thing happened before my A-level exams.'

'And what about at university? You took exams there?'

'That was worse,' she admitted as she began to shred her napkin. 'I stopped revising two weeks before the exams. I put a note on my door banning any conversation about studying and past papers and avoided anyone who started to discuss them.'

'And despite all that anxiety,' Saul said, 'you still got your degree?'

'First class. But my friends were creeped out about my behaviour, they said it was odd, and so...'

'You hid?'

'I pretended I wasn't in when they knocked and kept my door locked.'

Saul felt as though a mist had cleared in his brain. Now he felt he understood her use of botanic euphemisms and why she'd kept such a big secret from him – it was all down to fear. She'd always been alone, or at least had felt alone, and had coped as best as she could despite her anxieties. 'You just have baggage, like everyone else. Like me.'

Then she raised her head and looked him straight in the eye. 'You don't think I'm weird?'

'No.' Not any more... 'I hid today too,' he added,

hoping to make her feel better.

'It's funny, isn't it? Choosing the same place.'

'It is. Shall we see if this truce can last longer than the last one?' He wasn't ready to forgive her for spending the night with him without telling him she was pregnant with another man's child. But he was prepared to be understanding. Realising there appeared to be no malicious bone in her body stirred warm and tender feelings towards her again, and he wasn't sure that was a good thing.

And then she beamed at him. And his heart melted, against his better judgement.

Chapter 25

late August

It was the night of her due date when Perdita's eyes sprang open. There were strange sensations from down below, and, at first, she was scared she was bleeding. But with her bedside light on and the duvet thrown back, she was relieved to see the fluid was clear, like water. Clutching her nightdress between her legs, Perdita felt weight bearing down as she hobbled to the bathroom in a gait suggestive of someone who'd spent her first day on a horse. Since it seemed her time had come, she knew she must shower. It wouldn't do to be whiffy when midwives got stuck in down below, doing whatever it was they had to do.

It was three in the morning when Perdita rang the maternity unit, with a deep ache in her pelvic region that went down into her thighs. She was told to come in, so called for a taxi. It was when she was tiptoeing downstairs with her hospital bags that Saul's bedroom door opened.

'Are you all right?' He appeared anxious as he knotted the belt of his grey towelling robe. 'I heard a lot of moving about up there and then the water running.'

Now was not the time to gaze at Saul's naked calves or try to guess whether he was wearing anything underneath his dressing gown and, if he wasn't, what the view would be like. She regretted she'd not taken a good look when she'd had the chance. She might never know what Saul's dangly bits looked like. What any man's dangly bits looked like, for that matter. She hadn't had any glimpse of Tony's and was no longer curious to see his anyway. And neither man had seen her very private parts; she'd made sure of that.

'Are you all right?' Saul repeated.

Perdita nodded. 'I phoned the hospital to tell them that my waters broke – just over an hour ago. I'm not having regular pains. But they said to come in, so I booked a taxi.'

'Why didn't you call me?'

'You never suggested I should,' Perdita said.

'Cancel the taxi. I'm taking you. Wait for me downstairs, and I'll bring the bags when I'm dressed. I'll let Violet know we're leaving, and then I'll help you out to the car. You just rest.'

Sometimes Perdita thought Saul was overbearing, but just now she welcomed his taking charge. It was a relief that he would be with her, but was there any way she could avoid him seeing her bare bottom?

The pad that she'd put on proved pretty useless against the steady stream as she could detect some overflow. It was lucky that she'd left armed with another hand-towel. She placed it strategically between her legs, worrying about spoiling Saul's leather seats and arriving looking like she was incontinent.

Saul stopped the car by the drop-off point outside the Central Delivery Suite. Perdita was grateful for his supportive arm as she shuffled towards the buzzer to alert staff to her arrival. Soon she was being pushed down a corridor by a hospital porter with the towel firmly wedged in the V of her legs. Visions of her leaving wet trails along the floor began to disturb her.

Even now, Perdita could detect the faint bleach odour and wondered whether the porter could smell it too. If Saul had any doubt in which way to head after parking the car, he would only need to sniff the air and peer at the floor if her giant stand-in sanitary towel did not hold out.

Perdita eased off the wheelchair in the assessment room, concerned her wet buttocks had left marks on the seat. But she needn't have worried as the porter withdrew promptly, taking any evidence with him.

Although she'd already written a germination plan with the help of a midwife, there was still paperwork to be done, and the plan was briefly discussed again with another midwife who helped her clamber onto the bed.

'The man who brought me – Saul – isn't the father. We're not a couple. I don't want him to see my bottom,' Perdita said.

'Not even when the...' The midwife squinted at Perdita's care plan, '... seedling is born?'

'No.'

'We'll do the best we can,' the midwife said. 'But sometimes there are emergencies, so we can't guarantee to keep you covered. Do you still want him with you?'

Going through the germination without Saul was a very scary prospect. The thought of him sitting by her side, perhaps holding her hand, for several hours was a very pleasing prospect. 'Yes.' Then the midwife put down the folder and began to put on gloves. The kind that meant that something unpleasant was about to happen.

'Please could you take your pants off? I need to examine you.'

This hadn't happened in her outpatient appointments.

'Legs apart, please. I need to give you an internal

examination.'

'That's the kind of view of my bottom I was talking about.' No one had prepared her for the pain she felt as fingers probed deep inside her. She pulled away. The midwife straightened, both hands visible, and Perdita panted madly, clamping her legs shut. 'I didn't like that. I didn't like that at all. I don't want you to do it again.'

'I need to find out how much fluid you have left and how many centimetres you are dilated. Let me give you gas and air to breathe as it will help with the pain.'

'What about the epidural? It's in my care plan.' She knew she was a wimp.

'We'll discuss it after I've examined you,' the midwife said, handing Perdita a mask, and then there was a hissing sound and the flow of something against her skin. Perdita inhaled deeply, bracing herself for the next assault.

When Saul walked in, Perdita screeched something into the mask as he was greeted by splayed limbs and a naked and exposed pelvic region. Perdita hoped the most vital area was shielded by the midwife's hand.

'Saul, please could you sit on the chair by the bed?' the midwife said. 'Although we'll do our best to keep Perdita covered, please keep your gaze above the line of Perdita's waist while you are supporting her.'

Perdita removed the gas mask for a moment. 'I don't want you to see my bottom.'

Squinting at Saul while the midwife was emerging from down below, Perdita wondered whether there could be a less alluring view a woman could give a man. But then the alluringness stage had passed. Was that why flowers shed their petals like unwanted cloaks? Because they'd been pollinated and there was no more use for them – or the bees? But what did she care? She wasn't really in her body at all; she was floating around the room like an oversized insect that bobbed in the air on outstretched wings.

'Perdita, you can let go now.' The midwife was attempting to remove the mask from her face. 'I've finished the examination. Please let go.'

Perdita lowered the mask but did not let go. 'I might want it again.' The voice sounded like Mickey Mouse's or Donald Duck's or some other cartoon character. It definitely wasn't hers.

'I'll hang the mask here, and you can take it when you need to. You don't need it now.'

Reluctantly, Perdita released her grip. The spaced-out, woozy feeling was still there. She turned and smiled widely at Saul. He was here. That was all that mattered.

'I've never seen you drunk,' Saul said. 'But I've got a fair idea as to what you'd be like under the influence.'

'Perdita,' she assured him serenely, 'does not get drunk.' Then an unwelcome image of her on the vast hotel bed with Tony after too much wine flashed on her internal viewing screen, and she said, 'Oh.' She had a fair idea too. 'Well, only the once.'

'Once was all it took,' Saul muttered.

Perdita held his gaze. 'I know. Please hold my hand.' Saul's hand enclosed hers in a warm grasp and she felt safe.

After the midwife restored Perdita's modesty, she said, 'Perdita, as you have lost a lot of fluid and you have had a show, we will need to induce you to speed up labour as we don't want you to get an infection.' Then the midwife explained she was going to check on the availability of the anaesthetist.

At first, Perdita felt like cheering – she was going to get her epidural. But then her spirits plummeted. She knew from her antenatal classes – when she'd not been rushing out to vomit down the toilet – that when a woman was induced her contractions got suddenly worse and very powerful. The fact that the midwife was going out to arrange for Perdita to have an epidural without her having to ask for it again suggested she was definitely going to need it.

But, to Perdita's disappointment, when the door next opened the midwife was back on her own. She was going to set up a drip, and there was a queue for the anaesthetist so Perdita would have to wait. If her contractions became too painful, she could have some pethidine.

'You'll be fine,' Saul reassured.

'That's easy for you to say considering you're not the one on the bed.'

'You're in good hands.'

The midwife poked a cannula into a vein in the back of Perdita's left hand and taped it securely in place. 'I may be in good hands,' Perdita said irritably, 'but that doesn't mean I won't be in pain.'

Once the drip was set up with whatever chemicals were needed to speed things along and the midwife had left the room, Perdita recalled the CD she'd brought with her. She asked Saul to find it in her bag and put it into the CD player provided.

'Is this the one?' he asked doubtfully, holding it up.

'Yes.'

'Here goes,' Saul said as he pressed the button for play.

She'd seen the CD in a charity shop, and since it didn't have any upsetting pictures on the case cover or, indeed, on the CD itself, she'd decided to give it a go. It had been specially created to help in situations such as this.

'You like these sounds? I'm not sure whether to call

it music but I guess if pushed it would go into that category,' Saul said.

Perdita shrugged. She supposed it was as good as any sound to help her relax.

Saul returned to sit by her side and angled the chair to face her. 'Did you buy it from a vets' place? I ask because of the pictures of the dogs. And the title's a bit of a giveaway: *Relaxing Sounds to Help Your Dog Give Birth*.'

Perdita glared at him. The other kids' analogy in the orphanage had obviously made a lasting impression, and the CD was probably an ill-considered purchase. That or perhaps today she was more of a dog Perdita than a human Perdita. She certainly didn't feel at all herself. 'What goes on in this room, stays in this room, all right?'

'Woof!'

Perdita was doing her best listening to the sounds, but her pain wasn't easing. Then Saul said, 'Would you like a dash of lemon in your water? I noticed you have one in your bag.'

'Ha,' Perdita gasped. She'd forgotten about that. Why hadn't she hidden it in something?

'Are you okay? Was it a bad pain?' Saul was eyeing her closely.

'Yes,' she lied. 'But it's better now. And it's okay. I'll save the lemon for another day.'

'It looked a bit strange. The skin was scored.'

'I like the scent of citrus fruit as well as the taste.'

Saul went to the bag, retrieved the lemon and put it on the unit next to her. 'I hope the smell is strong enough for you to detect.'

She couldn't look at him. 'Yes. Thanks.' She'd got so accustomed to sleeping with a lemon every night, reminding her of Saul's aftershave and, by association, him, that she'd been unable to come to hospital without her comforter.

Then he picked the lemon up again, sniffed it and said, 'It's a bit like my aftershave.'

Perdita raised a brow, tilted her head and said, 'Really?' She held out her hand, and Saul passed the fruit to her. After inhaling the aroma, she popped the lemon back on the unit as though she hadn't noticed anything about Saul's aftershave.

About an hour later, Perdita was screaming, 'I want the epidural now!' She made to swing her legs over the side of the bed. 'I'm getting out of here. I want to go home. Saul, take me home.'

The midwife was offering her some pills and a small container of water. But Perdita was trying to get the line out of her hand.

Saul grabbed her wrist to stop her. 'Take the pills, Perdita. They will help. And you can have gas and air as well.'

Then there was an urgent sensation, so urgent it could not be ignored a second longer. 'I need to poo,' Perdita wailed, afraid she was going to have an accident.

'Take the pills, and then we will sort that out,' the midwife said.

'I don't want Saul to come.' Perdita's feet were already on the floor, and she obediently swallowed the pills.

'It's okay,' he said quickly. 'I'm quite happy to stay here.'

As they emerged from the bathroom, Perdita pulled the door shut behind them wondering whether Saul had already detected the foul air. The midwife was inhaling deeply as though she'd been holding her breath in the bathroom. Approaching the bed, Perdita said to Saul, 'What just happened in there was very impressive.'

Saul grinned. 'I know. I heard.'

Just as she was getting back on the bed, Perdita was gripped with an enormous space hopper clutching pain that squeezed her so tight she couldn't breathe. Those pills hadn't started to work yet. And where was that anaesthetist?

'Pant,' the midwife said.

Saul let his tongue loll out, and he panted to show her what to do. Although Perdita knew he was trying to make her laugh, she didn't find it in the least amusing.

'Shall I restart the CD?' Saul asked. 'The beat might have been specially set up to time with panting.'

Perdita bared her teeth and growled at him, but Saul just woofed back and handed her the gas and air mask. When he caught the midwife's eye, Saul said, 'Perdita's a dog lover. The CD was made for dogs.'

About to reprimand him for making fun of her in her hour of need, Perdita took a few more breaths of gas and air before removing the mask. The stern words she'd intended to inflict floated away and dissolved into nothingness, and she just gave a quiet woof and put the mask back on.

Saul took her hand in his and stroked it. The midwife said she would check on Perdita later and suggested she tried to catch up on some sleep.

To her surprise, Perdita found that she had drifted off because she was suddenly aware of a contraction that was so intense, she thought she was going to die. Saul was asleep next to her in a reclining chair, but he still held her hand. She tugged at him and shouted his name and told him to press the buzzer for the midwife. Then Perdita stuck the mask back hard onto her face.

'You'll be fine,' Saul soothed. 'You can do it.'

What the heck did he know? She felt that familiar rising panic and knew she was losing control.

'I have every faith in you,' Saul said. 'You're doing really well.'

'You patronising–' But Perdita didn't get to finish the sentence. She swung over to the side of the bed, away from the drip, and vomited over Saul's shoes. After he'd given her tissues and water to rinse her mouth, walking around the room in his socks, she spat, 'Yes, I'm doing really well, aren't I?'

Not long after, Perdita lay with one foot on the midwife's hip and the other on another midwife's hip, her knees bent. Saul held her hand with his back to the midwives and she pushed and pushed and pushed. And trying to breathe in as much gas and air as she could, conscious of a burning pain deep inside her.

'I can see the head,' the second midwife exclaimed.

'Can I see?' Saul asked.

'No!' She didn't want the image of whatever it looked like etched into Saul's memory where he could revisit it at will. After all, Saul was not her husband, her boyfriend or even her friend. He was her... landlord. 'I don't think... it would be appropriate... for my landlord to see my bottom.'

'He's your landlord?' The first midwife's head snapped up.

'Yes. Although... would he actually be... my landlord... since I don't pay him rent?'

'We don't need to go into that now,' Saul said. 'I won't look at your bottom, I promise.'

'I thought he was a friend,' the midwife said. 'I'm not

sure that we would allow–'

'Well... as I don't pay him rent... perhaps he isn't my landlord... It is his house... but I do things... instead of paying rent.'

The midwives gasped.

'That's not helping,' Saul said. 'Perdita looks after my aunt. Don't you, Perdita?'

'Absolutely,' Perdita huffed as she removed the mask from her face again. 'His aunt.'

'Stop pushing now. The head's almost out. Can you give a little cough?' the first midwife instructed. 'We want the head to be born as slowly as possible.'

Perdita coughed delicately, and the head slid gently out. Then its body followed with the next contraction. It felt like her insides were sliding out with it.

'It's a girl!'

A pink scrawny wrinkled seedling was delivered onto Perdita's tummy. Her lovely, delightful, girl seedling, who opened her tiny little lungs and wailed. 'You can look at her,' Perdita said to Saul who'd released her hand. She was already missing the feel of his skin against hers.

Saul looked and then smiled back at her as the wailing body was removed for examination and a clean-up. Perdita felt she was in need of some intervention with soap and water as well.

There was a discreet knock at the door, and then a woman walked in wearing blue hospital clothing. 'Someone wants an epidural?'

Perdita had a strong impulse to pick up her plastic container of water and hurl it across the room. But the second midwife abruptly left with the anaesthetist, despatching her to another patient.

'Do you have a name for her?' The remaining

midwife held a pen poised over the identity bands.

As Perdita told her, Saul bit his lip as though suppressing a smile.

The midwife hesitated. She checked that she'd heard correctly and then asked Perdita to spell it out before dutifully writing it down. As the midwife fixed the bands to the seedling's wrist and ankle, Perdita glanced back at Saul. Was he thinking, as she was, that if things had been different they'd have chosen the name together? Would he have vetoed her choice? Or would he love it as much as she did?

As though reading her thoughts, Saul said, 'It's a lovely name. Really cute.'

When the roots were successfully delivered, a nursing assistant arrived with a trolley and asked for Perdita's flannel and soap so that she could wash her.

'This is my cue to go.' Saul's eyes were moist and shiny. 'I'll let Violet know the news. Let me know if you need anything.' He squeezed her hand and left the room. And Perdita felt bereft and abandoned and wondered if she would ever be as close to Saul again as she had the hours previously.

Having been washed, the midwife put Perdita's feet into stirrups. She didn't think they were going horse-riding. With grave misgivings, she watched the midwife put on gloves and wield a needle and thread. 'There's a tear that needs to be repaired,' she explained.

And Saul wasn't here to hold her hand. Perdita started to cry.

Chapter 26

A few hours later, when Perdita was settled on the maternity ward, the cot at the end of her bed, she reached for her mobile. Opening a new message box, she tapped *Germination complete*. Then she sent the message to Luke and copied it to Gavin. Moments later her mobile vibrated.

The message was from Luke. *Congrats. How did it all go? Are you okay? What sex is the seedling? Does it have a name? L & G.*

I'm okay. Saul was with me. You will have to guess the name. I'll give you three goes. Perdita smiled. Contact with the boys always cheered her up.

There must be a good chance of us guessing then. Caveman fallen in love with seedling?

Perdita tapped in, *I wish*.

When Luke and Gavin arrived, Perdita was sitting up in bed cradling the newly arrived bundle. The boys bent to kiss Perdita and then made use of the two chairs near her bed, drawing them closer.

'Let's have a gander then.' Luke leaned in.

Perdita pulled aside the material the seedling was swaddled in.

'I hope they got all the roots out okay. I heard it can be nasty if any are left inside.' Luke sounded concerned.

'They said it was complete. Now, guessing time.'

'You called her some Latin derivative of seedling,' Gavin said.

'I did think of that. But when I did a search on the Internet, I gave up on the idea.'

'Oh?' Gavin said.

'It came up with the word semen.'

'How about Italian for seedling?' Luke suggested.

'Semen-something or other,' Perdita stated. 'Same theme.'

Gavin sniggered. 'I can understand why you dropped the idea.'

'Yes,' Perdita agreed. 'The Italian dictionary said it was a masculine word.'

The boys stared at her.

'I think,' Luke said seriously, 'that germination has addled your brain.'

'I was only kidding.' Perdita gave him a playful slap.

'But you actually looked up the word seedling online? Doesn't that worry you?' Gavin sounded incredulous.

'No,' Perdita said defiantly. 'Don't all names have meanings? Yours, for example, means white hawk. And Luke means bringer of light.'

'Well, he's certainly brought light into my life.' Gavin blew Luke a kiss.

'Second guess?' Perdita prompted.

'Polly,' Luke said. 'From pollination.'

'Good try.'

'So we're on the right track?' Gavin asked.

'Mm.' Perdita rocked her hand mid-air.

'How about Petal?'

Perdita glared at Gavin. 'How did you manage to guess that?'

Gavin laughed. 'I had a chat with one of the midwives on the way in.'

'You mean you chatted her up,' Luke said disapprovingly.

'I saw the way you were flirting with her.'

'Means to an end, that's all.'

Scowling, Perdita shook her finger at them. 'Cheats.'

'Why don't you have two names for her? Rose Petal,' Gavin suggested.

'Why don't you shut up?' Perdita snapped.

'Can I hold her?' Luke asked.

'You can. But she's a bit whiffy at the moment. I need to change her.'

'Go ahead,' Luke said. 'We can learn how it's done.'

'I came ready.' Gavin produced a peg from his pocket.

Perdita burst out laughing. Mindful of her stitches, she eased her legs over the edge of the bed. 'Did you really bring that especially?'

'No,' Luke said. 'He's been hanging out the washing in the garden and there was a peg left over.'

Gavin said, 'Hey, the military could extract nappy smell and use it in chemical warfare.'

'Yep. Powerful stuff,' Luke agreed.

'I was round a friend's house once when he had to change his boy's nappy,' Gavin said. 'Minging, it was.'

Laying Petal down on the changing table, Perdita said, 'Well, you two won't be my number one sitters then.'

'We're made of strong stuff,' Luke assured her. 'You can count on us.'

'But Gavin said it was minging,' Perdita pointed out.

'Isn't everyone's poo? I can cope with it. I'd be happy to do it.' Luke looked hopeful. 'Anyway, it shouldn't smell much at all. It'll still be the meconium.'

'The what?' Gavin asked.

The nappy was open now. The boys gathered round.

'Jesus,' Gavin exclaimed. 'What have you been

feeding her on? Tar and vegetables? I've never seen anything like it.'

'That's the meconium,' Luke informed. 'It's been in Petal's tummy all the while.'

'How the hell did that get in her tummy?'

'Tell him, Perdita.'

'No, you seem to be doing a great job.' She was washing Petal's bottom now with balls of wet cotton wool.

'It's mostly from what she swallowed when she was in the uterus – womb to you, Gavin. It's from the Greek word for poppy because it looks like raw opium preparations.'

'How do you know it looks like raw opium preparations?' Gavin asked.

'That's what it says in Wikipedia. I looked it up.'

'Why would you go and look up the word meconium?' Gavin asked.

'Why wouldn't I?' Luke frowned, dropping his gaze.

Mm, Perdita thought. Gavin was right. It was strange. Why had he?

'Do you have enough to feed Petal on?' Luke asked. He seemed genuinely interested. 'It takes a while for full milk production, doesn't it? After the colostrum?'

'If you need more, we'll order some extra for you.' Then Gavin's brows puckered. 'Luke, how come you know about what ends up in nappies and breast feeding?'

'Oh, I just picked it up. As one does.'

'Then how come I haven't "picked it up"? How come I don't know any specialised language such as – what was it now? Colstrum?'

'Colostrum,' Luke corrected.

'Gavin has a point,' Perdita said. 'I've been reading

special magazines.' But, before getting stuck in, she'd gone through the entire publication covering up all the upsetting images with Post-it stickers. And she'd only read them before a meal was due, just in case. 'I've made a study of the subject. How do you know words such as meconium and colostrum?'

She'd finished changing Petal and was wrapping her up again. Luke's arms were out ready. But Perdita held back. There was a mystery to be solved first. 'Well? How do you know those words?'

'I've been reading them too,' Luke confessed.

'Special magazines?' Perdita asked.

'Yes.'

'I haven't seen you with any magazines,' Gavin commented. 'Well, not that kind.'

'They're in my locker at work.'

'Why are you reading pregnancy magazines at work?' Gavin asked. 'Have you got clients who are pregnant?'

'Yes,' Luke said briskly and then, 'No,' more quietly.

'Have you, or haven't you, got pregnant clients?' Gavin asked.

'No. Not that I know of.'

'Then why...?' Perdita couldn't understand it either.

'Because I think it would be wonderful to be able to make a... seedling. The power women have. Amazing. I wish...'

'Yes?' Perdita prompted.

'I wish I could make one.'

'You wish you were a woman?' Gavin squeaked.

'Oh no, I like being a man. I just wish I could be a woman too. Experience being pollinated and... germination... and have a seedling...' Luke started to sniff, 'of...' tears began to form, 'my...own,' he sobbed.

Gavin staggered back to the chair.

Perdita had never known Luke to cry. Why, he hadn't even shed a tear when Gavin had reversed the hearse over his foot by mistake. Perdita put Petal in the cot, guided Luke to sit on the edge of the bed and delicately lowered herself down next to him. She put her arm around him. 'Tell me, how long has this been going on?'

'Ever since I found out you were pollinated.' Luke sniffed. 'I couldn't stop thinking about it.'

She did remember now Luke's habit of staring at her bulge. She kissed his cheek. 'Well, you can be Petal's uncle or godfather. How's that? You can seedling-sit her and, when she's older–'

'Teach her football. I'd like to teach her football.'

'Well... yes... that sounds good.' Perdita hoped Petal would be football mad. She glanced across at Gavin to see what he thought of it all. He was sitting statue-like, his eyes popping out. 'Luke, would you like to give Petal a cuddle now?'

Luke nodded, wiping his eyes.

Perdita reached into the cot and handed Petal over. Luke stroked her cheek and smiled longingly at her. Perdita surreptitiously gestured to Gavin to give some supportive input. But he just shook his head in bewilderment.

'I think you and Gavin need to go home soon and have a little chat, don't you? Talk about your feelings?'

'Yes,' Luke said, 'that would be nice.'

Chapter 27

Three days after the boys had visited, Perdita was discharged, and a midwife carried Petal to Saul's car. Perdita struggled to hold back her baby blues as Saul drove them home to Westbridge. In the end, Perdita fished out a baby grow and bawled into that since she'd used up all her tissues on the ward. And a whole lot of toilet paper too.

'Are you all right?' Saul asked.

Of course, she wasn't all right. 'Fine,' she hiccupped and blew her nose into a leg of the garment. 'Never better.' Her breasts were so swollen she wondered if she could be the sole supplier of milk for Westbridge Primary, and the pain was excruciating every time Petal latched on. Hence her use of the nipple protector a midwife had slipped her.

It hurt every time Perdita sat down. Her stitches had burst open from trying to pass rocks – after midwives had administered doses of laxative – and she had to bathe the gaping wound in salt water three times a day. Every time she applied ointment to her tender piles, she pictured a bunch of grapes. She dreaded every step she took due to the chafing massage the fruit of her bottom received and had to keep reminding herself not to scratch – especially when with company. And she hoped that her ongoing blood loss would not leave her exsanguinated. She was also a tad short on sleep. Like four nights' worth.

'So, crying in the back of the car is your way of expressing extreme happiness?' Saul asked.

Wiping her eyes with a sleeve of the baby grow, Perdita sniffed. 'I think if you'd been through what I've been through the past four days, you would understand.' It was then she remembered her squishy stomach that felt like risen dough and the shaky lines on her skin as though an enthusiastic toddler had performed purple pen quality control tests.

'What have you been through the past four days? Or at least, since I last saw you?'

'More than you could imagine.' She blew her nose in the second sleeve, looked at Petal sleeping and, with an effort, composed herself. She had to be strong now.

When they arrived home, Violet rushed into the hallway and said, 'I must have a cuddle.' But when Perdita put her arms around Violet, she murmured, 'Although I'm happy to have a cuddle from you any time, I was referring to Petal.' Violet's speech was almost perfect now.

'Oh,' Perdita said. 'I'm to take second place now, am I?'

Saul said he'd take her things up to her bedroom and then disappeared. The rest of the day went in a blur as Perdita did little but soothe Petal, change nappies and get milked.

The day after Perdita and Petal arrived home, the community midwife came to see them.

'Aren't these stairs too much for you at the moment?' The midwife was huffing and puffing up the two flights with her heavy-looking bag.

'They're fine,' Perdita said. Apparently, Perdita couldn't have her appointment on the ground floor as the midwife needed to examine her. Perdita had lost count of the number of people who, from the time of her hospital admission, had needed to inspect that private area she hadn't wanted Saul to glimpse. Had she known just how much of a fairground attraction it was going to be, she would have maintained neatly trimmed hedges. 'Petal sleeps downstairs in the pram during the day and, at night, I'm up here with her. Where I go, she goes.'

Night after night, Petal bawled. Perdita's slippers were worn and leaked fluff all over the carpet from walking around so much with Petal snug against her shoulder. Perdita wondered if someone had let on about the Guinness World Records book and whether Petal was hoping to be entered for non-stop crying.

When Perdita looked in the mirror, the image staring back at her could have been considered for casting in a horror movie: the skin under her eyelids was almost black, her cheeks were sagging, cracked lips looked as though they didn't know how to smile, and the expression in her eyes was empty as though she no longer inhabited her own body. Although naps helped to keep Perdita going, they weren't enough to bring the zing back into her life; she'd morphed into a mummy automaton. She'd seen Saul watching her, chewing at his bottom lip. But he never said a thing about it and never chided her over neglecting Violet's needs, however reduced they had become. He'd picked up the slack without comment.

It was when Petal was three weeks old that Perdita gave in to tears as she paced and patted with Petal held fast against her. While Perdita was doing her best to give a tuneful rendition of a nursery song, she thought of slumber, cocooned in her soft cosy bed. It was gone two in the morning, and the way things were going, she'd be seeing the sun rise again without having had a wink of sleep. Although the nightlight was on, Perdita had kept the curtains open so that she could see the moon. She felt too lonely without it.

At the sound of a gentle tap, Perdita opened her door to find Saul in his towelling robe. He held out his arms. So far, Saul hadn't shown any interest in Petal, passing the pram without as much as a peek. But Perdita handed Petal over.

'Do you know, *The Wheels on the Bus*? It's one of her favourite songs – maybe you're better at singing than I am?'

'How does it go?'

Perdita sang the first two lines and noticed a slight creasing of the skin around Saul's eyes. Had that been a wince?

'Can't say I do. How about, *Twinkle Twinkle Little Star*?'

Perdita nodded, and then Saul gestured towards the bed. Gratefully, she snuggled under the duvet.

When Perdita groggily came to she became aware of sniffles and grunts. Checking her alarm clock, she saw that it was just before six. And there was no trace of Saul. Had she dreamt him coming in? The grunts changed to wailing, and Perdita knew from the pressure in her breasts that they were ready to be milked again. When she heard a faint knock at the door, Petal's breakfast was in full flow. 'Come in.'

Saul appeared carrying a tea tray laden with toast spread with marmalade, a napkin and a mug of something. Probably tea as she couldn't smell coffee.

'Saul, how kind.'

He threw her a wry smile as though to acknowledge he could have been kinder. But he had been there for her during germination, and he hadn't booted them out. Yet.

'Thank you for helping with Petal. I can't remember the last time I slept for so long.'

'I heard you walking about and, since I was awake...' He shrugged.

Perdita guessed what it must have cost him, cuddling Petal, becoming involved.

'Well, I'll leave you to eat. It's time I left.'

She gave him her brightest smile. 'Thanks.'

Later, she found Violet in the second living room. Perdita offered to make her a cup of tea, and Violet followed her to the kitchen.

'Saul's looking tired this morning. He's working too hard,' Violet said sitting down and peering at Perdita across the kitchen table.

'Yes,' Perdita agreed, doing her best to stop the heat rising in her face. 'He's doing most of what I used to,' she added guiltily thinking of all the shopping he was doing. She knew from the packaging that Saul now bought meat from anywhere but David Murphy's shop. Lamb had lost its extraordinary appeal, and she could eat anything. Even chicken. 'I'm so sorry that it's worked out like this, Violet. I'd no idea Petal would be such hard work. I hope it won't be long before I can take care of you again and relieve Saul of the extra chores.'

Violet nodded. She knew more of what went on than either Perdita or Saul supposed. The morning Petal's father, Tony, came to the door for instance.

Saul had been uncharacteristically cheerful as he'd helped Violet with her tea and toast before he'd left to go shopping, and she'd suspected then that he'd spent the night with Perdita. Having let Frank in, Violet had been sitting by the open window, behind the net curtains, and had seen the man, who turned out to be

Tony, driving in. There had been little point in showing herself as she'd still lacked the power of intelligible speech. So she'd decided to leave it to Perdita to answer the door.

The man had harassed Perdita, threatened her position in the house. And when she'd come in after Tony had left, eyes wide with fear, to ask Violet where Saul was, she'd ignored the girl, incensed by Perdita's stupidity. It was clear as day that she'd allowed Saul to bed her without revealing her impending motherhood.

And Violet knew that something else had happened last night. And it wasn't just Saul's bleary eyes that had given the game away. Now that she could climb stairs, she was back in her own room, next to Saul's. And she'd been lying awake, listening to Petal and the sound of Perdita's movements, when she'd heard the careful opening of Saul's door, his soft tread on the stairs, the creaking of the top step and the deep timbre of Saul's voice.

Change was afoot, and she was not about to scupper it.

Chapter 28

Earlier than last night, Saul tiptoed up the flight of stairs that led to Perdita's room, this time remembering to avoid the noisy top step. He didn't want Violet questioning him about his nocturnal visits especially while he was still working out how he felt about the situation with Perdita and Petal.

He'd gone to bed at nine o'clock, exhausted. The wakeful hours spent with Petal had caught up with him, not to mention the other hours he'd lain awake wishing he'd had the courage to climb that mountain. Now that the barrier of the stair-climbing activity had been broken there was no stopping him. No matter how much it hurt. Like a moth to the flame, he supposed; holding that delightful baby in his arms made him feel closer to Perdita, the woman he would not, could not, touch.

If things had been different, he'd have got stuck in straight away like any proud father would. But that was the problem. He wasn't the father. Nor was she his woman. Tenderly, he tapped a knuckle against her door. When it opened, his heart bucked as Perdita gave him one of her sweetest smiles. Shyly, he grinned back and stepped into the room that smelled of baby products – and lemons.

Tonight, there was no instant oblivion, no rapid descent into that other world. Tonight, Perdita savoured the sounds of Saul whispering to Petal, telling her she was beautiful and confiding secrets about the world outside that she would discover when she was older. And singing, *The Wheels on the Bus*. Had he learnt the song from the Internet?

Perdita wondered what Saul made of Petal, how he felt about her special smell. This, she thought, was how it could have been, working as a team. Could she hope that Saul would do a complete U-turn and make them into a family?

As she felt her limbs melt into the mattress, her sense of the immediate was blurring. Now she was imagining herself snuggled up against Saul's chest, his arms around her, soothing her. It was a very comforting image and the last she remembered before sleep overcame her.

Regarding the double bed enviously, Saul wondered if it was possible to lie down without disturbing either Perdita or Petal. They were both deep in slumber now, and he was rather hoping he could join them. The feeling of being refreshed from his short sleep had been transitory.

Like last night, Saul did attempt to put Petal back into her cot. But unlike last night, she'd started to fret the moment she was released from the security of his arms, and he'd picked her up again. After two more tries, he decided not to take the risk of popping her back in. Perdita needed a good block of sleep to re-energise. It would defeat his purpose if she got disturbed. She looked so peaceful now, and he felt proud that he'd been able to give her the gift of rest.

She lay curled up and, judging by the bulge under the duvet, had kept to one side of the bed. He wondered whether she ever slept in the middle like he did. He liked to command his space, stretch out in all directions. There was no chance of that here. But what did he care if Perdita was lying next to him?

Gingerly, he lowered his buttocks, shifted further in, swung his legs up and lay back, Petal on his chest. But something was digging into him. Imitating a contortionist, Saul felt around and plucked a lemon from under the duvet. His lips twitched as he tucked the fruit under the bedding next to Perdita. She had some weird habits. As he felt drowsiness stealing over him, he tried one last time to put Petal back in the cot, and this time she settled. He decided to stay up here just in case she stirred again. He eased himself back onto the bed. Very soon he, too, fell asleep.

Violet, stretching her limbs in her bed below, smiled when all became quiet and there wasn't even the sound of soft padded footsteps retreating from the room at the top of the house. And she knew what that meant. Things were still on track.

Suddenly, Perdita sat up to look in Petal's cot and found it was empty. With a gasp she spun back, searching the room and was astonished to find Saul partially propped up in bed next to her with Petal, like a limpet, lying on top of him, his hands cradling her against him. Saul smiled at Perdita. When she looked at her watch, she saw that it was just after six. 'I'm surprised she's not hungry.'

'She started to whimper a little while ago; it woke me, but I didn't want her to wake you. I wanted you to catch up on as much sleep as you could.'

'Thanks.' Perdita yawned and longed to shuffle closer to Saul but instead just put out a hand to touch

Petal's tiny fingers.

Saul looked up at the ceiling. 'This used to be one of the guest rooms. When I was a boy.'

'Where did you sleep?'

'Next to the first-floor bathroom. But when I became a teenager, I asked to move up here. It's bigger, and I liked to play my music loud.'

'So how come you moved downstairs again?'

'I'd come to terms with the loss of my parents and decided it made sense to claim their room rather than let it continue to age; it hadn't been touched since they'd left, and it was damp. I had an en suite put in and redecorated up here as part of the general upkeep of the place.' He pulled an apologetic expression. 'I lied to you about my parents. They hadn't gone Christmas shopping. My mother was leaving us to join her lover in London. She wanted her freedom. A divorce from us both. My father chased after her and with the crash and the speed they were probably doing...'

Now Perdita understood. First he'd found his mother had cheated and then his ex-girlfriend. No wonder his distrust ran so deep. And then she'd let him down...

'I couldn't understand why my mother had left me, hadn't wanted to take me,' Saul murmured as though speaking only to himself.

It must have been a long-standing riddle for Saul, Perdita thought. 'She was probably madly in love,' Perdita said. 'A temporary aberration before she came back down to earth. There was no reason for her to cut herself off from her son.'

'No,' Saul agreed. 'Only she didn't get the chance to change, to make things better. And she took Dad with her. Why, I've asked myself time and time again, couldn't he have been content with me? He should have stayed to comfort me and gone after her later.'

'Did he know where they'd be? Could he risk losing her?'

'I don't know,' Saul said. 'That's the trouble. I wish I knew what had gone on in their minds, how they'd felt, why my mother had left, why she'd become involved with another man in the first place.'

'Doesn't Violet know?'

Saul shook his head against the pillow. 'Unfortunately not. And she didn't know then I'd heard the shouting, my mother saying she was leaving. She thought I was in the garden, but I'd come in and heard Mum say she wasn't ever coming back and that Dad couldn't stop her. She was going without saying goodbye.' Saul sighed. 'Then Dad rushed for his car keys, and I guess chased her up the motorway. Violet had been staying with us that weekend, and she told me the story about them having gone Christmas shopping, like I told you. I'd been too shocked to tell her I knew it wasn't true, and then, when I heard they'd died, the secret got buried deep. Until my teens.'

'I'm so sorry, Saul. It was a dreadful thing to happen. To lose both parents like that must have been devastating.'

'Then there was Teri. She cheated on me with a work colleague.'

'How did you find out?'

'She said she wasn't free that evening because of a work event. We'd been through the cinema listings to pick a film to see on the weekend. As she'd discounted one I fancied seeing, I decided to spend that evening at the cinema. Automatically, I aimed to sit where we usually sat, right at the back and, as I approached, I saw a man and woman kissing. When they broke off, the light from the adverts fell on their faces, and I recognised them. When I edged closer, they became aware of me, and all I could see was their guilt. This is why I can't stand lies. I need you to be honest with me in future.'

'I will,' she promised.

'Trust, once broken, can't be fixed.'

'I understand.'

Petal woke grumbling, and Perdita plucked her off Saul. Propping herself up with pillows, Perdita positioned Petal for her feed, feeling self-conscious. 'There's something I've got to do, Saul. Within the next month or so.' It was a good opportunity to ask, while they were being matey like this.

'Oh?'

'I want to offer Tony the opportunity to meet Petal. Would it be all right for him to come here when he's working close by?'

'Yes. But let me know when. Remember, I don't like surprises.' Then he swung his legs off the bed saying, 'I'd better get ready for work,' and was soon gone.

Chapter 29

late October

Snuffling sounds disturbed Perdita. As she lifted heavy lids, she consulted her watch by angling it in the direction of the nightlight. It was just after four in the morning. Saul was lying next to her as he had done for at least some of every night for the past month.

Saul offering to remain until after dawn, on the premise that Petal might become unsettled again, was why Perdita had delayed so long in contacting Tony and arranging Petal's baptism. But it was time Perdita did both. And she fretted over how it would affect this unspoken arrangement with Saul, this other secret life that happened in her bedroom at night.

Perdita studied what she could see of Saul's features as he lay on his back. It was not often that her gaze could linger on his face like this without being discovered. Then she moved her fingers across the pillow to touch Saul's hair. He didn't stir. She became bolder and rested her hand on his head. And then she lightly stroked his cheek down to where it became rough with stubble before tracing a finger around the side of his eye.

Since Saul had started sharing Petal's care, he'd become so aware of movements and noises in the room he was easily alerted. He became aware of something touching his head. Saul remained still when he felt the touch of her fingers create a warm trail down his cheek and then around his eye. Fighting against sleep, he waited in the expectation that Perdita would stroke his skin again, but she didn't, and he guessed that she'd settled back down. He wished he'd seen the expression in her eyes when she'd caressed him because he wanted to know the truth. He wanted to know how Perdita truly felt about him and whether it was the same as how he felt about her.

Pretending to turn over in his sleep, he flung his arm around her. Perdita shifted closer so that his front was pressed against her back. He breathed in the apricot scent of her hair. He was about to let go of the world and let oblivion overcome him, when something else happened.

When Perdita felt Saul's arm fall across her she nestled into him. And then she thought that, if Saul could move his arm in his sleep, surely her hand could move in her sleep? Soon her fingers found his, and she took a longer sleepy-sounding breath to help cover up the fact she was awake. When Saul's hand enclosed hers in a strong grip, she smiled to herself. She couldn't tell whether he'd been pretending to be asleep also as soon his grasp softened and he began to snore. But she wasn't sure that mattered.

At breakfast, Perdita was downing some toast and coffee in the kitchen. Saul was nowhere to be seen despite it being a Sunday. Violet was keeping Perdita company, cradling Petal.

'How did you sleep?' Perdita asked politely.

'Oh, don't worry. I don't hear a thing.'

'Excuse me?'

'Out like a light. As I am every night. That's what I

meant.' Violet's unwavering gaze held hers.

'Did you just say something about your hearing?'

'Pardon?' Violet fiddled with an ear. 'Do you know, I think I might be getting a build-up of wax.'

Did Violet know that Saul helped with Petal at night? Perdita regarded Violet suspiciously and then peered at her closely with raised eyebrows.

Violet must have sensed she'd been rumbled and capitulated. 'I'm not senile, and I'm not deaf. But I'm minding my own business. If Saul prefers your room to his, I'm not going to interfere with his treating you to his company.'

A crumb of toast went the wrong way and Perdita coughed… and coughed… and coughed.

'Is everything all right?' Saul walked in as Perdita was retching into the sink from all that hacking. 'I heard you from my study.'

Perdita took a deep breath, coughed again and cleared her throat. 'Just choking.'

'Need some help?'

'I seem to be doing… ugh… quite a good job… ugh… of it on my own,' she croaked.

'I meant, shall I pat your back?'

Perdita took a deep breath before coughing again. 'No need,' she wheezed and then cleared her throat. 'I think I must have sorted it out.'

'Did something happen?'

Perdita exchanged glances with Violet. 'No, nothing,' they said, aiming innocent expressions at Saul.

'You're doing that thing again, when you look at each other and share something silently,' Saul complained.

Perdita began to speak but then had to clear her throat again as another frog had jumped into it. She wondered how many more were to come. And what was the collective noun for frogs? 'When I choked, Violet happened to mention she thought... hem hm ...her ears might have a build-up of wax.' It was as though Perdita had drunk a jar full of tadpoles as she had to clear her throat yet again. 'Oh, is that the time?' she exclaimed. 'Must dash or we'll be late for Mass.'

Rushing to the far side of town, whilst pushing Petal in the pram, reminded Perdita of the egg and spoon races she'd competed in on Sports Days. She needed to go as fast as she could yet had to be mindful of the precious cargo that was moving along with her. Which was why she limited her speed to a brisk pace. Although she was cutting it fine, she should make it to the finish line on time – it wasn't the done thing to be late when she wanted a favour from the priest. It was a relief when the quaint church was in sight, and she saw David and Catherine Murphy waiting for her with their children.

When Perdita entered the porch, a teenager handed her a hymn book, the Order of Mass and the newsletter. A man helped her and the Murphys find somewhere to sit together.

Father O'Connor was middle-aged and jocular, and quite short with a round red face. Perdita considered him down-to-earth as his homily was tinged with humour and resulted in a few titters from the congregation. She hoped he would regard her situation with gentle understanding.

At the end of Mass, Father O'Connor stood outside the door greeting everyone. Catherine sidled up and introduced Perdita.

'Ah, I've heard about you, Perdita,' Father O'Connor exclaimed. 'And would this be the little girl? And what's she called, now?'

'Petal.'

Uncertainty flickered across Father's eyes. 'Oh...That's a fine name. It's a pleasure to have you both at Mass.'

'It was a pleasure to come, Father, I enjoyed it... Father?' Perdita said.

'Yes, my child?'

'Would you baptise, Petal?'

The priest smiled. 'It would be a pleasure. Come and have a chat with me. Would tomorrow suit? After morning Mass?'

Morning Mass was at eight. Perdita knew that it would be a struggle to be there on time. 'That would be... great, Father.'

'Or would you prefer I come to you? Would she be keeping you awake at night?'

'She is.' Relief flooded through her. Despite Saul's visits, she was still permanently tired.

'You tell me what time's best for you, and I'll see if I can fit it in. Give me a call this afternoon when I've my diary to hand.'

Perdita called Father O'Connor after lunch, and he said he would come at seven the following evening. Now she had to tell Saul. And there was something she'd been putting off asking, afraid he'd say no.

That evening, while she and Saul were clearing supper away, Perdita took courage and said, 'I saw Father O'Connor to ask if he would baptise Petal, and he said he would.' Saul stopped stacking the dishwasher. 'He said he could come tomorrow evening at seven to talk about it. Would you be Petal's godfather? I really hope you'll say yes.'

For a moment, he stared at her dumbly. 'Um. I don't know. This has taken me rather by surprise. I'm not

Catholic. Don't you need to have a Catholic godfather?'

'As long as one of the godparents is Catholic it doesn't matter apparently. Strictly, you'd be called a special witness. Catherine's agreed to be godmother and, of course, she's Catholic.'

'Isn't there someone else who could do it?'

'I will ask Luke to be a special witness. But I hoped you would be one too.'

'Luke?' A cloud darkened Saul's expression.

'Yes.'

'Why Luke?'

'He likes Petal.'

'And Gavin doesn't?'

'Not in the same way.' Gavin was not at all keen on Luke's idea of adopting – the result of their little chat following the hospital visit after Petal's arrival. Perdita thought it might help Luke if he was formally involved with Petal.

Saul turned to take in the view of the garden, but Perdita doubted he was appreciating the plants or the squirrels. 'I can't do it,' he said, raising his hands as though she'd been holding a gun to his head.

'That's okay,' she said softly. It was what she'd expected, after all, but she'd wanted to ask anyway. Just in case.

'I need to–' Saul ditched the tea towel he'd been holding, swivelled on his heel, and then strode out. A second or so later she heard the opening and shutting of a door. Presumably the one that led to his lair. He was being a caveman again.

Chapter 30

The next day, when Saul was having supper with Perdita and Violet, Perdita reminded him that Father O'Connor was coming later. 'Perhaps you've changed your mind about being godfather?'

Saul hadn't visited her last night, and he wondered whether he could bear going any other night now. That dreadful pain of someone else being Petal's father had resurfaced. 'No.' He averted his gaze. 'I can't play Happy Families with you, Perdita. And that's what we'd be doing.' When he glanced up, he saw her hurt stare.

'That's a game I've never played.'

'I'm not responsible for that.'

'Will you meet Father O'Connor?'

'I've got to go out this evening.'

Fifteen minutes before the priest was due, Saul made his escape, wondering whether he'd made the right decision. Of course, he had. Didn't Perdita realise that asking him to be godfather to that child of hers was like sticking the knife in and twisting it?

As he trudged on the gravel, intent on getting to The Dick Whittington before Father O'Connor arrived, Saul tried to think about work; anything to get his mind off Perdita and that delightful daughter of hers. But, before he'd even got to the end of the drive, he saw the dog collar and the black clothes through the leaves of the bushes. Instantly, he ducked low behind the gate, hoping the greenery was sufficient to screen him. He should have worn camouflage clothing. When Father O'Connor came through the opening, he would be looking straight ahead, so Saul could sneak out masking the sound of his own movements with the priest's footsteps.

Damn. The priest had stopped to retie his lace. If he so much as turned his head by a margin, his peripheral vision would pick Saul out in his charcoal coat. Why hadn't the priest had the decency to at least turn up on time if he couldn't oblige by being late?

'I'm a great lover of nature,' the priest said in an Irish accent.

Saul started.

'And I've seen many a strange thing in my lifetime. But not stones that can grow a man.'

Shit.

'Sure, I can understand why you don't want to see me. I'm your conscience.'

Saul eased himself upright. What the hell did the priest mean? Conscience? 'Dreadful these laces,' Saul improvised. 'I see you had trouble with them too.'

The priest smiled. 'Terrible. Aren't they always letting you down when you least expect it? I'm Father O'Connor.' He held out his hand.

'Saul. Saul Hadley.' He took the proffered hand and shook it. 'Pleased to meet you.'

'That's why you'd be hiding in the bushes, now?'

Saul felt heat suffuse his face.

'A guilty conscience?'

'No,' Saul said. 'I don't have anything to be guilty about.'

'You are the fellow Perdita lives with?'

'Yes, but–'

'And are you not the baby's father? The whole

town's buzzing with it. I'd prefer to perform the Rite of Baptism after the Rite of Marriage, you know, although that seems to have gone out of fashion with the young these days.'

'I'm *not* the baby's father.'

'There's nothing to be ashamed of. But think of the little girl. Little girls need their daddies. It's good for children to have both their parents.'

'I'm sure that's true. If I were Petal's dad, I'd be there for her. But I'm not. Check with Perdita; she'll tell you. Now, if you'll excuse me, I've got an appointment to keep.' With a pint of beer.

Skirting around the priest, since Father O'Connor did not move aside, Saul abruptly left, wishing he and Violet had never met Perdita.

When Perdita heard the sound of the knocker, she rushed to the front door. 'Come in, Father. It's very kind of you to come to me.'

'No problem. Actually, I've never been here before, and I must admit I felt some curiosity.' Father O'Connor looked around the hall appreciatively.

'We're in here, Father.' Perdita gestured to the second living room. Petal was lying on her play mat, swiping at a mirror dangling from a frame that had rattles and squishy things hanging down to keep her stimulated.

'This is Violet,' Perdita said.

'So pleased to meet you. And how are you?'

Violet smiled. 'I'm getting on very well, thank you. Perdita's been wonderful in helping me recover from my stroke.'

'That's why I came to live here. To help care for Violet,' Perdita explained.

'Well now, and I thought it had something to do with the man I met hurrying down the drive.'

'Oh. Saul?'

'That's the name he gave.'

'He's my nephew,' Violet informed with a proud ring to her voice.

'It was through Saul I heard about what had happened to Violet, so in a way he is the reason I am here,' Perdita said.

'He says he's not Petal's father.'

'No.'

'Town gossip says he is. How do you think that's come about?'

'People jump to conclusions. I came to help out, that's all.'

'And who would the father be then?'

'Someone I worked with a while back.'

'And he couldn't come tonight, Perdita?'

Feeling sudden tension, she exchanged looks with Violet. 'I didn't ask him, Father.'

'Wouldn't the baptism of a child be important enough?'

Perdita's airways were becoming constricted. 'It isn't that. He wouldn't be interested, I'm sure.'

'If I'm to talk to you about Petal's baptism, her father must be informed, don't you think? Would he not have a mind of his own?'

'Yes. You're right. I'll ring him later this evening.'

'Good. And what about godparents? Is he going to have a say in that?'

'I'll ask him, Father,' Perdita murmured meekly. 'I'd like Catherine to be godmother.' Then she asked about Gerry and Luke being special witnesses.

When Father O'Connor left, Perdita said to Violet,

'So, I wonder what Tony will say.'

'Ring him now. While Saul's still out. I can stay with Petal.'

Perdita called Tony's mobile from the kitchen, and it was answered after only three rings.

'Hello?' It was a soft female voice with an upper-class accent.

'Oh. I think I might have the wrong number. I was hoping to speak to Tony Crawley.'

'He's popped out. I could take a message. Get him to call you back?'

'Oh, yes of course. Could you tell him Perdita rang? It would help if he called me straight back.'

'If it's work-related, can't it wait until the morning?'

'It's not work-related. It's personal. It can wait, but–'

There was a bang in the distance, and Perdita heard a male voice in the background say, 'Who is it, Jessica?'

'Someone called... Perdita.'

There was a pause, and then Perdita heard Tony say, 'Perdita?'

'Yes.'

'Can I call you back? It's not convenient now.'

'It's about–'

'This is something we can sort out at the office tomorrow, Perdita.'

He didn't want to talk in front of *Jessica*. 'Okay, I get the message. When then? I want to talk to you about the baptism of our–'

'Oh, I see. You mean you need to get back to the client tonight? Let me think. I could see him Wednesday evening. Would that be any good?'

'Yes,' Perdita said.

'Around seven-thirty? I'll pop in on my way back

from Exeter.'

'Okay, fine.' Perdita would let Saul know.

'I'll see him at home. Same address? I hope he appreciates this and puts some business my way. Make it worth my while.'

'Tony, I've already told Jessica it's personal, not business. She won't be taken in by this.'

'Listen, Perdita. I don't appreciate business calls at home. I'm surprised Jessica didn't hang up on you. This isn't the first time– You what? You told her it was personal? That's a cheek.'

'You could show a little more interest in your–'

'Well, you might find it's once too often. You're still on probation, remember, and that may well end after this.'

Perdita's phone went silent.

Chapter 31

Hallowe'en

Time permitting, Saul enjoyed a walk after his lunch before going back to the office. This was the third day in a row he'd chosen the same route which happened to include passing a jewellers' shop. But it was the second day in a row that Saul had lingered to admire rings. Engagement rings. Perhaps seeing the priest two days previously had affected him.

Saul suspected that not having Perdita and Petal as part of his family were responsible for his strange gut sensations – like he had maggots from hatched housefly eggs crawling around and nibbling at his innards. It had been made worse when Perdita had asked him to be godfather as he so wanted to be that little girl's daddy instead. Then the maggots had been upgraded to fantastic alien parasites determined to populate a new planet using him as a prime host – and giving him bouts of diarrhoea in the process.

It was too painful to be with Perdita and too painful to be apart. Indecision was ripping him in two – or, rather, shredding him as he recalled those parasitic aliens. Becoming engaged might purge them from his system. There would be the added advantage that he wouldn't have to remain within a short radius of a toilet.

Despite wanting to move things forward with Perdita there remained that cautious gremlin inside his head warning him about untrustworthy women and betrayal. Perdita had deceived him once; he wasn't yet sure whether he was ready to trust her implicitly again. Was her love true or was she merely looking for a home, a family and a father for her child and he'd just happened along? What kind of muppet would it make him if he got it wrong, if Perdita were using him as a meal ticket? And, even if he did decide to trust, it would be nice if Perdita picked her own ring, if they shopped together. So, he turned away from the display window and headed back to the grindstone. And the loo, he thought, as he suddenly felt a need to quicken his pace.

Back at his desk, Saul saw the last two clients of the day. Just before 3 o'clock, Violet called to say the heating had stopped working. He decided to head home. When he couldn't get the boiler to restart, he worked on finding someone to take a look. After four calls, he found a repair guy who was able to offer emergency assistance. Saul hoped that the boiler could be repaired that day, before Perdita returned from the mother and baby clinic. There was a distinct chill in the air, and he didn't want Petal to catch cold.

It was mid-afternoon when Elliott Bletch pulled his van to the side of the road to answer his mobile. He'd just finished repairing a leak and was considering whether to take a spare part to The Dick Whittington in Westbridge or wait until the following day so he could knock off early. He was his own boss. It wasn't an urgent situation; the radiator valve didn't demand instant replacement. And now that his phone was ringing, with the possible advent of another job, he was quite prepared to put off the pub for another day in favour of a more lucrative call from elsewhere. However, he was delighted to find that his caller also lived in Westbridge, past the pub in fact, down

Westbrook Lane.

'No probs,' he told the caller, 'Be there in twenty minutes.' He would go to the pub after. And maybe enjoy a pint before driving home to Mother.

Swinging his van rather too fast around the corner onto the gravelled driveway, he worried over the spray of stones and what they might have done to his paintwork and signage.

It was a fancy looking house. When he knocked loudly the door was opened by a tall man. 'I'm here for the heating, mate,' Elliott said and then gaped, feeling his eyes almost pop out of his head. He'd often wondered what had happened to the man in the store and whether he'd chucked that Perdita girl out.

'The boiler's in the kitchen.' The tall man led the way.

'What exactly is the problem?' Elliott noticed the enormous pram as he walked through to the kitchen. Was Perdita still here then?

'The flame keeps going out.'

'Let's have a look,' Elliott said, removing the cover. 'It's likely the thermocouple's burnt out.'

'What does the thermocouple do?'

'It stops the gas flow if the pilot goes out – and keeps it flowing as long as there's heat.' Elliott gained access to the inner workings of the boiler. He whistled under his breath. 'A bit tricky this, some of these screws are hard to get at... There you are,' Elliott exclaimed at last, holding out a long piece of metal which was charred at one end. 'There's the culprit.'

'How soon can it be fixed?'

'Now, if I've got a spare.' He went to rummage in the back of his van but had no luck. 'Hello?' Elliott called as he walked back down the hall, casting a sideways glance at the pram. It was no use; he couldn't tell if it was occupied. It faced the wrong way, and the hood was up.

'Yes?' the man said. 'Have you got one?'

'Sorry, mate. First thing tomorrow.' Elliott lingered, noticing the slight puzzled frown on the man's face. Was he trying to remember where they'd met?

'Can't you do it today? We've got a newborn.'

Aah. 'And how is the baby? And your wife?' If Elliott had been vindictive, he'd have also mentioned the three non-existent children.

'Fine thanks.' The man looked even more puzzled until suddenly his face cleared. 'As you see, we've er... had another one.' The man's gaze faltered.

'Yours is it?' Elliott asked in surprise.

'Well,' the man said, 'she is my wife.'

'You married her then?' Elliott was confused.

The man scratched his head. 'Don't you remember? Wife, three children.'

Elliott now knew they were at cross-purposes. 'She wasn't your wife then even if she is now. She told me.'

'Told you?' The man's voice went up a few tones.

'And that baby she had, isn't yours.' Elliott was sympathetic, especially when he saw the man swallow hard. 'You didn't know she had a boyfriend?' Poor guy.

'Boyfriend?'

'The father of her baby. Perdita's. Nasty piece of work,' Elliott said, shaking his head.

'You've met him then?'

The man's face was becoming grey, but Elliott didn't hesitate. He didn't hold with keeping secrets. 'In a restaurant. Begging him to marry her, she was. But he was having none of it. By the looks of things, he couldn't stand the sight of her. Felt sorry for her until I saw who it was. She didn't tell you then?' he finished sympathetically.

'No.'

'He refused to find her a place to live. Didn't want to pay what was due, didn't want them living with him. Didn't want much of it at all, I'd say.'

'When was this?' It was a strangled whisper.

'Ooh, couldn't say. I remember it was warm. But it was before my summer holiday which was in June.'

The man nodded distantly, as though remembering a certain day it could have occurred. 'Just the once you saw them together?'

'Yeah. She said you'd throw her out if you discovered she was pregnant.' The man was looking very much as though he wished he had thrown her out. 'You married her?'

'We're not married. I just said we were because I'd told you that in the store. Perdita didn't say she'd met you, talked to you. Or that you'd met… Tony.'

'Well, she wouldn't, mate, would she? Women don't like to give much away; they play things close to their chest.' He winked at the man. He'd listened to Mother, his friends and had watched TV. He liked to share his wisdom with not so enlightened men whenever he thought they could benefit from his vast experience, albeit second-hand. 'You look like you need a drink, mate. Led you a dance, has she?' There was one born every day. Though it was the first time he'd got to meet such a big mug.

Returning to the crisis at hand, the man said, 'Can you get our heating fixed today? I'd appreciate it.'

Elliott sucked in his breath between his teeth. Since this was a customer with a difference... 'I'll be back this evening.' He could pick up a new thermocouple on his way home and come back after he'd had his tea, with Mother. Then there'd be no rush. He might even get another glimpse of Perdita.

Chapter 32

When Perdita arrived home, she was puzzled to find Saul in a taciturn mood. Had something gone wrong at the office? And why had he come home early? 'Is everything all right?' She laid a bag containing three pizzas on the table.

'Fine.'

But Perdita knew every nuance of his expressions, and things were definitely not fine. And it seemed that whatever the problem was, it involved her. 'Gosh it's cold,' she said, rubbing her hands together. 'Petal will have to stay wrapped up.' Perdita had popped Petal in the pram on her way to the kitchen.

'The boiler's bust. The heating guy's coming back to mend it tonight. Interesting fellow.'

'Is he? When did the heating stop?'

'This afternoon.'

'And you managed to get someone so quickly?'

'Yeah. I was certainly lucky,' Saul said dryly. 'My usual one was tied up on a big job, so I tried someone new.'

Perdita frowned as she met Saul's gaze, but he didn't enlighten her. There was a look in his eyes that unnerved her. 'Don't forget, Tony's coming this evening,' she said in case there had been any possibility of his forgetting. She switched the oven on.

'Did you ever want to marry him?' Saul ventured.

Was that why he was harsh and prickly? Perdita laughed. 'No. Whatever made you think that? After what I told you?'

'Did you want to live with him? Have him support you?'

'No! Although I do expect some financial support, since I'm likely to need it. Saul, what's this all about?'

'I'm just getting the facts straight before I meet *Tony*. I thought perhaps you might be hedging your bets, backing both horses at the same time,' Saul sneered.

Perdita slumped into a chair. 'Why are you saying these things? What's got into you?'

Saul shrugged and left.

Perdita ate her pizza with Violet in the kitchen, but Saul took his to the study. Having cleared up, Perdita took Petal to the second living room to play on a mat on the floor, well away from the electric fire that had been switched on. She was wearing white tights and a frilly pink dress with a white cardigan for the special occasion of meeting her dad for the first time.

The closer it got to seven-thirty, the more sparking tracks of trepidation ran up and down Perdita's legs and the pressure in her head was steadily increasing to the definite regular thump of a headache. When she heard the sharp rap of the knocker, she forced herself to amble to the door and open it in one smooth motion to show a serene face to Tony.

But it wasn't Tony. She blinked as she recognised Muscle Man dressed in shabby clothes. 'Yes?' She reduced the gap the door had made. 'What do you want?'

'I've come to mend the boiler.'

It all clicked into place. Saul had said the heating man had been here that afternoon. Muscle Man, aka Elliott Bletch, must be that person. Why wasn't he a road builder or a grave digger? Someone who didn't need to go into people's houses?

They must have discussed her, Muscle Man and

Saul. What had Muscle Man said to have had such an effect on Saul? Then, as she recollected the night in the restaurant with Tony, her heart missed one of its rapid beats and then another. Oh, God, what had she done?

'Excuse me. I haven't got all night.'

Muscle Man brushed past her, and then she saw Tony in the open doorway. He was dressed in a suit, daringly light for everyday wear. Especially in the bad weather they'd been having. 'Come in,' she said. Tony was looking over her shoulder, wide-eyed, so Perdita turned around and saw that Muscle Man was staring back at Tony with a similar expression.

'Excuse me,' Saul said as he brushed past Muscle Man.

Perdita placed a hand on the wall to steady herself.

'I'd like to clear a few things up while we're all here together,' Saul said. 'Has Perdita ever asked you to marry her?'

Tony opened his mouth, caught Muscle Man's fierce expression and then said, 'Yes. But I'm not going to.'

'Did Perdita ask to live with you?'

Tony glanced towards Muscle Man again. 'Yeah, but that's never going to happen. And I told her.'

Saul turned empty eyes towards Perdita. She'd seen that look before, when he'd found out she'd been pollinated. She wanted to shout out that it was all a misunderstanding, that she'd play-acted that night to protect herself and Petal – and the developing relationship she'd had with Saul. If she explained in front of Tony, then Tony would know she'd played games with him. And Saul would know how badly she'd behaved, and she didn't want that either.

'Well,' Saul rasped, 'you can rethink having her live with you and marrying her. You can have them both:

mother and child.' His blazing gaze rested on Perdita. 'I want you out of my house. I'll give you a week to find somewhere, and I'll give you money for the deposit. You won't be homeless even if...' He gestured towards Tony, 'he doesn't change his mind.'

'Saul?' She felt faint.

'You heard. We can manage perfectly well without you.'

'I can explain–' Later, she wanted to tell him. She could explain later.

'This is one explanation I don't need.'

'But, Saul...'

Saul grabbed his coat, slamming the door behind him. She checked an impulse to run after him. Partly because Tony was blocking her exit and it gave her a second to recall why he'd come and partly because Tony would undoubtedly follow her and hear it all. She aimed an accusing glance at Muscle Man who suddenly seemed to remember he had work to finish on the boiler.

'I'm not taking you anywhere,' Tony said. 'You're not coming with me.'

'I know.'

'So, you are involved with that man. You told me you weren't.'

'I met you months ago. Things change,' Perdita said. 'And, no, even now I couldn't say I was involved with him as such, and it definitely won't happen now, will it? But you would have liked it to as it would have relieved you of the responsibility of Petal.'

'Petal? You called her Petal?' Tony asked.

She pressed mutinous lips together.

'Why the hell did you call her such a pathetic name?'

'I think it's a pretty name.'

'Pretty awful, you mean.'

'What would you have called her then?'

Tony glowered at her. 'Make sure you don't tell anyone who knows me what you've called her.'

'We're in here.' Perdita opened the door to the second living room. Violet was dabbing at her eyes. Perdita felt a rush of guilt and wondered if she was going to be sick. 'This is Violet, Saul's aunt. And,' Perdita said, gesturing to Tony, 'this is Tony, Petal's dad.'

Tony winced. He took Violet's hand and shook it. 'So sorry about the investments not working out. Perdita was very worried about them, you know. I reassured her that she'd done everything in accordance with the rules. It wasn't her fault, you know.'

'I know it wasn't Perdita's fault that I lost my money,' Violet said tremulously. 'But what went on out there was definitely down to Perdita.' She sniffed and shot Perdita a smouldering glance. 'Now, if you'll excuse me...' Violet slipped out, shutting the door behind her.

Perdita sank onto Violet's chair and signalled for Tony to sit down. Petal was struggling to eat her toe but only managed to stretch the leg of her tights which flapped with her kicking. Tony only gave her a fleeting glance.

'Well, what is it that you want?' he asked, sitting down. 'What was so urgent that you had to call me at home? Money?'

'I want to ask if you can make Petal's baptism. I've spoken to the priest, and he said it would be good if you could come.'

Tony gave a sharp laugh. 'No way. I think it's best if we break all contact. I've spoken to a solicitor. And he said I should make it official.' He removed a folded envelope from his pocket and extracted two pieces of printed paper. 'I want you to sign these now. One's for me, and one's for you. And then I want no more to do with you or your... whatever it is you call her.'

'Petal. You've barely looked at her. Don't you want to pick her up? Give her a cuddle?'

Tony's gaze flitted towards the floor and then back again. 'I've had a look. Now I want out of here.' He held out the papers and a biro. 'I want a clean break, and I don't want anyone chasing after me for money. Have a look at how many noughts there are. It should please you.'

Perdita gave an ugly laugh. 'You think everything boils down to money?'

'Believe me, it does. Don't be so naïve, Perdita. You need this. Admit it.'

'Why are you doing this? You're not the generous type.'

He bowed his head. 'I've met someone.'

'Jessica. You've fallen in love?'

He couldn't maintain eye contact with her. 'She's my new boss's daughter.'

'Ah. You're going to marry her, aren't you?' Perdita almost laughed. Of course, it wouldn't be a simple case of falling in love for Tony that would make him want to marry. There had to be a financial incentive.

'Read it.'

Perdita began to read. When she saw the sum, she double checked. 'It is generous of you. What do I say to Petal though, when she asks where her daddy is?'

'Tell her I died.'

'I won't do that!' Perdita exclaimed

Tony shrugged. 'I don't care what you tell her as long as it keeps her away from me and my wife. You understand what it is I'm asking? What the money's for?'

'To keep me quiet.' Perdita felt drained, broken. And

she and Petal did need the money, had little hope without it. 'Okay.' And it meant she could afford to leave the house today.

Tony didn't hang around once Perdita had signed. She wrapped Petal up warmly and popped her back in the pram. Perdita could barely see the tread of the stairs in front of her as she went up to gather some things, eager to leave before Saul returned. She couldn't face him, knew he'd be in no mood to listen, and his tossing her aside so carelessly, so easily, was not something she could forgive.

Perdita called Luke and Gavin's landline. 'Luke, is that you?'

'Perdita? What's up? You sound upset.'

Through gulping sobs, she said, 'I need somewhere to stay. Until I find somewhere to live.'

'Aren't you living somewhere right now?'

'Not… anymore. Saul… told me to get out.'

'Bastard. Where is he?'

'I don't know. But I want to be gone before he's back.'

'We'll come to get you. You're in no fit state to drive. Gavin can bring your car back.'

After carrying some essentials downstairs, Perdita went in search of Violet. Muscle Man had left and the boiler was working at full pelt, the radiators making banging noises as they filled with hot water. Violet was sitting at the kitchen table gripping a mug of something between her hands and dabbing at the corner of her eyes.

'You have been so silly. You should have told Saul what you told me... It has to come from you.'

'I know. But he's given me up so very easily that I don't feel like it now. I'm sorry, but we're leaving soon. Luke and Gavin are coming to get us.'

Violet began to cry in earnest now, and Perdita put

her arms about her. 'I really don't want to go, but I must. I can't live like this, with Saul always believing the worst of me and being cold and unfriendly. I started to hope... But that's over now.'

'Never give up. Just give him time.' Violet's expression became more urgent. 'I want you to make me a promise.'

'What promise?' Perdita asked guardedly.

'I want you to promise that if you ever get the chance to put things right with Saul, you will take it. No matter how hurt or embarrassed you feel, you must make him listen. It might be your only chance.'

Perdita was not sure she wanted to make things right. Saul had let her and Petal down by his knee-jerk response. How could love grow if there was no trust? If he didn't believe in her? 'I don't think there will be a chance.'

'All the same, promise me.'

'Okay, I promise,' Perdita said. 'And when I'm settled, I'll come back for more of my things, when Saul's not here.'

When the door knocker sounded, Perdita kissed Violet goodbye and went to let Luke and Gavin in. Perdita ignored their outstretched arms so that she could pick up Petal. 'Just get me out of here,' she said with a catch in her voice.

Perdita cried throughout the journey to Clifton, and she didn't stop even by the time she was in bed in Luke and Gavin's spare room. Luke helped her soothe Petal and offered to punch Caveman. For a moment, Perdita was tempted. 'No,' she said. 'I hope he'll punch himself when he realises how rash he's been.'

Chapter 33

March, five months later

It had been through Sister Margaret's insistence that Perdita had scoured the Internet for a post-sixteen teaching job that required no initial formal teaching qualification; Perdita's mathematics degree would be enough. Due to a maternity leave vacancy that had not been filled, she was welcomed into the arms of a sixth-form college and set to task mainly on getting students through GCSE and A-level retakes while the Head of Department undertook the education of the high-flyers, who also happened to be the best behaved.

Instantly, Perdita had been expected to be fully cognisant of four years' worth of subject material. Had her students been pleasant to teach, it might have helped sweeten the pill of the mind-boggling workload. But her GCSE retake students preferred talking, texting and making paper aeroplanes to buckling down and mastering algebra, probability and trigonometry. So far today, five months after she'd been booted out of Saul's house, she had a collection of six mobile phones, three notes and two paper aeroplanes in her capacious bag – especially purchased for the job.

Glancing up at the clock, Perdita willed the bell to sound probably as much as the students. Twenty minutes remained; twenty painful minutes sharing this room with a bunch of very reluctant learners. How she was going to get them to knuckle down and achieve a respectable pass was a revelation for which she still awaited. But she would give it her best.

A swift movement caught her gaze. She focused on what two lads were doing. One of them had given a fleeting look in her direction and then had equally quickly bowed his head towards his work. If it was work. As she approached, Perdita saw Shaun screw up some paper and bury it in his vast midriff. She put out her hand and waited patiently. Honestly, did they think she navigated around the room using sonar? Did they think she did not have eyes that could see? Or perhaps they thought she was ancient enough to have developed cataracts?

'I'm waiting,' she told Shaun.

'For wha', Miss. The bus?'

A few of them sniggered.

'For your next fatal error.'

''ardly fatal, Miss. Unless you're gonna murder me. And there are witnesses, Miss.'

'I think it might be your dad that has that doubtful pleasure. Hand it over.'

''and wha' over?'

She raised her brows and glared.

'Miss?'

'Stand up now, Shaun.'

'What's 'e done, Miss?' Shaun's friend asked.

'Stand!' she barked. Shaun stood. 'Now, hands up in the air. Let's see how far you can reach towards the ceiling.'

'Don' be ridiculous, Miss.'

'Do it,' she snapped.

Everyone else was looking her way. But she ignored them. In a few more weeks, she hoped to knock these miscreant teens into the shape of polite young adults who did as they were told and gave up messing her around. And got their GCSE maths.

Shaun slowly brought his hands up in an awkward manner that involved slipping whatever he was hiding under one armpit.

'Both arms. Make them straight.'

'I can't, Miss. I've injured my arm.'

'NOW!' she bellowed. This was something to which she'd had to gradually build up. As the weeks went on, she'd relished freeing some of her pent-up frustration by making sounds of a volume she'd not produced since her own school days on the hockey pitch.

As Shaun lifted his second arm a ball of paper dropped to the floor. Perdita picked it up.

'I'm sorry, Miss. Please don' read it. Please. I'll never mess about in your lesson again. Just please don' read it,' Shaun begged.

Perdita was intrigued. Unfolding the paper, she took in the four words written there and couldn't understand what all the fuss was about. Had he spelt it wrong? Was that why she didn't recognise the word? Or was it some kind of slang that had not been bandied about at her school?

Shaun was sitting down again now, his head buried in his hands, his face filled with shame. 'Please don' report me,' he begged.

'Stay behind at the end of the lesson, and we'll discuss it then.' It bought her more time. There was another twelve minutes to go.

Returning to the desk, she got out her mobile. Keeping her phone below the students' line of sight, she tapped out, *What does, Miss is a MILF mean?* and sent it to Luke. There was more chance of him answering than Gavin as Gavin had to switch his mobile off during funeral services.

Moments later, her phone vibrated. She read the message in horror. *MILF stands for mother I would like to f–* She couldn't read the whole sentence. She'd got the gist of it.

Bingo. This provided grounds to have Shaun removed from her class now, surely? Sexual harassment? Saul would know. But she couldn't ask him. She mentally harrumphed to herself. Shaun thought he could stop her from telling? Dream on. She was a tough-nut teacher now. And teachers who caved in to students' demands were walked all over. You didn't dis Perdita and get away with it.

Checking her watch, Perdita saw that the bell was due to ring. 'You can pack up now. Chairs on the desks, please. And you can leave as soon as the bell goes.' Perdita looked at Shaun. 'Apart from you, Shaun Gibson.' Shaun wore a pained expression. The bell sounded, and Perdita called, 'Have a good Easter,' as they hurried out. Most of them were polite enough to say it back.

Leaning against the front of her desk, Perdita beckoned Shaun to approach. 'Do you have anything to say, Shaun?' she asked, when he stopped three feet away.

'Sorry, Miss.'

'That's it?' She waited.

'I didn' mean anythin' by it,' he said. 'I was just 'aving a laugh.'

'The problem is, Shaun, that although you might find it funny, I don't.'

'Wha' are you gonna to do about it?'

'I intend to take your note to the Head of Year. Do you realise that if you'd done something like this in the work place, you would have probably been fired? If not taken to court for sexual harassment? It wouldn't be a good start to your career, would it?'

'Please can you drop it? I promise tha' I won' mess around again. My dad will go ballistic.'

Judging by the size and attitude of Mr Gibson when she'd met him at parents' evening in January, Shaun's dad might well go ballistic. But Shaun probably needed some home discipline too.

'I deserve to be treated with respect, Shaun. You failed to give me that respect. You are almost an adult now, and it's time you took responsibility for the consequences of your actions. It's called growing-up. And I think you've got rather a lot of that to do.' She knew all about growing-up; she'd done a great deal of growing-up the past year herself. 'You can give me a letter of apology as soon as you're back after Easter. And your dad will, I am sure, hear from the Head of Year later today. You can go now.'

Soon Perdita was left in an empty classroom. She'd give the others five more minutes and, if they weren't here by that time, then it would be just too bad. One by one, she lined up the mobiles she'd collected that day on her desk.

The first tentative knock came at the open door. 'Yes?' she said.

'I've come for my phone, Miss,' a girl said meekly.

Perdita held out her hand, and the girl placed a note on Perdita's palm. It read:

Dear Miss Riley I am very sorry I was text my boyfriend in the lesson. We broke up yesterday and when he text to say sorry I wanted to say sorry to. From Becky

'Describe your phone to me.' Perdita stood shielding her telecommunications display.

'It's pink, Miss. In a flowery case.'

Perdita moved aside and watched as Becky selected her mobile.

The next letter, from Richard, read:

Sorry I used my phone in your lesson. My little brother was at home sick and my mum had to be at work and I said I would check on him when my brother text me I was worried there was something wrong and so I text back Richard

Darren's letter read:

My dog was put down yesterday and I was upset and so was my sister. I text her to ask if she was OK cos she was crying at break time. Darren

Sophie's read:

Dear Miss Riley my gran died last night and...

All the notes contained emotional angst. Either the students she taught were very unlucky or they were making up sob stories to make her feel sorry for them.

The first week she'd taught at the college, last November, she'd believed all that the brief missives given to her had mentioned. Now she believed none of it; yes, their lives might be full of turmoil, but Sophie had killed off just about everyone in her family. If her phone got confiscated again and another member of her family died, she'd be purporting to be an orphan with no near relatives. No one could be that unlucky in one year in Britain in this day and age. It wasn't as though there was a civil war or a rampant plague and everyone's families were being wiped out.

But it was easier for Perdita to pretend that she believed all that the notes said; she was tired and wanted to go home. And it was time to pick up Petal from the childminder. Via a quick dash to the Head of Year's office. He always worked late, and she needed to drop off the evidence of Shaun's behaviour now so that it could be dealt with before the start of the new term.

Before she left the building, Perdita's phone buzzed. It was still on vibrate mode. She plucked her phone from her bag and read the message. It was from Violet. *Frank ill. Please call. Love Violet x*

Frank had been left with Violet so that she would have some company and he a much higher standard of living. From a feline perspective, Westbrook Lane was Paradise. It was Paradise from Perdita's perspective too, but she'd been banished from that particular Garden of Eden.

She pressed the call button. 'Violet?'

'Perdita?'

'Yes. I just got your message. What's wrong with Frank?'

'He's been off his food a bit lately, but now he won't eat at all.'

'Oh dear. Okay. I'll come over and take him to the vet. Is there a surgery in Westbridge this evening?'

'Yes. It's drop-in between six and seven.'

'Can you keep him with you until I get there?'

'Yes, of course. Perdita?'

There was a change in Violet's tone, and Perdita steeled herself. 'Yes?'

'I've asked Saul to be at home tonight. I want you to stay for supper. It's time you both sorted this out.'

'The fact that he doesn't trust me?'

'Everything.'

'Does he know you're inviting me?'

'No.'

This subterfuge would probably backfire, and Perdita felt uneasy. 'I don't know.' How would she feel if she came home unexpectedly and found Saul there, with no warning? She'd be delighted. But he wasn't likely to feel the same way. If he missed her, surely he would have done something about it? If he cared for her at all, would he not have checked that she and Petal were okay? Violet would have told Perdita if Saul had asked about her. 'I'm not sure it's a good idea, Violet.'

'Do you have a better one?'

'No.'

'I'm entitled to have a guest.'

'Yes, but it would be awkward.'

'It would be convenient. You have to come here anyway.'

'Let me sort Frank out first, and then we'll see,' Perdita prevaricated. 'I'll be with you in about an hour.'

The last time Perdita had been to Westbridge was for Petal's baptism. Sister Margaret and Gavin had come as guests, and Catherine, Gerry and Luke had carried through their promises of becoming godparent and special witnesses. Instead of going back to Violet's as originally planned, they'd gone to Gerry's for tea and sandwiches. Saul hadn't been there. Perdita hadn't seen him since she'd moved out. And she'd felt furious that he'd absented himself from Petal's baptism.

Petal had missed him. It had been just as Sister Margaret had said to her: seedlings could recognise who was holding them, and Petal had wanted Saul's cuddles at night, settling less easily again in his absence. So Saul had not only hurt Perdita, he'd hurt Petal as well.

The prospect of seeing Saul later that day gave Perdita shivers of nervous excitement. It could be the start of something rekindled or an excruciating disaster. But, if her attempts at reconciliation failed, it might give closure to the idea that there was any chance of a possible relationship with him. It would give Perdita the push, perhaps, to look elsewhere. Eventually.

But what if Saul had already done that himself? Surely Violet wouldn't have arranged supper for them all tonight had that been the case? But Violet might not know if Saul had moved on, and then it would be yet another humiliating experience.

Later, as Perdita drove up the driveway with Petal buckled in the back, Perdita saw Violet waiting for her by the open doorway. As Perdita made her way up the steps carrying Petal, Violet said, 'Let me look after Petal while you go to the vet.'

'I was hoping you'd say that. She needs something to eat; she's getting grizzly. I've brought food for her – and here are her toys.'

As they entered the kitchen, Perdita saw Frank's pet carrier.

'Oh, you didn't need to bring that in – I'd have gone to the garage to get it.'

The items of hers that had been stored in the garage were still there. Her flat was too small to take everything considering all the gear Petal had.

'It was no trouble. Honestly. Frank's in the living room. I wasn't sure how long you'd be so thought it kinder to give him room to move about in.'

Perdita took the cat carrier into the main living room and shut the door behind her. Frank was curled up in Violet's armchair. She went to stroke him. He began to purr. Carefully, she lifted him up and gave him a cuddle. She'd missed him terribly. Then, very gently, she eased him into the cat box.

Chapter 34

Perdita groaned inwardly when she saw the line-up of patients waiting for the clinic door to open despite the fact that she was early. Just as there were sounds of a key grating in the lock, someone arrived with a greyhound. Did greyhounds make dog walking into dog running? Curious, Perdita raised her gaze to assess the athletic prowess of the owner of the dog and then wished she hadn't. Jim The Gardener always had a collection of snide remarks at the ready when she was within sneering distance, and Perdita quickly turned her back to him before he recognised her. She'd once suspected Saul of being involved with Jim's mean personality, but now she knew it was just down to Jim's own nature - having discovered that he was nasty to most people.

The queue at the nurse's desk soon shortened. Then it was Perdita's turn. She was asked to fill in a registration form.

'Oh, I know the people who live there,' the nurse said when Perdita handed her the completed paper. 'Westbrook Lane. The big house.'

'Hey, I work there. I know you,' Jim said and sniggered.

Perdita ignored him.

'Cat go' your tongue? Hey, Burt,' Jim called across the room. 'This is the woman who used to live with Saul Hadley an' his aunt. Before she got 'er marchin' orders.'

Perdita glared at him.

'Ooh. Did I let the cat out the bag? 'As tha' put the cat among the pigeons?'

'Mr–' the nurse began in a stern voice.

'Okay. I get the message.' Addressing Perdita, Jim said, 'But remember, you're no' the cat's whiskers anymore.' He gave an evil laugh.

Finished registering, Perdita shouldered past the growing queue and claimed a seat next to a wiry woman with grey frizzy hair. She looked like she'd been electrocuted.

'Take no notice of 'im, love,' Electra said. ''e's just jealous as 'e's got no one of his own: old and lonely and crotchety.'

'Hardly surprising if that's what he's like.' Perdita scanned the room. One of the hounds was trembling. He'd been here before then. She presumed that the other three canines were newbies as they looked relaxed. A woman was holding a cardboard box with something jumping around inside, and there was a couple of cat boxes.

Peeking into her own cat box, Perdita discovered Frank was cowering at the back. She turned the carrier with her foot so that Electra's dog wouldn't be in Frank's direct line of vision, but as there were peep holes all along the sides, Perdita wasn't sure how much it helped. The clinical smell that she'd noticed on entering had all but disappeared, being overpowered by doggy smells. When Electra's dog decided to rest its pointed chin on Perdita's thigh, its snout aimed at her crotch, she guessed where the overpowering odour was coming from.

As she was about to shove the sniffer dog away, Electra said, 'Look, 'e likes you. 'e doesn' do that with everyone.'

Perdita smiled weakly. 'I'm not really a doggy person.' She pushed Sniffer's face away and crossed her legs.

Sniffer nosed forward again and planted his nose squarely towards the apex of the V her legs made.

'Well, 'e's really taken a fancy to you,' Electra said.

'He wasn't the only one,' Jim drawled from his corner seat the far side of the room.

The dog was now drooling and dribbling over Perdita's work trousers. Well, at least they were machine washable.

'You've got enough to worry abou' without the likes of 'im getting involved with *cattiness*,' Electra stated tartly at stage volume. 'We all feel for you,' Electra went on. 'A man like Saul Hadley should shoulder 'is responsibilities. We were all shocked that 'e didn' marry you, love. I've heard it said that people have gone to that other solicitor instead of 'im. By way of solidarity.'

Perdita was appalled. 'No, they mustn't do that. It was all my fault. I messed up.'

'It takes two to make that kind o' mess, lovey.'

Titters went around the room.

'It does,' Perdita agreed. 'But he wasn't one of the two. Honest.'

'Really? Well, what were you doin' livin' with 'im then?'

'Violet needed me.'

'Mmph.' Electra didn't sound convinced. 'So why did you leave?'

'And then she didn't need me.'

As though the vets had practised synchronised manoeuvres, both clinic doors either side of the nurse's desk were opened at the same time and each vet called in a patient. One of the dogs who hadn't been called tried a spot of queue jumping, but the vet wasn't having it. The offender was hauled back out, and the lead passed back into the hand of the apologetic owner.

Desperately trying to avoid Jim's mocking gaze, and Electra's understanding smile that didn't understand a thing, Perdita pulled her bag onto her lap. Using it as a shield, she gradually eased it towards her knees, making Electra's hound back off before anyone in the room suspected her secret. If Sniffer's nose had remained glued to her crotch a moment longer, she bet the other owners would put two and two together and make it that time of the month.

After only ten more minutes of humiliating agony (Most Humiliating Experience Number Eight), feeling Jim's gaze sear into her, Frank was invited into a consulting room.

'Hello.' The vet beamed as she lugged the pet carrier over the threshold. He was in his thirties, had dark hair and a day or so's stubble. She thought of Saul's smooth face after he'd had a shave. And the lemony tang.

Perdita explained that Frank was off his food while placing the carrier on the hip-high bench. The vet unlocked the gate and tilted the box until Frank came sliding out. The vet pulled the box away and passed it to Perdita. She put it on the floor.

Frank crouched low, his tail tucked in tightly. The vet took hold of him and popped him on the scales. 'Well, his weight is within normal range.' The vet felt Frank's belly. Frank gave a low growl. 'Nothing untoward here. Feels normal.' The vet held Frank's tail up and stuck a thermometer in. Frank struggled as Perdita held him. 'Normal. Well, if you drop him back in the morning, I'll take some blood and we can do some tests. It'll have to be under general anaesthetic otherwise I'll be clawed and chewed. No food or drink after midnight. So nice and sharp at nine tomorrow. I'll see to him first, and then he'll be ready for you to take home before we close up for the rest of the weekend.'

As Perdita left the consulting room, Jim shouted, 'What was up with 'im? Was he *cat*atonic?'

Electra, who had just finished paying for her dog's consultation, shouted back, 'Maybe it's time you 'ad those *cat*aracts seen to, Jim.'

'You need a *cat*alogue of things seeing to. Including your manners,' another yelled.

Jim folded his arms. 'Keep your claws in.'

'Wouldn' it be a *cat*astrophe if you lost your job over this, Jim?' Electra crowed. Jim reddened. 'See. You dish it out bu' you don' like to get it back,' Electra pointed out. 'You'll be joining the *cat*egory of the unemployed when Saul and Violet get to hear o' this.'

Jim threw a worried glance at Perdita who gave him a withering look. 'You'd be *cat*erwauling then,' she said and left with Frank to a round of applause.

Perdita's heart lurched when she saw the Merc parked outside the house. It didn't help knowing that there was visible Sniffer slobber on her trousers. In the wrong places.

Releasing Frank from his box, Perdita picked him up. Cuddling and crooning over him, she strolled towards the house. Just as she reached the bottom of the steps, she saw the front door swing open, and Saul emerged. Slamming the door behind him, he descended at a brisk pace appearing furious. At the last moment, he sidestepped her. Frank struggled from her grasp and darted towards the rear of the property with surprising agility and energy for a sick animal.

Saul stopped and turned to look at her. 'I might have known you'd be back. Why didn't you take the damned cat with you?'

'Hello, Saul,' Perdita murmured. 'I didn't take Frank with me because I didn't have a suitable home to give him, and Violet's taken to him. You know that.'

'It's so that you could keep your ties to the place and use him as an excuse to return.'

'What's really the problem, Saul?' Perdita bit harshly.

'You're my problem.'

'Okay,' she said, placating hands held up in surrender. 'I'm going to pick up Petal and leave.'

'Don't ever come back.'

Whirling round on her heel to face him again, Perdita declared, 'Does that mean you'll take Frank to the vet's in the morning? He needs tests.'

'I'm busy.'

'Then, if you don't want to see me again, I suggest you aren't around at eight-thirty, when I come for him. And damn you, Saul. You see evil where there is none. And you judge without a proper hearing. You were judge and jury to me when you asked me to leave last year.'

'I trusted you!'

'Then why didn't you show it before listening to one side only?'

'I'd had enough of the lies you tell.' He crunched down the drive away from her. If he'd been going any faster, he'd have been running.

Biting back a stinging retort, Perdita decided to leave Saul be. She could do striding and crunching too, and she strode and crunched in the opposite direction, towards the kitchen and Petal. She knocked on the back door and let herself in. 'Violet? It's me. I'm back.'

'I know you are, dear. Frank came in long ago. What kept you?' Violet had paid a man to put in a cat flap for Frank.

Petal was on Violet's knee checking out pictures in magazines. As soon as she heard Perdita's voice, the magazines lost their appeal, and Petal kicked her legs in excitement, her mouth in a joyous grin.

Planting a kiss on Petal's head, Perdita said, 'I ran into Saul. He's not happy I'm here. We should go.'

'Oh no,' Violet protested. 'What about supper? It's all prepared.'

The aroma of something good in the oven only now caught Perdita's attention. 'It will make Saul angry.'

'You're my guest, Perdita. I am entitled to invite you for a meal. And if he's too stubborn to join us, that's his bad luck. I can't eat a whole lasagne on my own.'

'Okay. But I won't linger. I should get Petal ready for bed soon.'

'Seedlings happily sleep anywhere. Please, spend the evening here. It's something I've wanted for ages.'

Perdita capitulated; she'd missed Violet's company dreadfully. 'All right. You know, I need to come back early tomorrow to take Frank back to the vet.'

'Why, what's wrong?' Violet sounded surprised.

'Well, as the vet couldn't find anything amiss he needs to do blood tests – under a general anaesthetic.' Perdita's voice wobbled.

'Oh, I'm sure it's nothing serious.'

Perdita focused sharply on Violet's expression. 'There's no need to look guilty; it's not your fault that Frank needs an anaesthetic.'

Violet waved a hand downwards. 'I'm sure there's no need for him to go through that.'

'Something must have happened to put him off his

food. The strange thing is that he jumped out of my arms just now as though he was full of energy. It doesn't make sense.'

'Perhaps he ate something that disagreed with him. Perhaps he's already on the mend.'

While they ate supper, Petal sat on Perdita's knee banging a small wooden spoon onto the table in between sucking at one or other of its ends.

Violet lightly touched Perdita's hand. 'Perdita. He loves you. Talk to him. For me. He's too proud to make the first move.'

'I did try. He wouldn't listen.'

'Make him listen, Perdita. For all our sakes.'

Chapter 35

After a hasty breakfast, Perdita grabbed jeans and a jumper for herself and leggings and a football top – gifted by Luke – for Petal. Once their outdoor clothes were on, Perdita bundled Petal into the car seat and drove to Westbridge.

Noting Saul's Merc tucked close in the corner, by the bushes, Perdita considered it prudent to knock at the front door. She didn't want to anger Saul by taking, what he might call, liberties and bumping into him unannounced.

When Violet opened the door, Perdita said, 'If you take Petal, I'll get Frank's box from the car. Is he in the front room again?'

'Oh, no.' Violet held out her arms for Petal. 'He's not turned up. I can't find him.'

'But if we can't find him, he can't have his tests.'

'No...' Violet said and then added, shrugging, 'Well, that's that then. I'll put the kettle on.'

'There's no time for that, I've got to find Frank. We'll be late.' Perdita descended the steps, frantically calling his name, concerned he was too ill to come home. She hunted around the gardens and searched the garage. But there was no sign of him. Bursting into the kitchen, her heart pounding, Perdita moaned, 'It's no good, I can't find him.'

'Well, leave it for now. I'm sure he'll turn up.' Violet was at the kitchen table with a mug of tea, studying the

Radio Times with Petal.

'But it's so unlike him. What if he's too ill to get home? What if he's locked in somewhere, and there's no food or water for him?' Perdita plonked herself down opposite Violet. Petal beamed at her. Perdita beamed back. Pulling out her phone she searched for the vet's number and called to cancel.

'I'm sure Frank'll be all right.' Violet's gaze zoned in on Perdita. 'But there's someone in the study who isn't. Go and sort it out. While you have the opportunity.'

'So, Saul's not gone out then?'

'No.'

'He said last night that he didn't want to see me again. I'm too scared to go in. He might shout at me.'

'Perdita, he's waiting for you.'

'How come?'

'Because I told him that if he didn't stick around to see you, I would be very unhappy. I told him he had to give you a chance. And I'm not the only one.'

Perdita's brows furrowed.

'He's had people call the practice and leave messages with his secretary about taking their business elsewhere. They think he treated you shoddily.'

Perdita warmed to the idea. 'Yes, he did,' she agreed. 'Very shoddily.'

'Just because I'm on your side, it doesn't mean I don't realise it's six of one and half a dozen of the other,' Violet rebuked. 'You both need your heads banging together. You're both at fault.'

'I know,' Perdita admitted despondently.

'And David Murphy and Father O'Connor have seen Saul to try to get him to settle the issues between you.'

'Has there been a petition?' That's what people did when enough of them got together to agree to disagree with someone else.

'No,' Violet said sarcastically, 'unless you'd like me to start one? Don't be ridiculous.'

It was as though Petal suddenly found something highly amusing as she banged her hand down hard on the table and gave a loud happy laugh.

'I think Petal's just seconded the motion that you go in and sort it out. And I don't want to see you until you've made him see sense.'

Slowly, Perdita got to her feet, her heart battering her ribs. The stakes were high, and Perdita was not sure that she liked the odds. But the fact that Saul had agreed to stay in his study augured well.

'You'll need this.' Violet proffered a key.

The odds had suddenly lengthened. Perdita met Violet's gaze as she passed the small lump of metal. Perdita tiptoed to the study door and listened. Would Saul still be in there, she wondered, or might he have escaped through the window?

Giving a gentle knock, Perdita heard Saul's commanding tones from within. 'I can hardly invite you to come in when the matter's out of my control.'

It was hard to get the key to fit in the lock as her hand was shaking so much.

'Unfortunately,' Perdita heard Saul say, 'I can't offer to help you get the door open. You'll just have to rely on your personal resources. And the key, of course, that Violet took.'

All of a sudden, the key fitted and turned smoothly. Perdita held her breath as she eased the door open, unsure whether Saul would come storming out like stampeding wildebeest. He didn't. He was sitting at his desk, a pile of papers in front of him, and his expression was glacial.

'Why did you come back?' Saul asked.

Perdita sat on the seat opposite his desk. 'We need to talk.'

'Do we?' His glance slid back to his papers.

'Yes,' she urged. 'There are two sides to every story.'

'I don't like stories.'

'You'll like this one,' she enthused.

'I don't think so. Especially since you've had so long to think this one up. It's bound to be a good one.'

'The truth always is and, yes, it is rather good.'

Saul behaved as though he hadn't heard her. Seeing him again yesterday and today made her realise that her feelings for him had not waned, and, if things could not be sorted to her satisfaction... it was to be the whole caboodle or nothing. 'You'd prefer me to walk out of here, never to see you again and, because of your misplaced pride, miss out on something that could have been so good, so lovely...?' She trailed off, unable to believe he would be so hard after all this time.

'I don't trust you, Perdita. There's no point.'

'There's every point. I love you!' And she did still love him despite the fact he had some rather unappealing traits.

'And I'm supposed to forget it all because of those three magical words?'

'Give me a chance to explain.'

'You've got ten minutes,' Saul said grudgingly.

Perdita saw there was a keen edge to his eyes. They looked tired and empty too. 'I meant to tell you everything when we woke up that morning, the morning when Tony turned up and insisted I meet him–'

'I know all this.'

'But you missed the ending. The ending is always of the utmost importance in storytelling. So, where were we?'

'You were meeting–'

'Yes, I was meeting Tony. Well, I decided the only way to get rid of him was to come on strong.'

'Why did you want to get rid of him?'

'Because he used me and uses all women. There isn't a shred of decency in him. I've regretted our... encounter ever since it happened. It wasn't even nice,' she said.

This seemed to please Saul who said, 'Go on.'

'He hates commitment and loves his money. I didn't want his values, or lack of them, affecting Petal's upbringing. And, I was so in love with you, I panicked. I didn't want things messed up. So, I dressed with padding up my clothes, waddled like a duck and generally made myself disagreeable to him – I was also concerned that he was interested in an action replay in bed with me. When he backed off from marriage, I pushed further and talked about the costs he'd have to share and mentioned him helping financially. By the end of the evening, he wanted to run a mile. The only hitch was that plumber, Elliott Bletch. He almost got Tony to believe that I was having an affair with you because Elliott Bletch mentioned I was married with three children. It could have spoilt everything.'

'What about when Tony came here the last time? To see Petal? He must have been interested in her then.'

Perdita shook her head. 'He barely glanced Petal's way. He wanted to get married.' Saul blanched. Perdita smiled wryly. 'To the boss's daughter. Tony wanted me to sign a contract relieving him of all responsibility. He paid me to free himself. He never wants to see either of us again.' Like Saul had said to her when he'd asked her to leave.

'And what did you do with the money?'

She'd guessed he'd ask that question. 'Most of it is invested. I accepted it for Petal's sake. For her future.'

'I'm sorry,' he said. 'I didn't mean…'

'I think you did, Saul. I'm used to little and can manage perfectly well–'

'Yes, I know you can.'

'I would have told you about my meeting Tony the day of your dinner party but you were in such a foul mood, and you weren't prepared to listen to what I had to say. Later, it wasn't relevant as we weren't a couple.'

'It was relevant as it shows that you're scheming.'

Perdita scowled. 'I did what I thought best at the time. If Tony really wanted contact with Petal for the finest of reasons my ploy would have given him the freedom to build bonds. Instead, he went to a solicitor to draw up a contract that would keep Petal out of his life.

'Do you think I'd have wanted a dad for Petal who was only around when it suited him, leaving her wondering what she'd done wrong between one visit and the next – if there ever was a next?' Perdita held Saul's gaze. 'Do you know how hard it was for Petal after we left here? She'd been used to being cuddled by you every night and wouldn't settle.' Saul's face was grey. 'Did you think she wouldn't notice, Saul? You'd spent hours and hours with her, and then, suddenly, you weren't there anymore. What I tried to protect her from in Tony, she found in you!'

Perdita watched as Saul's Adam's apple moved up and down. 'I missed her too.' His voice sounded husky.

'It's been months, Saul. Not even a phone call. You didn't care whether we had a roof over our heads. Earnings. That sort of thing.'

'Violet would have told me if there had been a problem. So, I knew you had to be all right.'

'I am now. I'm teaching. But I might not have been okay. Do you think you are the only one with pride?'

Perdita shook her head sadly. 'You aren't the man I thought you were. I thought you were constant, dependable. The kind of dad that would do Petal good. You didn't even come to her baptism.'

Saul covered his eyes with his hands. 'I know. You don't need to rub it in.'

'I need to say it. When I came here yesterday evening, you wanted me gone again. This might be my only chance.'

'I thought you'd betrayed me, so the sight, sound and smell of Petal was too much to bear. I wanted you both far too much. But I don't think a lack of trust can be put right.'

'You still mistrust me?'

Saul didn't answer and that was the limit of what Perdita could stand. She'd thrown herself at him, yet he was still his obstinate, obdurate, pig-headed, inflexible self.

As Perdita half-turned towards the door, she said softly, feeling as though her heart had been trampled on, 'Well then, that says it all. I'm going to go now, Saul. I need a man who will love us to bits and stick by us. You, Saul, are clearly not that man.'

Perdita had reached the door when a hoarse voice said, 'I am. I can be. Just give me another chance. And I do trust you – it's just that the past is so hard to forget.'

Turning, Perdita noticed how pinched Saul's expression was. He took a tentative step towards her. Sincerity filled his eyes. She felt her resolve soften. Just a bit. But he still mistrusted her despite what he claimed as he could not let the past go. How could she surrender until that was resolved?

'How do I know you won't change your mind back again?' Perdita asked. 'Your feelings seem to be on the fickle side. Someone comes to tell you a story, and you believe it without running it by me. I don't want to be hurt more than I already have been, and I certainly don't want Petal to be caught up in a yo-yo relationship.' She'd heard the girls at work. Their relationships were often on and off like light switches. 'And I'm not interested in a light-hearted dalliance,' Perdita said. 'I want the real thing, and if you can't give that to me, I will have to look elsewhere. Petal needs a dad. And I want–'

'A husband.'

She raised her brow, glad that Saul was catching on so well.

Locking his gaze with hers, Saul said, 'Marry me.'

His command was compelling, but did he really mean it or would he change his mind tomorrow, or the next day? She felt scared – and angry. A moment ago, he said he didn't trust her, and now he was popping the big question. And what kind of a proposal was that? 'Why do you want to marry me?'

Upturning his palms and sounding confused, Saul said, 'I thought that's what you wanted.'

'It depends.' Sidestepping him, she sat down again offering him a wounded glare on the way.

Saul sat down too. 'Do I have to prove it in some way? Is this a test?' Saul asked in disbelief. 'I thought I'd done the hard bit. I've said it.'

'Said what?'

'I love you.'

Perdita frowned. 'I think you might have missed that part out.' Leaning back, Perdita folded her arms. She was not a play-thing to be taken up and discarded at his will. But things had improved. Saul was chasing her now instead of she him. She wondered how she could get more of it. And make it last. She stared across the desk at Saul, and he stared right back.

'Things are never straight forward with you, are they?' Saul grumbled. Rubbing his lip, he regarded Perdita. 'Is it because I didn't go down on one knee?'

Perdita smiled sweetly. 'I believe it's traditional.'

Saul sprang to his feet and went to kneel by Perdita and clasped one of her hands. 'Perdita Riley, would you please do me the very great honour of becoming my wife?'

'I'll think about it.' Perdita delicately removed her hand from his grasp. But she was feeling the tension ebb from her muscles, and her jaw began to feel much more relaxed.

'What?' Saul's eyes were wide. 'You're the one who came to me...'

'Are you saying you thought I was "easy"?'

Saul shook his head and returned to the comfort of his seat in the manner of a chastised dog returning to his basket. Breaking the silence that hung between them, Saul said, 'I do believe that love will conquer all... love will prevail... Isn't that enough?' When Perdita didn't reply, he asked, 'Are you expecting more proof that I love you? Because I'm not sure I have any to give.'

'Shame.' Perdita stood up to go. She might have Saul hooked, but she still had to land him safely ashore.

'Wait,' Saul urged, and Perdita plonked herself down again, curious. Opening his laptop, Saul waited for the machine to wake up and then tapped some keys. After a short interlude, he reached for the phone and was soon speaking into the handset. 'Is that Father O'Connor? This is Saul Hadley... Very well thank you and you?... I was wondering when would be a good time for Perdita and me to come to discuss our wedding arrangements. We'd like to set a date... Yes, as soon as possible.' Saul caught Perdita's gaze.

She shrugged and nodded, trying to hide her delighted surprise, still wanting to keep the upper hand. But then she had an idea and raised a finger.

'One moment, Father,' Saul said. He covered the mouthpiece with his hand. 'Yes?'

'I'd like it soon,' Perdita whispered. 'But not too soon. It would be nice to have a boyfriend first. Or, at least, a fiancé for a while. Since I've never had one.'

Saul whispered back, 'I haven't either, so it's a new adventure for us both to look forward to.' Then he uncovered the mouthpiece and said, 'Father, can we come back to you on actual dates? And see you next week perhaps to talk about what we need to do?... Yes, thank you.... Thank you. Goodbye.' Hanging up, Saul looked triumphant. 'Proof enough?'

'Um...' Perdita wondered if she should milk the situation further or quit while she was ahead.

'And I want to adopt Petal. After we're married. Give her my name. Be her dad.'

Tears of joy welled up in Perdita's eyes, stinging her as she blinked. Saul pulled her to her feet and embraced her, and she felt like she'd come home. After a while, she pushed him away. 'You know, just to make sure...'

'Yes?' Saul's tone was obliging.

'How about an Agreement? Promise of intent, if there is such a thing... You like contracts.'

'Anything,' he said and kissed her hungrily before adding, 'There's something else. I want us to have seedlings of our own.'

She swallowed. She did too. 'Can that also go in the Agreement?'

'How many?' he asked. 'And when can we start trying?'

Although Perdita wanted to say this instant, she

considered her answer. Landed fish did sometimes make it back into the water. It was not necessarily a done deal until they were in the oven. Then, to top it all, she remembered how hurt she'd been, and how guarded she'd felt a moment ago, and decided self-preservation was called for. 'This time,' Perdita said, 'I think I'd like to do things the right way around – including not getting pollinated before I'm married. And as for how many... shall we see how it goes? At least two?'

'If you just meant what I thought you meant, short engagement after all?' Saul asked sounding hopeful.

'Summer? After I finish my job?'

Saul sighed. 'If that's what you really want.'

'Mm. Don't want to let the kids down by disappearing on honeymoon.' Then doubt beset her. 'There will be a honeymoon, won't there?'

'Absolutely.'

'August then. How's that? We've had quite a long break from each other. We have to get to know each other better–'

'In the biblical sense?' Saul asked hopefully. 'Did I read it wrong earlier?'

Perdita shook her head, and it was not without huge regret. 'In the social sense. You can get to know my friends, and I can get to know yours – and so can Petal. We have a lot of ground to cover. I'm a sensible girl now, making sensible choices.' Keeping something back for the wedding night was sound insurance, surely?

'And you're set on this course of waiting?'

Perdita nodded. 'I wouldn't have. But the way things worked out, I don't feel comfortable not waiting.'

'Well, in that case, how about we start from scratch? So that I woo you up until the wedding day?'

'And beyond?' Perdita asked hopefully.

Saul grinned. 'Sounds like a plan. Will you move in?'

Perdita sucked at the inner side of her lip as she considered. 'Not until after the wedding. I have my own place, and it's closer to work.'

Saul pouted.

'You're the one who kicked me out,' Perdita pointed out reasonably.

'I know.' Saul groaned. 'And don't I regret it?'

'I would like to experience your wooing skills from my own place. And I'm not having you haul me out of another home until I'm ready to come.'

'Ouch...' Saul winced. 'But I deserve that.'

He'd been prepared to send her away again today. So it made sense to be cautious. And Saul seemed ready to accept her terms. Being cradled in his arms, she felt loved and at peace with the world, protected and secure.

'I'm sorry I was a brute. That I wouldn't listen.'

'You've got at least until the wedding day to show me just how sorry you are,' Perdita said.

'I'll use the time wisely then,' Saul said as he nuzzled her neck. 'The fear that you really were going to move on brought me to my senses. I won't let you down. I promise.'

It seemed a good time to kiss him again.

'And I don't want you to feel lost anymore,' Saul said, pulling away. 'You have a home here whenever you give the word should you change your mind, as well as a place in my heart.' He caressed Perdita's cheek. 'And I want to get that first ring on your finger as soon as we can get to a jeweller's. Keep any other rivals away.'

As if.

Feeling as though her heart would burst with unaccustomed happiness, Perdita exclaimed, 'We must tell Violet...'

Chapter 36

As Perdita led Saul into the kitchen, their hands clasped together, Violet rattled her tea cup on the saucer and grinned. Petal, on Violet's lap, rocked back and forth, raising her arms. Saul looked at Perdita enquiringly as he stepped into Petal's view, and she nodded. She wondered whether Petal recognised Saul or the sound or smell of him. How long were seedlings' memories?

'Oh, how I've missed you,' Saul said to Petal and planted a big resounding kiss on her cheek. She squealed in delight. He picked her up and cuddled her close.

'At last.' Violet smiled. As though a burden had lifted from her mind, her body slumped. 'You've made me a very happy woman.' She pulled something out of her pocket. 'And you'll have a very happy cat if you use this.' She held out her hand, and Perdita took the offering.

'Why have you just given Perdita my car key?' Saul asked as he planted a kiss on the side of Perdita's head. 'She's got my heart; is she to have my car too?'

Understanding dawned, and Perdita said, 'Frank's not ill at all, is he?'

'No.' Violet chuckled.

Saul was catching on fast. 'Where's the Tesco delivery that was coming? The big van I had to get my car out of the way for?'

'That's not coming either is it, Violet?' Perdita asked.

Violet laughed. 'No, it's not.'

'You've been scheming rather a lot the last couple of days,' Saul observed.

'Oh, I can't take all the credit. Only a third of it.'

'Would you care to explain to my future wife?'

'And to my future husband?'

'It's a bit like the Holy Trinity,' Violet said. 'Sister Margaret, Father O'Connor and myself. There was a bottle of wine that helped the ideas flow.'

'I'm surprised,' Perdita said with mock sarcasm, 'that David and Catherine Murphy didn't join you as well.'

'They were late because their babysitter let them down. But the plot had their seal of approval.'

'I'm so glad it did,' Saul said. 'That makes me feel immensely relieved. And how will you inform them of the success of this... plot? Drums? Smoke signals?' Now he was bouncing Petal on his hip; she was loving it.

Violet fished her phone from her pocket. 'I've been keeping them updated.'

'You've had a very full pocket this morning, Violet,' Perdita said. 'I hope being that full hasn't stretched the material.'

'*Immaterial,*' Violet said, 'compared to what might have been lost. Now my hard work has paid off.'

'You mean about Frank?' Perdita asked.

'Everything,' Violet replied triumphantly.

There was more? Perdita looked at Saul to see if he was any the wiser.

Violet sighed. 'For two supposedly intelligent people, you can be very dim.'

'Perhaps you'd care to enlighten us dimwits?' Saul suggested.

'I'd been trying for months to find you a suitable wife before I met Perdita,' Violet said.

'*You* find me a wife? How?' Saul laughed.

'The number of organisations I'd had to call – insisting each time that I only had a woman visit as I was old and vulnerable – before Perdita came – you wouldn't believe.'

'Seems like I'm not the only one with stories to tell,' Perdita said, pulling out a chair opposite Violet.

'...And each time Perdita came,' Violet continued, unabashed, 'I made late afternoon appointments but you, Saul, kept being late home from work. It was that last time, about eighteen months ago, that I managed to get Perdita to stay on longer, and there you were. But had you come home when you were meant to, you could have had a cup of tea with Perdita. While I'd gone to make it, the two of you could have got to know each other. It would have saved all this upset and bother. But you being late made my job a damned sight harder.'

'So that's why you talked so much about Perdita?' Saul asked. 'So that I'd be interested?'

'And you talked to me about Saul,' Perdita accused. 'You set me up. You made me think he was wonderful.'

Saul frowned. 'Aren't I? If I'm not, why on earth are you marrying me?'

'Well, my dears,' Violet interrupted, 'time was running out for me, and neither of you managed your love lives very well yourselves, did you? What's an old lady to do?' Violet shook her head. 'And you and your stubbornness, Saul, nearly messed it up.'

'Why did you think Saul would like me?' Perdita asked.

Violet smiled broadly. 'I have good taste. And when Saul met you, I knew he was interested when I saw his distinct lack of interest. It's his way of protecting himself. He frightens off the women that place him at most risk of falling in love.'

'What was I? A pawn in your game?' Saul asked.

'Don't take offence,' Perdita said. 'Look at the prize you've won. Admit it; you couldn't have done it without help. And I couldn't have got you to listen without Violet's help either.'

'Mm. I don't think I can advocate false imprisonment.'

'Well, you're certainly capitalising on the outcome of said false imprisonment,' Perdita said with an affectionate smile.

'Well, you can come and free me any day. As long as you stay with me.'

Perdita looked at him steadily. 'But I don't want to free you, Saul. I want to shackle you to me and throw away the key.'

'When you two love birds have finished shackling yourselves to each other, don't you think it's time you liberated Frank?' Violet said drily.

Perdita sprang to her feet and skipped out of the house towards Saul's Merc. Frank was meowing frantically at the back windscreen, his front paws resting on the glass. In fact, in the sunshine, she could see paw marks over every window of the Merc. When she opened the car, she saw a cardboard box that appeared chewed and scored, presumably from Frank's efforts to escape it. She would find some window cleaner when she went back in. And perhaps two cloths? Saul could help: their first task to be completed together as an engaged couple. And then, she thought with a thrill, he could drive her into town to buy a ring.

Chapter 37

early August

It was the first Saturday in August. As the white Mercedes pulled up outside St Mary's Catholic Church in Westbridge on the day of her wedding, Perdita spotted the black vehicle parked ahead of them. She turned to Luke who was seated next to her in the back. 'Is the hearse something to do with Gavin? Because if it is, I don't find it funny. It's meant to be a happy day where people have happy thoughts and not be reminded of death, gravesides and burials.'

Luke appeared sheepish. 'Gavin left his car at work as he was too emotional to go back to the office to do the switch. I was to drop him off on the way to yours, but he was running late. So, I came in mine and–'

'Gavin brought the hearse,' Perdita said.

'Yes.'

'He could have been a bit more unobtrusive,' she grumbled.

'Doesn't fit into a car park space. He'll get away with it here, parked outside the church. Traffic warden will pass him by. Sorry. It had been a bad night, you know. I had to comfort him. Stress of the job.'

When the uniformed chauffeur opened the door, Perdita clutched at the skirt of her chiffon ivory dress, careful not to damage the floral creation she was also holding, and guarded the clipped half veil as she eased her way out of the limo. Catherine and Gerry were there to greet her, wearing full length pale lemon dresses and holding small cream and yellow posies. Petal was with them in her buggy wearing a frilly confection of lemon chiffon. Catherine was going to carry Petal down the aisle as she hadn't yet mastered walking.

As Perdita waited in the porch for the signal to get things rolling, she thought of her parents and wondered if they could see her now. She blinked hard. Petal would not have the lonely life Perdita had had. Petal would have siblings, family and family friends as well as friends of her own. She would grow up steeped in love.

As the organ started to play, Perdita slipped her hand into the crook of Luke's arm and they entered the nave. The scent of flowers was distinct above the usual smell of wood polish and incense. The church looked beautiful with floral arrangements at the end of every pew and, even from this distance, Perdita saw that the altar had massive displays of yellow and white flowers. Making her way slowly, doing the special wedding walk, she cast about her and was astonished to see the pews fuller than they had been on any Sunday morning she and Saul had attended Mass here – on Father O'Connor's orders as an extension of their preparation for marriage meetings.

As she and Luke progressed down the aisle, the congregation turned towards her, and she didn't recognise any of the people. But they seemed to know her as they were all smiling at her. So, she smiled back. As she approached the front, she recognised more faces. Even Jim The Gardener was here. He seemed to have left his cap at home and, as her gaze met his, he touched the side of his forehead. Perhaps he was grateful he'd kept his job. Perdita had confided about him to Saul but had asked Saul to let Jim stay, and he'd been let off with a warning.

Then Perdita glimpsed Violet – in a beautiful pale rose outfit with a becoming pale rose hat – with Sister Margaret. David Murphy, Gavin, Faith and Hope, her former neighbours, were there too. But her eyes now sought Saul. Looking ahead, Perdita could see him in a new grey suit and a new grey tie, standing next to Bruce. Both men beamed at her, but she was only interested in Saul who had never looked so handsome, so appealing, so... yummy, and she thought ahead to that evening. Perdita could not wait to break her celibacy.

Father O'Connor was ready at the altar. As Luke sat down, Perdita handed her bouquet to Gerry for safe-keeping. Perdita smiled at Petal, sitting safely in Catherine's arms, and turned to Saul as he took her hand and squeezed it. Perdita squeezed back.

She had opted for a simple ceremony rather than a full Mass which Saul had agreed to with some relief. It wasn't long before Saul slipped the ring on her finger, and when he bent to kiss her after they were pronounced man and wife, she felt a surge of happiness unlike any she'd known before. He was hers. All hers. For keeps.

Father O'Connor beckoned them to the vestry for the signing of the marriage certificate, and the organ struck up again as they left the altar. Father O'Connor shook Saul's hand heartily. 'Now, haven't I waited a long time for this day?'

'How come there is such a grand turn-out, Father?' Perdita asked. 'I don't know half those people.'

'Didn't they come to witness that Saul went through with the marriage? I had volunteers for bouncers – you know, keep him in.' Father O'Connor winked as he laughed.

Saul winced so Perdita took hold of his hand. The joke was a little too close to home.

'Don't you know, the whole town's been rooting for you?' Father O'Connor continued. 'It's been a-buzzing with stories of you and Saul for months now. Sure, they all wanted him to marry you. They all wanted a happy ending. For you both.'

'I'm so pleased I could oblige,' Saul said. 'Perhaps business will pick up again now.'

As they walked back up the aisle, to the sound of *The Wedding March,* Perdita wanted to skip lunch and just drag Saul away somewhere private. Very private.

'I'm sure you'll be very happy together,' Father O'Connor said as he joined them outside, giving Saul a hefty pat on the back. 'The power of prayer is a wonderful t'ing, but a little earthly assistance from your aunt goes a long way.' He chuckled and then suddenly put his hand to his forehead. 'Jaysus, I don't remember booking a funeral in after this.' He shook his head. 'My memory is not–'

'Don't worry, Father. It belongs to one of the guests. There's no funeral,' Perdita assured.

'Smile,' Bruce called as he aimed his camera and took the first snap. 'Lovely. That should come out really well. Now can we have everyone in the photo?'

At the end of the photo shoot, Perdita turned her back on her guests and threw her bouquet behind her. When she spun back, she saw that Faith and Hope had caught it together, holding the flowers aloft triumphantly. Bruce snapped the moment.

After that, they drove to The Berkeley Square Hotel where they'd booked a table in The Square Kitchen. Perdita had assured Saul that she had no lasting bad feelings about the place. And it did not matter that they didn't have their own private room as the numbers had been whittled down to a handful; rent-a-crowd from the church hadn't been invited to join them. And Saul and she were planning to leave as soon as the meal was over. No fancy after party. They had other plans.

The long table in the centre of the room had been decked out very prettily with cream and yellow carnations, a crisp white linen cloth and cream and yellow napkins artistically folded into swans. The wedding breakfast menu had been sent to guests in advance for pre-ordering so that lunch would run smoothly. When Saul sat down beside Perdita, at the centre of the table, she hooked her foot around his ankle. He grasped her hand and kissed her on the lips before whispering, 'I am so looking forward to having a wife in my bed.'

Blushing, she whispered back, 'And I'm looking forward to having a husband in your bed.' They'd had days out as a family; evenings out and evenings in as a couple. But they had not spent the night together. And she'd learned to trust that Saul wouldn't turn against her again.

'I think,' Saul murmured, 'since we've tied the knot, we should call it our bed.'

'Good idea,' Perdita said, doing her best to ignore the butterflies that flitted around her insides whenever she thought about making love with Saul again.

As the waiters arrived with the first course, Perdita scanned the diners, a contented smile pulling at the corners of her lips, but then did a double take. It couldn't be. It was impossible. But when her gaze was held by his, she knew she hadn't been mistaken.

Muscle Man. Oh, goodness. She hadn't seen Elliott Bletch since the day he'd come to mend the boiler, and now here he was again. In the same place he'd been when she'd dined here with Tony. Was this his favourite restaurant then? She'd envisaged pub grub being more his thing. And who was that he was with? The woman looked enormous. An older version of him? Yes, it had to be; Muscle Man's mother. Perdita's jaw dropped. And what was that around her neck? In disbelief, Perdita recognised the red and gold paisley scarf as one she had nearly bought in the department store, the day of her abduction. So, Muscle Man must have seen it, liked it and given it to his mother as a gift.

'Is something wrong?' Gerry asked, from her seat opposite.

'No. Everything's fine.'

'Then why were you looking at that man like you know him, and why's he nudging that old bag with him? Now she's craning her neck to have a good nose.'

'It's the plumber.'

'Oh?' Gerry didn't look any the wiser.

'You know. Muscle Man,' Perdita hissed.

'Did you say I've got big muscles?' Saul asked, as he finished his conversation with Bruce, opposite.

Perdita smiled tightly. 'Let's just eat, shall we?'

Gerry leaned forward. 'Perdita says it's the plumber over there. The man who–'

'I haven't forgotten,' Saul said.

'They're taking a big interest in us,' Gerry said.

Saul turned in the direction Gerry had indicated with a toss of her head and groaned.

'Shall we just eat and ignore them?' Perdita suggested.

At that moment, Bruce stood up. Tinkling his fork against his wine glass, he declared, 'I'd like to propose a toast. To the bride and groom!'

Obediently, everyone at the table lifted their glass and proclaimed, 'To the bride and groom.'

'He's laughing now!' Gerry scowled across the room. 'Oh, good. The waiter's just giving them the bill.'

Perdita brightened and concentrated on her food. As she ate, her gaze found Petal who was sitting on Luke's lap, tucking in to the food they'd brought from home.

'Excuse me.' A deep, growly voice sounded to Perdita's right. Almost cricking her neck as she swung sharply round, Perdita's mouth gaped as she saw Muscle Man tap on Saul's shoulder.

'Mm?' Saul was holding a napkin to his lips as he chewed.

'You two,' Muscle Man declared wagging his index finger between them, 'are the craziest couple I've ever met. She wasn't your wife when you said she was. But now she is. That's what comes of telling lies. Be careful. They just might come true.'

Recovering quickly, after a big swallow, Saul grinned. 'You're right. But all's well that ends well, huh?'

Muscle Man shook his head pityingly and turned to the woman next to him. 'Come on, Mother. Let's get you home.' The two lumbered off.

'Make sure that when the boiler next breaks down you find a different plumber,' Perdita muttered.

'Oh, but good plumbers are so hard to find these days.'

'It's me or the plumber,' Perdita said.

'Ooh, now that's a hard one... Ouch, that hurt.'

'Sorry. It was only meant to be a little kick. My pointy new shoes. Not used to them yet.'

'Any more surprises for today?'

Perdita almost choked on her food. 'We've had enough, don't you think?'

'Yes, but there's something in your tone that makes me think–'

'Later.'

'Why not now?'

'Later.'

A man's quick step nearby drew Perdita's attention. Her heart missed a beat. Tony spotted her, faltered, hit his brow with the palm of his hand and scurried back out again.

'Would you like to tell me what's going on?' Saul asked. 'I don't think later's going to work.'

'He texted me,' Perdita confessed. 'Last night. Said he needed to see me. I texted back and said no, I was getting married in the morning. That's all. I don't know what he wants, and I don't know why he's here.'

Saul kissed her cheek. 'How come life around you gets so complicated?'

Perdita smiled apologetically. 'He probably booked into this hotel as he stayed here last time.'

'Popular, isn't it? Don't worry. I'm not going to let anything spoil this wonderful day. And I'm the one who got you, not him.'

'You sound smug. But he didn't even want me as you well know. So, there was no competition over who was going to get me to the altar.'

Saul shrugged. 'Well, if he's changed his mind, we'll have to duel over you.' When Perdita stared at him, Saul chuckled. 'I'm just trying to let you know how much I care.'

'That is your role tonight, I believe.'

'And will you show me how much you care?'

'I can hear your conversation from over here,' Violet said in mock severity. She was sitting next to Sister Margaret, diagonally opposite Perdita. 'So other people can too. I think you need to rein in discussing your plans for tonight. Before it becomes X-rated.'

Perdita hid her face in her napkin, and Saul laughed. The waiters cleared away the remains of the first course and immediately produced the Moroccan chicken she and Saul had ordered.

After the dessert was eaten and the coffee was drunk everyone got up to leave. As they made their way into the lounge area, planting affectionate kisses on Perdita's cheeks, shaking Saul's hand and slapping him on the back, her guests bade them a good trip. Soon it was only Petal, Violet and Saul left with her, and they all made their way to reception where a cab was called. Saul retrieved Petal's carrier seat from where the receptionist had stowed it away.

When the taxi came, Violet sat in the front while Perdita and Saul sat in the back with Petal between them. Saul stretched out his arm, and Perdita felt his fingers caress her neck. She studied the sparkles on her left hand as the light caught the diamond: a single solitaire that stood proud of the gold. And now, there was a shiny new gold band next to it. Feeling fingers under her chin, she turned to Saul.

'Happy?' Saul asked.

'Ecstatic. Fairy-tale ending.'

'And,' he whispered into her ear, 'it will be a fairy-tale honeymoon.' His intense gaze promised plenty of passion. Saul must have sensed her tension as he whispered, 'Don't worry. I'll cherish you.'

Perdita smiled. 'Always?'

'Yes, always. I will prove it to you. Frequently.'

'Mm,' Perdita said, 'I'd like that. I have a poor short-term memory.'

'Starting as soon as we are alone,' Saul promised.

'I've tried very hard to close my ears to your murmurings,' Violet said. 'I don't wish to play gooseberry, so do you think you could leave these kinds of conversations until you *are* alone?'

'Sorry,' Perdita and Saul said, exchanging chastised expressions.

They were going back home to Westbridge to change into clothing more suited to catching a flight and to say goodbye to Frank who was going to be looked after by a neighbour. Petal and Violet were coming with them. It was what Perdita had wanted, and Saul had said he'd wanted it too. She and Saul would still have plenty of alone time and it would be more fun with all of them together exploring Vienna – and the nearby mountains. Perdita had never been abroad before. She began to imagine admiring scenery from up high with Saul by her side, holding her hand, sharing the experience of stunning views.

But when the cab crunched on the gravel of the driveway outside their home, Perdita saw the low sleek body of a red sports car and her spirits plummeted. As they stopped, Tony stepped out, his hands making a supplicant gesture. 'I know I shouldn't be here. It's your wedding day. And I'm sorry. But it can't wait.' His eyes were beseeching, and his feet were stomping the gravel like an impatient horse.

'We'll go to the kitchen,' Saul said, as he held Petal, and walked with Violet into the house. Perdita supposed Saul wanted to get Petal out of sight so that Tony wouldn't become smitten by her.

'What do you want, Tony?' Perdita demanded. 'I thought you never wanted to see me again.'

'I know, I know.' Tony looked around. 'Can't we go in to discuss this?'

Perdita frowned. 'I've a plane to catch. It's my honeymoon.'

'It won't take long. I promise.'

'I'm not sure that your promises are worth anything.' Perdita marched ahead and lifted the material of her dress as she sprinted up the stone steps. Tony followed. 'In here.' Perdita led the way into the main living room. 'Now, what is it? What is it that's so important you have to turn up on my wedding day?'

'I was wrong. I don't want to break off contact with you and Petal. I got the papers from your solicitor–'

'Oh.' Perdita lowered herself onto the sofa. Tony chose to remain standing even though she'd proffered Violet's armchair.

'I don't want to give her up. I can't let him adopt her.' He began to pace around the room.

Her heart not only fell to the floor but sunk to the sub-floor as well. 'He's already been a far better father to her than you ever could.'

'I'm sure. But it's all changed now.'

Perdita snorted. 'How come?'

'Jessica's left me.'

That didn't surprise her. 'You were unfaithful?'

'Actually, no. She was.'

'What?'

'Apparently, she's like me. When I told her dad she'd cheated, he said we deserved each other. I'd done him a favour by taking her off his hands. It was a set up. I was used.'

'I'm sorry it didn't work out for you. But what's that got to do with Saul and me?'

'I should have married you, not her.'

Perdita sighed. 'Tony, I wouldn't have married you anyway.'

'But I thought that's what you wanted?'

'No.' Perdita spoke softly. 'What kind of father would you have made? You would have let her down like you let me down. You use people, Tony. I don't like that about you.'

'I've learned my lesson. I actually loved Jessica.'

Perdita shook her head. 'I hardly think so. If you did, you wouldn't be running straight back here. You wouldn't have even considered marrying me.'

Tony sighed and sat on the sofa next to her. Perdita shifted over so that their thighs weren't touching. He took hold of her hand, and she pulled it away.

'I don't want to be left out,' Tony said.

'You paid me to leave you out.'

Tony winced. 'A guy can change his mind, can't he? Petal's the only thing that's important now. I know that. Honestly.' Tony was wringing his hands together. 'Look, you needn't even tell her who I really am. Call me Uncle Tony if you like – until I've proved myself. And I can see that you're right. Your husband would make a far better dad than I would. But I am her dad, and there's room in her life for the two of us. You can call the shots. I just need to know I haven't lost her entirely.'

There was no denying the sincerity in his voice. What was she to do? What was the decent, ethical, moral thing to do that would be best for Petal too? And what would Perdita have given to have had even one dad? She would have been ecstatic to have had two. 'Saul's going to be so disappointed that he can't adopt her. He loves her so.'

'Let me into her life, and I'll sign the papers. Saul can be her official dad. My bachelor life isn't suited to having a child. But let me in. I haven't been able to sleep for thinking about Petal. Ever since I got you to sign that damned contract, I've been seeing babies and pregnant women wherever I go. The shops, the streets, the TV, the films.'

Looking more closely now, Perdita noticed the dark rings under his eyes and the gaunt, haunted appearance of his face. He could be telling the truth. She hoped he was. And then, she noticed something had happened. At Tony's mention of babies and pregnant women, she'd felt no need to invoke the beautiful brightly-coloured flower waving in a gentle breeze, on a hillside with lots of grass. But no one needed to know quite yet. She'd grown rather fond of her alternative terminology.

When Perdita led Tony into the kitchen, Saul and Violet glanced up sharply. Petal was sitting on Saul's lap, his arms around her protectively. Violet was sitting next to him, holding Petal's fingers.

'Tony's come to say that he'll sign the adoption papers so that Saul can be Petal's dad,' Perdita said.

'Oh, that's great news,' Violet burst out.

But Saul looked wary.

'Petal,' Perdita continued, crouching down to her daughter's level, avoiding Saul's gaze, 'this is Uncle Tony, and he's come to say hello to you. Can he give you a kiss?' She plucked Petal from Saul's grasp and held her facing Tony.

Petal looked at Tony curiously before he kissed his daughter's fat cheek. When he straightened, there were tears in his eyes. 'Thank you,' he mumbled. And then he stumbled past them and left.

Saul raised his brows enquiringly.

'Every girl needs a daddy,' Perdita explained, biting her lip. 'And, if she can get two daddies, she's a very lucky girl indeed.'

'So, it's a daddy share?' Little crinkles showed around his eyes.

'It might be a very small share on Tony's part – but I can't deny Petal the opportunity to get to know him too. He's Uncle Tony until we say otherwise. Or so he says. But I think he'll keep his word. It's a big thing to sign away his legal claim to Petal, and he'll go ahead with that. He trusts me to do the right thing by him.'

Saul took her hand and said, 'And I do too. I believe in you.'

Perdita grinned at him. It had taken long enough.

Violet left the kitchen muttering something about needing to get ready.

'We must get a move on, too,' Perdita said.

Perdita changed Petal into her travelling outfit and then sought help from Saul in getting out of her wedding dress.

'There's something I've been wondering about,' Saul said as he finished opening the buttons at the back of Perdita's dress.

'Yes?'

'Now that we're married and we'll be sharing a bed every night, do you think you could manage to sleep without a lemon?' Saul helped her step out of her gown.

Perdita took a sharp breath. 'How…?' She turned to face him wearing only white underwear.

Saul took in her appearance appreciatively. 'I became painfully acquainted with the fruit when I was helping out with Petal, in those early weeks. Care to explain?'

Perdita didn't care to explain and placed fingers over her eyes. As Saul drew her close, his arms encircling her waist, she moved her hands to his shoulders.

'No more secrets? This feels like a secret.'

What did it matter now? 'When we were on the labour ward and you mentioned the lemon I'd brought, I pretended I hadn't noticed that your aftershave smelt of lemons. But it was one of the first things I'd noticed when we were in the back seat of your Merc – the day you made me agree to come me here. Sleeping with a lemon was the closest I could get to sleeping with you.'

'You substituted me with a lemon?'

'Don't get all bristly. It was your aftershave I substituted, not you.'

'So you don't consider me a worthless lemon?'

'I wouldn't have married you if I did. Although you did occasionally behave like a lemon.'

'You're right, I was an idiot.'

'But you're *my* idiot.' She hugged him closely as she spoke.

Saul chuckled. 'You're the most adorable woman I've ever met.'

Winding her arms tightly about his neck, Perdita showed his lips just how adorable she really was.

Printed in Great Britain
by Amazon

60122809R00190